CHRISTOPHER MURPHY

WHERE THE BOYS ARE

CHRISTOPHER
MURPHY

First edition

ISBN: 9781686801136

*This book was professionally typeset on Reedsy.
Find out more at reedsy.com*

To my family, my husband,
and anyone who has overcome the odds.

Praise for Christopher Murphy's Debut Novel,
WHERE THE BOYS ARE

"Have you ever been told you look like someone? In Where The Boys Are, Murphy takes readers on a journey full of unforgettable twists and exhilarating surprises that will keep you on the edge of your seat trying to solve the mystery..."
– Truniece White

"Murphy expertly weaves in surprises that upset expectations, and then makes the read all the more satisfying when he brings everything together in the end."
– Theresa Kostelc

"This is a mystery/crime thriller that lives up to the definition. And there is plenty of Murder, Martinis and Mayhem! I found the storyline very unique and it weaves several stories together into the ultimate finale, which without giving anything away, the ending is... highly satisfying! Christopher Murphy has a bright writing future and I hope we see more novels like this one, and maybe even some of these characters in another story!"
– Will Smith

MURDER, MARTINIS AND MAYHEM...

BOYS WILL BE BOYS.

WHERE THE BOYS ARE

CHRISTOPHER MURPHY

PROLOGUE

A strange breeze whispers through the curtains of Vaughn Parker's ninth-floor flat. It brings with it the smells and clamor of the outside world. The sweet yeasty odor of flour and sugar from a nearby French bakery along the promenade below. The roguish laughter of children running between tourists on the sidewalk. Forks and knives being dropped by a busboy at a sidewalk bistro. Foreign tongues and syllables of another language filling the air. It makes its way through an unsuspecting window open in the handsome, historic Viollet-le-Duc edifice above, filled with residents starting their day. It carries through the open window, fluttering past the silk curtains and stirring about the room.

It comes like a warning.

It comes like an omen.

Adam's eyes snap open as he jolts awake, covered in sweat. His arms thrash against the silk sheets until he's pushed himself upright. He blinks away tears, wincing to find the bedroom full of light and the pillow next to him abandoned.

He tries to catch his breath as he examines both sides of his hands, then curls them over to check his fingernails.

No blood.

It was just another dream.

A noise from the open window calls his attention. *What time is it?* Adam sighs and leans against the cream tufted headboard that stretches to the ceiling. He glances at the empty pillow beside him, silently cursing himself for sleeping so late.

The bedroom looks untouched. Like a staged showroom or a page from *Insider Homes*.

The décor is a bit too Country-French-meets-Liberace-on-acid for his taste, with its pale Parisian-pink drapes and matching chaise in the sitting area. Fresh hydrangeas and the latest *French Vogue* are on the coffee table. There are two matching lamps and chairs, a silk upholstered footstool, and a built-in bookshelf on the far wall with hundreds of books he's figured out are mostly for show. A few gold frames sit before rows of hardcover books, anchored by plaques and awards Vaughn has collected during his career. Prized gold and silver statues of little bald men without eyes or expressions, given in his honor. They stand there, solid, like soldiers. Keepers of the books.

The hardwood floors have been refinished, but just enough Adam correctly suspects to hold their original "rustic charm". Then there's the overly ornate crown molding that lines the walls like sugary piped icing, the gold leaf ceiling that makes the sun's glare more intense during the day, and of course, an over-the-top chandelier that drips over the center of the bed. Iron and crystal daggers dangle precariously above Adam's head.

A closet sits off to his right. A large walk-in behind two French doors with gold hoop handles. He's peeked in once to discover it half full of Vaughn's suits and shoes. Vaughn's only moved to Paris two months ago. Most of his everyday clothes are still in Chicago because his assistant hasn't shipped them yet.

Nondescript watercolors and pastels cover the bedroom walls. Dull artwork that might easily be found in any office waiting room, except Adam knows they must be expensive. Likely commissions from some artist he's never heard of – not that he's much of an art connoisseur to begin with. He knows what he likes and what he doesn't. That about sums it up.

Still, there they are. Hanging proudly in spite of his ignorance, in the exact spots they were created to occupy.

Yes. Everything is just-so and in its place. In fact, the only thing out of place… is Adam.

Adam Walker. Five-feet-ten inches of perfect dark chestnut hair, skin and teeth, wearing merely a pair of barely-there briefs. He's from a small town in the middle of nowhere-you've-ever-heard-of, where once upon a time he would have laughed to hear he'd awake in Paris one day.

Yet here he is.

Despite humble beginnings and years of braces, he's now a sophisticated beauty, dangerously handsome with bright, intelligent green eyes and all-too-kind genetics that allow him to look five to ten years younger. It's something that's kept Vaughn guessing and intrigued. That, and Adam's quiet magnetism and gift for conversation. Navigating his way around older men has always been a talent though. Adam has "a way" about him, he's been told. A way that came treacherously early and easy to him, but at a steep price.

He runs a hand through his thick brown hair. Hair like his father's.

The memory of his father creeps back into his mind and he's reminded of their last encounter. He can still smell the tobacco on his father's breath and if he closes his eyes tightly enough, he can picture every detail, down to the dirt under his father's nails from working around the farm.

Before the memory fully resurfaces, his thoughts are cut short. Vaughn's up and clanking around the kitchen, which brings a tiny smirk to his face.

Vaughn Parker, the COO of WorldTek France is making him breakfast in bed.

He sheds his black designer briefs like snakeskin and glances at the clock on the nightstand.

Eight thirty-seven. *Where has the time gone?*

He composes himself, hops out of bed, and messes up the covers. The cold hardwood floor bites at the soles of his feet as he strolls through the open French doors that lead to the living area.

Vaughn is at the stove, plating something, with his dark brown eyes glued to the TV in the kitchen.

Thankfully, Adam notes, the kitchen and living space look far more modern than the bedroom. It's as if Vaughn's flat has a split personality… Nothing but moody pink fluff in the bedroom, while the kitchen houses masculine stainless steel and glass surrounding an oversized island. The living room furniture is sleek and modern without much fuss: A gray sofa with steel legs. Two matching chairs. A white mid-century coffee table. Sparse artwork on the walls and two tall matching silver lamps. A shag rug sprouts from the wood floor, making the space almost cozy.

There's a door that leads to a small second bedroom Vaughn uses as an office with only a desk and paperwork to be found there. Then, another door that hides the bathroom and a plunge tub they christened on their third night together. Every time Vaughn walks by, he remembers their splashing and the suds on the floor. Adjacent to all this is a small wrought-iron balcony. It's barely large enough for two people but offers a decent view of the city and busy cobblestone street below. You can even see the very top of the Eiffel Tower over the stone rooftops if you lean far enough in the right direction.

The sun is out, but it's starting to rain, which reminds Adam of something his grandmother would say in this case.

"The devil's beatin' his wife..." She'd say this lightly and shake her graying head as if the devil and his wife actually lived next door and she could hear them cursing and fighting through the walls.

Vaughn peels his eyes from the news as his peripheral vision catches Adam's naked flesh saunter by. He watches Adam open the double doors and stand in the rain, baring it all on his balcony for the world to see.

"*The fuck are you doin'?*" Vaughn's voice is rash and scolding, but in the end, he can't keep that shit-eating grin off his face. Like the rain, he bathes Adam's body with his gaze. It washes from the hollow of Adam's neck, down through the peaks of his chest and past his chiseled abdomen, dripping down to the mass of weight that hangs between his thighs.

In the daylight, the faint discolored web of scars scattered along Adam's chest and thighs are visible. Adam's told Vaughn they're from a motorcycle accident when he was sixteen, that he was on the back when his older cousin skidded and flipped the bike off the side of the highway. But that isn't true. He knows the true story behind his scars is more than Vaughn can stomach.

Adam tilts his head back and exhales into the sky, tasting the rain on his tongue.

5

Vaughn's jaw draws tight, realizing this little show might indeed be noticed by Ms. Prouvaire, who constantly waters her plants on the next balcony. She's one of those rich widows who shows her age by waking up at six every morning to vacuum and clean house, all for company who never visits. Adam has only passed her in the hallway once to know what she looks like, and doubts she'd recognize him should their paths cross again.

According to Vaughn, her first husband was loaded.

Old money.

Real estate.

They had six kids who grew up to be trust fund brats, scattered about the globe now. A daughter in Marrakesh who married much too young but seems happy. A son in Miami who runs a porn studio, or at least that's the rumor. Another son in Jersey with a nasty coke habit who's twice divorced. The rest she's lost track of.

Adam glances over at her overflowing terrace, taking in the bright blooms she cares for in place of her absent children. She's managed to birth beauty out of seeds and dirt and sheer determination, and in return, they've given her something to take care of. They give the old girl something to look forward to in a house devoid of family and the rumblings of sticky-fingered grandchildren running about.

Adam frowns weakly at the thought of this, then throws Vaughn a wicked smile. He leans back against the railing, daring Vaughn to come get him.

Vaughn shoots Adam an annoyed glare before stomping over and snagging him inside. "Babe, come eat. Your waffles'll get cold."

Store-bought waffles. He acts as if he's made them from

scratch. Adam smiles anyway and accepts the warm plate of dry waffles, egg whites, and what he guesses to be turkey sausage. Early on, he noted Vaughn to be especially sedulous concerning his diet. Vaughn would labor over his menu at restaurants, calculating carbs and calories as Adam idly watched, savoring his icy martini. When Vaughn does cook at the flat, everything is either low-fat-this, organic-that, sugar-free or just flat out tastes like Styrofoam.

The old fitness magazines in Vaughn's bathroom tell the story of a forty-four-year-old man desperately fighting gravity. Adam thankfully has the metabolism of a teenage boy on speed. He can eat anything by the boatload and not gain an ounce. He has no idea where these good genes come from. He figures that science and the gay gods have smiled upon him, granting him favor. His muscular frame and abs aren't going anywhere soon. Vaughn, on the other hand, seems to have jumped on this health kick a few years too late. Plus, the pills in his medicine cabinet tell Adam what he hasn't offered to divulge. High cholesterol. Low libido…

Men like Vaughn hold tight to their secrets, thinking their flashy lifestyles and bank accounts are evidence enough of who they are. He's rich and powerful. What else does Adam need to know, right?

The first time Adam saw him, during a press conference for WorldTek's new Paris headquarters, he nearly dropped the remote.

Vaughn has a face the camera loves. A bald head and smooth skin the color of bitter dark chocolate. Regal features, thick lips over white teeth with salt and pepper seasoning his razor-sharp beard. His large, solid build reminds Adam of an old teddy bear. Soft and cuddly in all the right spots, which is a nice way of saying he has a gut.

Still, Vaughn's attractive – and he knows it.

It didn't take long for the two to be introduced once Adam arrived in Paris. Nor did it take long for Vaughn to invite him to his flat for a nightcap that he never made and conversation that soon turned to pillow talk.

Vaughn doesn't believe in wasting time with formalities. Adam liked this about him immediately.

They met at a gala at the Musée du Louvre, a fundraiser for Juvenile Myelomonocytic Leukemia, which Adam didn't realize is a thing but apparently is.

WorldTek was a major sponsor for the event and Vaughn had just relocated to accept the role as the Paris division's COO. In a sense, it was also his coming-out party, his first public event among his peers since accepting the role.

Vaughn stood out in a sea of tuxedos that night. The alpha. Hated by his new male colleagues, who held tight to their bourbons and scowls, and wanted by a number of women in the room, who strutted by like glittering peacocks. Game faces on. Pouty red lips. Fuck-me pumps. Plunging gashes in their sequin gowns that threatened wardrobe malfunctions.

The majority of his peers were simply curious about Vaughn. *Who was this handsome American with the beautiful dark skin?*

The women nursed their martinis and whispered among themselves.

"Handsome and *no ring…?*"

"Must be gay."

"Sabine, you think everyone's gay."

Meanwhile, the men were just as gossipy.

"There goes Mr. Big Shot. That's one smug motherfucker."

"What makes him so damn special?"

"I hear he never loses. There isn't a deal he can't close."

The high six-figure offer raised eyebrows on the board, and the move had happened fast – so fast that Vaughn quickly found himself working between Paris and Chicago, and had yet to fully transition to the new flat when he met Adam that night at the gala.

The spark between them was undeniable. Vaughn took Adam home that night, after Adam knocked into him, spilling a deep blood-red Shiraz down his shirt. They made it a few feet in the door before getting tangled in each other and collapsing on the floor. Vaughn was forceful, almost savage in the way he removed Adam's tux with the smell of expensive wine on his breath and 8-hour-old cologne lingering at his collar. His appetite was voracious – violent – but Adam barely flinched when Vaughn grabbed him by the throat and started to squeeze.

Adam grinned back, egging him on. Thinking of all those stupid women from the party who never stood a chance.

The next morning Adam awoke in his own hotel room. He assessed the damages in the bathroom mirror – a little bruising and a few inflamed scratches – then wrapped a scarf around his neck and met Vaughn at a café near Le Marais for roasted strawberry tartines and coffee. That was the beginning of their romance.

After a few dates and rounds of death-defying sex, it was official. Vaughn Parker was hooked.

Now, in what Adam cynically calls "the honeymoon stage" of their relationship, the two meet whenever Vaughn has a free night or weekend off, which is rare. There's not much time for a relationship when you're overseeing one of the largest solar technology corporations in Europe, one could argue – as Vaughn often does.

Adam often calls to find him in a meeting or about to hop on a conference call, and it's pointless leaving a message with his assistant. His best strategy is to wait it out and allow Vaughn to feel guilty for his own absence.

In the beginning, during what Adam called the "interview period," there were numerous canceled dinner dates and promises. There were times when Vaughn had to fly back to Chicago suddenly, without explanation. There were times when Vaughn didn't call for days, but Adam never launched complaints. He's been careful not to exhibit a burning need for a boyfriend, something so many of Vaughn's past conquests craved, ultimately leading to their demise. They had all been much younger and clingier – eager to enjoy the lavish lifestyle a man like Vaughn could provide.

When his schedule allows, Vaughn tries to make good on his broken promises the best way he knows how. He takes pride in introducing Adam to Paris and teaching him little phrases like, "Combien cela coûte?" – which Adam pretends to not already know as they browse boutiques along the Rue Saint-Honoré. Their time together always proves exciting, and amidst the glittering dinner dates and private opera booths, Adam has discovered a different side of Vaughn Parker. Sure, he's the only person he knows who always wears a suit (no matter where they go, night or day), but Vaughn's reputation as a hard-edged corporate shark quickly subsides when they're together.

Vaughn makes bad jokes.

He melts at the sight of kittens.

He loves cartoons.

He cries when people win on game shows.

He really *does* want world peace!

Remarkably, Vaughn can be incredibly goofy and affectionate when he wants to; so much so that Adam sometimes forgets, just for a moment, that the man runs an international dynasty – with all the stress of managing thousands of employees and billions of dollars right at his fingertips.

"How'd you sleep?" Vaughn's words suddenly cut through Adam's thoughts.

He falters for just a moment, then produces a smile. "Like the dead."

"You've barely taken a bite."

Adam frowns at the lukewarm breakfast, realizing he's lost track of time again. He looks back to meet Vaughn's gaze, thinking fast. "Actually, I think I'd rather have a bite of you." He adds a wink for good measure.

Vaughn grins, satisfied with this. It feels good to be wanted at his age and nice to know that he can still bed a guy like Adam. He could hardly believe his blind luck when Adam bumped into him at the gala. It felt like kismet... but there was also something theatrical about it at the time... like something Vaughn has seen in a movie somewhere.

Had Adam meant to bump into him?

Adam glances at the time on the stove and sneaks a hand inside Vaughn's robe.

"Mmm..." Vaughn hits him with that signature grin of his and kisses him hard on the mouth as they abandon their plates. They quickly make their way to the bedroom and melt on the expensive sheets like butter in a hot skillet.

Adam unties Vaughn's robe and allows himself to be pinned to the mattress like a butterfly under glass. Vaughn's breath is heavy on Adam's neck, like the weight of too much cologne.

Adam closes his eyes and waits for what must come next. His heart races as he feels Vaughn's weight shift and his lips inch closer. He thinks about how many times he's done this. He thinks about the very first time and how difficult it all had been. Although he'd known what to do, it didn't make the job any easier. The anticipation had been too much – so much that he'd worked himself into a frenzy. Now he knows how to stay in control. Now it all feels like second nature.

The air in the room abruptly goes still, as if time has stopped. Adam senses the distance growing between them and opens his eyes to find Vaughn squinting down at him, as if seeing him for the first time. "Babe, what is it?"

Vaughn smiles softly and strokes Adam's bottom lip with his thumb. "I know it's only been a few weeks, but—" He makes a tortured face. "You mean a lot to me. I'm so glad you bumped into me that night. Even if you did ruin my shirt."

Adam manages a smile.

"I think I'm falling in love with you," Vaughn says.

Adam's breath catches in the back of his throat, but he's careful not to react as Vaughn leans in with a stale kiss that seems to last forever. Finally, he hears the wet sound of their lips breaking apart. He exhales and opens his eyes, just as the front door explodes open with a bang.

• • •

"Vaughn!"

They both look to find a woman standing in the doorway with her fists dug into her hips, sheer horror smeared across her twisted face.

"*You son-of-a-bitch!*" She charges them. She grabs the closest thing in reach (the vase of flowers in the sitting area) and chucks it across the room!

It's clear that this is no random psychotic woman who has wandered into Vaughn's flat and interrupted their breakfast-in-bed.

This woman has a key.

She also has a ring. A three-carat yellow stone on her finger that flashes at Adam like a warning sign.

Not a girlfriend.

Not a fiancé.

This is most certainly something more.

Vaughn only confirms this by hopping up to cover his hard-on. He suddenly looks like a wide-eyed toddler caught with his hand in the cookie jar. Inanely trying to hide the evidence.

"So, this is your new Paris client that's keepin' you so busy, huh?" She cocks her head to the side and rakes her eyes over Adam.

"Tonya, wait, wait – *baby…*" He arches his eyebrows. "It's not what it looks like."

Tonya and Adam both roll their eyes at this. *Caught in the act and that's the best he can come up with?*

She reaches toward the bookshelf, launching books and anything she can get her hands on in their direction. She curses the air and screams like a banshee as Adam ducks a picture frame, caught in the crossfire. Vaughn's words are lost in the storm. Whatever he's saying has no effect. *"How fucking stupid do you think I am?"* She pauses as if waiting for an answer to her rhetorical question.

Vaughn looks as if he might answer. *Should he answer?* She's completely thrown him by showing up like this. He quietly wonders what time she left their brownstone in Chicago to get to Paris. He imagines her on the plane, fuming in first-class for hours.

Now that foreign objects are no longer hurling through the air, Adam gets a good look at Tonya.

She's American. She's beautiful. Even through the anger in her smoky eyes, he can see this. Her makeup is flawless over skin like maple syrup in the sunlight. She wears a designer dress that stops short to show off a set of killer legs and impossibly high heels. Her long dark hair ends in blonde ombre tips, curling down her back. Her nails are bubblegum-pink claws with rhinestone nail art. Bejeweled talons that clutch tightly at one of Vaughn's awards. It looks heavy but ready for liftoff. Ready to make contact with one of their skulls.

She's attractive. Still, she doesn't look like a woman you might imagine a man like Vaughn being married to.

Married!

She looks young and flashy. Not quite reality TV housewife material, but more like a basketball player's wife with her oversized earrings and yellow Hermès bag hanging off her skinny arm. "There's a naked man in our bed!" She bellows and turns her attention to Adam, pointing the bronzed statue. *"I don't know who the hell you are, but—"*

"Your problem is *not* with me," Adam bites back. "I had no idea this was your husband!" He glares at Vaughn, who's shrunk two sizes by now.

"Like hell your ass didn't!" She reaches into her bag with her free hand.

Shit.

Did she bring a gun?

She digs deep and comes out pointing something in their

14

direction.

It's *pink*.

Not a gun.

A Taser?

It flashes at them as strikes of light burst from her pink phone case.

"Goddamnit! Enough!" Vaughn covers his face in vain, making a move to grab the phone.

Tonya sneers and raises her arm with his award, set to throw.

"Baby, look, let's all just sit down and talk about this. Alright?" His palms are out, trying to calm her. He offers a smile. That winning smile again.

Ugh.

She flings the statue. It shoots past Adam's head, barely missing, and bounces off the headboard with a sickening thud. She lashes out and clocks Vaughn across the face. Before he can recover, she pummels her fists into his chest.

Adam takes this as his cue to leave as Vaughn tries to restrain her and himself from fighting back. Tonya's throwing punches like a heavyweight now. Likely something she's learned at some random cardio kickboxing class while Vaughn was at work. She never fathomed she'd have to use it on her cheating husband one day.

She fights and struggles against him. Tears ruin her makeup as she screams, "How could you *do* this to us? Why?! Wasn't I enough for you?!"

Words like *lawyer* and *divorce* are thrown out as Adam steps into his briefs, grabbing his clothes on the way out. Vaughn shoots him a look full of embarrassment as he tries to control the situation, but Tonya is a ticking bomb that he doesn't know how to defuse.

There's something else in his frantic eyes. It's almost as if they're pleading for Adam to stay, despite Tonya's tirade. Stay, despite the fact that a wife has materialized and caught her husband with another man. His eyes plead for Adam to stay through the blast and not give up on him, despite the mess he's made.

Adam already knows how this will play out.

Of course, Vaughn will do whatever it takes to appease her and keep this out of the press. Gay skeletons in the closet are bad for business. He'll pay her whatever she wants, give her their home back in the States and maybe the beach house in The Hamptons if her lawyer is any good. But he really isn't fazed by getting caught with his pants down.

Not really.

Should Adam resurface in a few weeks, or even months later, he'd be right there to wine and dine him back into his life with pricey bottles of champagne and romantic French phrases. He'd fix up the flat again, and replace the broken pieces and furniture. No. He'd buy a new place *for the two of them*. He'd let Adam pick it out – perhaps some urban chic penthouse this time. He'd let Adam decorate and move his clothes into the other half of the closet. He'd try to pick up where they left off with frozen waffles, rough sex, and I love yous as if he's never been caught.

Adam takes one last look at the scene. Tonya is hysterical, like a wildcat. Distraught and ruined. Vaughn's eyes fix on Adam as he holds tight to her wrists, fending her off.

Adam glares back with cold green eyes and watches something shift in Vaughn's expression. He sees Vaughn doing the math in his head... calculating what will happen to his career if the pictures Tonya just took go public... calculating how much a divorce of this scale could actually cost… calculating the number of schmucks at WorldTek who'd rally for his dismissal at the first sign of a scandal…

Adam watches callously as Vaughn crunches the numbers, carries the one, and concludes that he stands to lose it all. Including the man he loves.

It's the coup de grâce to the morning as Adam blinks and slams the door on his way out.

● ● ●

Adam dresses in the elevator, escaping the scene of the crime. It's an archaic freight elevator that doesn't lend much privacy as he descends through the spiraling staircase, where a couple and their daughter are walking up, likely on their way back from church.

Not knowing what else to do, he dares to wave at them, shirtless and in his underwear. They've probably heard Vaughn and Tonya arguing upstairs, their razor-sharp words echoing and falling down the stairway like lightning. *The devil and his wife…*

He zips his jeans and quickly exits the building, making his way across the street and down a few blocks. Never looking back. Once out of view of Vaughn's balcony, he stops to collect himself. He bums a light and a cigarette from a handsome street artist with kind eyes. He's blonde and looks barely twenty, unpacking his paints and brushes for the day. He says his name is Émile and asks in hurried French if Adam wants his portrait done. There's something familiar and beguiling in the way he asks. Adam declines but tips him anyway. He can feel Émile's eyes follow as he strolls away, down the sidewalk of sightseers. He takes a long, much-needed drag and pulls the hood of his jacket over his head.

It's still drizzling outside.

Finally, after walking a few blocks, he settles into a small pub. The wood sign that hangs over the door is peeling, and he barely makes out the name, *Villes Jumelles*, scribed in faded blue paint across the weathered slab of wood. It's an inconspicuous, rundown bar that's usually empty, apart from the locals who come for the cheap beer. Inside, it's hard to make out the faces of the shiftless shadows who drink from their mugs, eyes fixed on the football game playing over the bar. PSG is behind by two goals.

Adam tears his eyes from the game with a scowl and plops down at the bar. A pencil-thin man with a wide smile slides a napkin over. He looks like a Tim Burton character with his dark oversized eyes, thin hair, and ghost-white complexion. The sleeves of his dark gray shirt are rolled up, ready to mix and concoct dangerous elixirs and potions garnished with maraschino cherries. "What can I get for you today, sir?" He asks in a bad American accent. The words come out like an '80s French-to-English cassette tape brought to life.

It occurs to Adam that he must look a bit touristy amidst the bar's patrons. Out of place once again.

He peers at the array of bottles that line the top shelf like sparkling artifacts, and orders a vodka with St-Germain on the rocks in perfect French. It doesn't make him feel any more like a local or do much to impress the bartender, who makes his drink without comment and promptly returns his attention to the game.

"Beaucoup." Adam nurses his drink and wonders what's happening at Vaughn's flat. How much will Vaughn confess about their time together? He imagines Tonya torturing the details out of him. Slow twists and jabs, demanding a full confession.

Will Vaughn tell her they frequented Chartier, one of her favorite restaurants?

Will he tell her Adam has a key?

Will he tell her he's fallen in love with Adam?

He instantly frowns at the thought. It's been years since anyone has mentioned the "L" word to him, and *that* had ended so badly he didn't think he'd ever recover. The idea of someone being in love with him, even just hearing the words, was more than he was prepared to deal with that morning.

Adam nearly spills his drink as the room suddenly erupts, cheering for a goal on the T.V.

He sighs and closes his eyes, pulling at the charm at the end of his necklace – a pair of sterling silver cherries with the initials A.W. engraved on the back.

He suddenly misses home more than ever.

· · ·

Roughly an hour later, Adam hears the door open followed by a rush of cool air. He's been daydreaming while the weather outside took a turn for the worse. The sky has finally opened, and people outside are walking by with umbrellas.

The door bangs shut, and Adam watches the bartender's expression dim. He says something under his breath, too quick for Adam to translate, and turns from the game to greet the new arrival with a fresh napkin on the bar.

The room has grown quiet again, except for the occasional sports-induced uproar.

Adam ashes his cigarette into his empty glass and turns to see Tonya sitting one stool away at the bar. Her curls and makeup have been defeated by the storm outside, and her clothes are completely drenched as if she's been walking in the rain like a zombie. She stares dead ahead, eying her reflection in the mirror behind the bar.

The bartender leans forward, panicked by her appearance, and asks if she's alright, forgetting to speak English. Adam doesn't know how much French Tonya actually knows, but she seems oblivious to him.

Adam clears his throat, and she comes to life, blinking out of a trance. "A shot of Patrón." It sounds more like a declaration than a request.

She tosses the shot back, and Adam watches as she dutifully reaches into her bag to produce a thick #10 envelope. She sniffs, wipes at her nose, and places the envelope on the empty barstool between them.

PSG scores again, and the room screams at the television.

Tonya makes a wasted attempt to fix her hair and clears her throat, "I guess one day I'll have to explain this to the baby." She suddenly chuckles to herself amidst the chaos and hunches her shoulders. Then the tears come, filling her eyes as she bends and starts to sob. Real tears this time.

Adam quickly tucks the envelope inside his jacket without an answer. His blank stare is enough to put an end to her crying.

Vaughn never mentioned it, but of course Adam knew about the baby. A newborn is just one more detail, like Tonya, that he'd conveniently left behind in Chicago. He'd abandoned his family with the rest of his clothes and belongings, promising to send for them when the time was right. He told Tonya he needed time to establish some roots. He needed time to prepare things for their arrival... Time for their designer to complete the nursery, and so on. But somewhere along the way, he'd lost track of time... with Adam.

"It's all there," Tonya says softly with as much dignity as she could muster.

He doesn't insult her by counting it. "I thought you were gonna take my head off back there, you know." He smirks and zips up his jacket.

An ironic little smile makes its way to her lips, followed by a pause. It's clear now that they've reached the end of their contract. Adam's job is done, and he'll be onto his next client, Tonya realizes. She exhales sharply and extends a hand. "*Thank you, Michael...*" Her smile fades. "For everything."

It feels like a back-handed compliment in a way. A bitter-sweet show of gratitude for dismantling life as she knows it.

Adam kills his cigarette in the glass of half-melted ice. It hisses before dying as he stands to leave.

"Just doin' my job." He shrugs and firmly shakes her hand.

He leaves the pub, saying goodbye to Tonya and the city of Paris. He says goodbye to Vaughn Parker and the memories they've created. The rough sex, the pretty lies tied up neatly with satin bows, and the man Vaughn had come to love – *Michael Reis*, an alias he'd given Vaughn at the beginning of his contract with Tonya. A character of sorts required for the job.

He leaves it all behind as he drops the fake driver's license from his wallet into a nearby trashcan and heads to the airport.

1 / THE HOOK

A moody melody hangs in the air, like incense, as *Quinn Harris* deflates onto his mat.

He's surrounded by a gang of sweaty blonde Stepford wives wearing ironic tank tops with sayings like SLAY ALL DAY. Behind them are a few stragglers mixed among the usual 5:30 yoga class.

He can't stop thinking about a dream he's had the night before. He vividly recalls being in Paris, where even the air itself smelled different – full of pastry flour. The entire dream was in black and white and he was speaking French, which is especially odd considering he doesn't speak French at all. It couldn't have been actual French, he realizes now. Just his mind's idea of what French might sound like in a dream. He's struggling to remember more details, struggling to weave the fragments into a clear picture. He vaguely recalls sitting in a bar at one point. There were televisions on the walls playing sports and the entire space was poorly lit but somehow felt comforting and safe, like a womb. It felt as if he'd been there before, although he's sure he hasn't. He's never left the East Coast, let alone stepped foot in France.

"Breathe in relaxation… exhale your tension…" Giselle whispers for the hundredth time, cutting into his thoughts.

The class lies completely still with closed eyelids, spread out like corpses on the bamboo floor. Bodies defeated by too many Downward-*Facing Dogs* and ready to be outlined with chalk. "Let your worries and stress from the day sink into the mat," Giselle's placid voice circles the room.

Quinn takes the opportunity to sneak a peek at *Tomas*. He lies across from Quinn looking peaceful and enticing with sweat glazing his arms. Tomas is one-part golden skin, one-part gray eyes, with dreadlocks he keeps tied up in a messy bun. His loose graphic tee and shorts do a poor job of hiding his toned physique. Every Downward-*Facing Dog* reveals strong soccer legs and granite abs. Every Balasana pose highlights his curvy glutes.

Quinn can think of hundreds of yoga-inspired positions he'd love to put Tomas in.

The Hidden Serpent.

The Naughty Ostrich.

The Raging Bull.

If only he had the guts to talk to him after class.

Tomas never makes it easy though. He usually rushes off, probably home to his boyfriend, Quinn imagines, who must be equally hot if not hotter. The two probably have crazy Tantric sex every night after vaping and eating a carefully planned organic GMO-free dinner that tastes bland but leaves them satisfied knowing the veggies come from their own garden. Quinn has imagined the garden. There are cherry tomatoes, cucumbers, squash, basil, blueberries, cilantro (that doesn't grow so well over the summer), sweet peppers, zucchini, and they're trying their hand at kale now. But it's not Tomas with the green thumb... more likely his hot boyfriend who's probably an oncologist by day and drives a red Prius with an

HRC sticker plastered on the bumper. His name's probably something stupid like Chet or Wilson.

Quinn's mind often wanders into deep waters like this, conjuring up the worst when it isn't occupied with work or other dealings.

It wouldn't take much to verify Tomas' relationship status, among other things. If Quinn truly wants to, if his conscience would allow him, he could uncover Tomas' entire life story in a matter of minutes. *If he has a boyfriend. If he's had any run-ins with the law. The name and current location of his fourth-grade teacher. The name and city of the hospital he was born in. A complete background check and credit score of the doctor who delivered him...* As an investigative journalist, this is what he does all day. Uncover the facts. And as easy as it would be to learn who Tomas is with a few mouse clicks, Quinn would rather let things develop naturally if they're to develop at all. There's something hopefully romantic about getting to know Tomas over coffee one day – instead of the instant gratification of cold facts on a computer screen.

Still, it's a temptation of the trade. Nearly everyone Quinn works with runs a full background check before first dates, and Quinn has been fighting the urge ever since laying eyes on Tomas.

Quinn's mousy brown hair is matted to his forehead, and he's a sweaty mess. It occurs to him that Tomas has only seen him like this, never dressed up. He may never see him looking his best or know how well he cleans up. He's actually quite striking when he puts in the effort.

"Let's have one more deep breath," Giselle says to wind the class down. She's a size-two sun-goddess blonde with perfect abs and a thin South African accent. The Stepfords would

24

hate her if she wasn't so nice to everyone.

Quinn jolts at the high-pitched sound of chimes slicing through the thickness of the air, signaling the end of class.

"Thank you for joining me this evening," Giselle purrs, "I hope you have a peaceful evening and to see you next time. Namaste."

"Namaste," they chant back on cue, like a cult.

A sigh escapes Quinn as he opens his eyes. The yellow fluorescent lights flicker on, transporting him back to life as he knows it. Back to studio B. He rolls over to find Tomas facing him. His gray eyes lock with Quinn's, and his lips shift into a sort of half-smile. Just a polite show of acknowledgment. Nothing more.

Quinn panics a little but returns the gesture.

This is it, he realizes.

He should say something.

Anything.

Introduce yourself, he thinks. Tell him you want to have his babies and you know how to grow cilantro. *Just say anything!*

Words begin to take shape but get tangled on his tongue, refusing to form a sentence.

Tomas stands to roll up his mat.

The moment is fleeting.

Tomas slips on his sneakers.

Going...

Tomas shoots Giselle a smile on his way out and holds the door for the person behind him.

Gone.

Well played, Quinn. He grimaces from his spot on the floor. He'll have to wait a whole week to try again. His job is demanding and idle time like this, for yoga or even a day

25

at the museum, is a luxury.

He's a journalist for *The Chronicle*, where lately he's starting to question his career choice.

"Seriously, Ren," he confided with his co-worker *Renaldo Davis*, a burly native New Yorker with an unruly afro who writes for the sports section. "I just interviewed a sixteen-year-old 'up and coming' rapper named Cinnamon, who could barely fucking spell cinnamon. Meanwhile, Justin gets sent to an immigration detention camp in Brownsville, where 1,400 migrant children are being held, separated from their parents. You tell me which story you'd read."

Ren merely scoffed and shook his head, his curly afro swaying in tow.

"I'm tired of landing these fluffy, human-interest stories. If I have to interview one more beauty queen, I swear I'll blow my fucking brains out on this desk."

"Just pass me the gun first," Ren said without looking from his screen. "I've been on the road for two weeks now. I miss my bed, and I miss my wife. I even miss those badass kids," he smirked, meaning his two-year-old twins. Judging from their adorable photos scattered on his desk, you'd never believe the boys are the terrors Ren paints them to be.

A longing crept into Quinn's green eyes. "At least you get to travel."

"To locker rooms that smell like balls, full of primadonna football players," Ren shuttered. "You can have it. Wait. Actually, that *is* your cup of tea, ain't it?"

"Touché." Quinn mused, "I hear Justin's getting the next cover story."

"His writing's mediocre at best. Man, you can write circles around that douche."

"Doesn't matter if no one wants to read it," Quinn said crossing his arms with a sigh. "I miss writing hard news."

Ren turned in his chair to give him a meaningful look, "You should talk to Marcus."

Marcus Styles is the new Editor-in-Chief at *The Chronicle*. A stout, distinguished-looking family man in his early fifties with mocha skin, a full gray beard, and orange rimmed glasses he's constantly pushing back in place. He's the magazine's first African American Editor-in-Chief, and Quinn, the son of a fiery Irish mother and hard-knuckled first-generation Italian father, is proud to work for him. Marcus is one of the smartest men he knows. Decisive. Woke. Always two steps ahead.

Surely, he's done his homework on Quinn. He must have read some of Quinn's better investigative work at *The Herald* and *The Voice*. Surely, he knows what Quinn is capable of.

Quinn may not be the biggest shark in the newsroom, but his instincts are razor-sharp. He has a gut for news. He graduated with honors from NY State, and quickly made a bit of a name for himself within New York's writing community, although writing hadn't always been his passion. He'd more so just fell into it and realized he was good at it… so he's never stopped.

Perhaps surprisingly, he'd aspired to be an astronaut when he was younger. Rocketing through the cosmos on deep-space missions, making scientific discoveries on distant planets. His parents thought it was cute when he was five, but as the passion persisted well into his teens, the horror slowly set in that he was serious.

He's seen nearly every vintage sci-fi film you can name, which now merely serves as a fun fact he throws out during icebreakers at networking events. *Deep Space Millennium. Battle of the Galaxies. Clones from Outer Space.* He can recite them from memory and has a beloved affection for the cheap special effects of '50s sci-fi cult films, often leaving him frowning at big-budget CGI movies. His knowledge of space exploration is vast. He can even name the crew from the Voskhod 1 mission, the first space crew with one pilot and two passengers. The capsule was so crowded that the crew didn't wear spacesuits. Afterwards everyone suffered terribly from space sickness.

He spent his teens with his head in science books, studying rockets and aerophysics. At night, he'd lay in his backyard and stare into the heavens, believing that one day he'd be among the stars.

By high school, he had it all figured out.

Step 1: Space Camp. He knew he had to sell his parents on this whole astronaut idea, so going was truly more of a P.R. tour. He had to show them he could do it. Also, what better way to start meeting real astronauts and get his foot in the door?

Step 2: He had to be in good health. Blanca Jimenez casually told him this on his third day of Space Camp, and he'd committed it to memory, like everything else the veteran astronaut told him. Physically, he knew he could meet NASA's requirements. Step 2 was the least of his worries. His 20/20 vision was a miracle since both parents and most of his family wear glasses. He's always been active. Fit. No history of family diseases or ailments that might raise a flag on a medical exam. He even ran cross country his freshman year to start building stamina, despite hating the muddy, hot days in the sun.

Step 3: A bachelor's degree in engineering, biological, or physical science. Grades weren't a problem, but he knew he'd have to get into a school with a good program. He wasted no time identifying the top three in the country and established a backup list. He rallied for his teachers to write recommendations and took the reins of his high school science club. The more feathers in his cap, the better his chances would be one day in a lineup.

Step 4: He knew he'd need at least three years of professional experience, which translated into becoming a test pilot. There's no way around 1,500 plus mandatory flight hours and he had no interest in joining The Air Force, so he set his sights on getting his pilot's license at sixteen. Back then, his mother worried enough at the idea of him getting his permit to drive, now Quinn wanted to fly a plane...

Everything hinged on how well he could fly.

The memory of this sometimes passes through the back of his mind, even years later as a journalist with his feet very much on the ground. How odd where life takes you. Now, instead of fighting for a place among the stars, he's fighting for his moment in the sun.

He decided to take Ren's advice and marched into Marcus' office. "I'm tired of writing fluff," he said flatly. "Interviewing the 'Ten Top Social Media Influencers' isn't what I signed up for." He instantly regretted that last part. He doesn't know Marcus well enough to tell if Marcus might fire him. There are thousands of journalists in New York who'd gladly take his place.

Marcus looked at him pensively, then pushed his glasses back onto his nose. "What would you rather be writing?"

It's such a simple question; it was almost insulting. "Real investigative work!" Quinn paced in front of Marcus' desk. "I want to get my hands dirty. I want to *travel*. D.C. sex scandals. Cold cases. Human trafficking. *Anything* but beauty pageants and celebrity chefs."

After thirty years in the business, Marcus found this amusing but kept a straight face. "You want to 'get your hands dirty, huh, youngblood?'" He leaned back in his chair and crossed his arms.

"I'm a big boy. I can handle the hard stuff. You know I can."

Marcus could send him to Tunisia to cover a fracking lead that came over the wire. The weather and the mosquitoes are especially miserable this time of year there. Then there's a rather nasty sex offender case in Phoenix everyone was buzzing about. Something to do with a past congressman. If the heat doesn't break him, the feeding frenzy in Phoenix will, Marcus thought. But then he caught something in Quinn's eyes that gave him pause. He saw a hunger that reminded him of his own former life as a journalist… Breaking and entering, secret rendezvous with his source at The White House, bribing the police. He's been arrested. He's been shot at. He's done things he would never confess to, even to this day, in order to protect his family. Marcus had been reckless at Quinn's age. He'd been fearless, and no cost had been too great for a story. He silently wondered how far Quinn is willing to go.

"What's the hook? Bring me a story," he said. "Something *new*. Something no one's doing right now. Something I can really sink my teeth into." He leaned across his desk and made his next words deliberate. "Bring me something that scares you."

Something that scares him.

Quinn has been banging his head against a wall all afternoon, looking for a story to help prove himself to be the writer he knows he is. He had hoped yoga would help clear his head, but Tomas, in all his glory, had distracted him.

He now leaves the yoga studio feeling lighter, although his mind is just as heavy as before. He cuts through Central Park, which is alive and green, with people picnicking and playing frisbee. He takes his time walking, soaking in the lushness of the trees in bloom before hailing a taxi to travel home. Once at his modest but affordable studio apartment in Brooklyn, he showers and changes into his favorite pair of ripped jeans, a navy cotton blazer with the sleeves rolled up, and a faded vintage tee he found at a thrift store in the Village. He squeezes some gel into his palm and wrangles his unruly brown hair into a pompadour of sorts. His hair never quite does what he wants when he wants it to. He gives up and fastens a weighty necklace around his neck – a sterling silver chain with a silver dog tag on the end. A birthday gift from his best friend, Bailey.

He quickly squeezes a glob of minty paste onto his toothbrush and checks his reflection. He's due to meet Bailey at SKY, a new bar near Broadway that reviews claim to be the remedy for tired, desolate gay bars everywhere. He can't wait to see what the fuss is about. Perhaps with his shitty luck, he'll be asked to review it.

He's rushing but doubts Bailey will be on time. He rarely is.

Quinn peers into the bathroom mirror and catches a glimpse of his father glaring back, like a sign of his future. Strong Italian features. Brooding eyebrows that cast a shadow over intense green eyes. A fading boy-next-door glow masked by a five o'clock shadow. He's attractive, but certainly not modelesque like Bailey. Bailey knows how to command a room. With his looks and charm, he can practically have any

31

guy he wants.

Quinn doesn't fault him for this. Only a select few are blessed with perfect bone structure. Meanwhile, it doesn't help that men are instinctively always looking for the next best thing.

The next more *handsome* thing.

The next more *chiseled* thing.

The next *wealthier* thing.

He spits into the sink and hits the lights on his way out, wondering what the evening will bring.

He's sure Bailey will be late. He'd bet his life on it.

He also has a feeling that SKY won't live up to the hype, but for a fleeting moment, he imagines running into Tomas there. He imagines all his suspicions about a boyfriend being revealed to be unwarranted, and a smile comes over him.

Perhaps there is no boyfriend.

Perhaps there is no garden.

He imagines their chance meeting as he steps onto the elevator. He envisions Tomas at the bar, turning with surprise coloring his face. Outside of yoga, his dreads are still up but he's wearing street clothes. He offers a real smile this time as he takes Quinn in, thinking, "Damn, he cleans up good. Who knew?!"

Quinn's mind wanders as the elevator doors close, distracted by the possibility of running into Tomas.

As he ventures out, he can't possibly fathom that the dream he's had about Paris carries any real meaning. He can't possibly know that life as he knows it is about to change forever… or that his past is about to catch up with him.

If only he knew.

2 / CHARMED

Bailey Langston Alexander.

With a name fit for a soap opera character, he's fortunate his looks rise to the task.

Bailey models for Harper Diam, which means he's obscenely handsome. Thick blonde hair. Icy blue eyes. Pouty lips. He's been called a young Guy Madison, who he had to look up, upon first hearing this. He nodded at his findings online, scanning through black and white images from Guy's Hollywood career that seem to justify the comparison. They share that same All-American dreamboat aura that makes Bailey easy to approach. Add in classic chiseled features and a thousand-watt smile, and it's a dangerous mixture.

Before life as a model, it had been a long road to building a real, viable career in fashion, of all things, in a city like New York. Bailey left his hometown of Savannah with one suitcase, two hundred and thirty-three dollars in his pocket and a prayer. He worked retail and a few unpaid internships to build his resume. During the day, he kept his stomach full with cheap Chinese takeout and fruit and muffins from hotel lobbies that offered a continental breakfast. For dinner, he'd simply go on a date, and whoever sat across from him would pay for the lobster and steak he'd wash down with champagne.

He made his way up working for a handful of up-and-coming niche boutiques on the Lower East Side as a fashion buyer, a fancy title for someone who predicts what will be on-trend. During Fashion Week, his days were filled with temperamental designers, manic models, glitzy fashion shows, and celebrity afterparties that inevitably stretched into sunrise. Then comes Market Week and meetings with PR and showroom reps, all to decide how much and which designers to bring into his clients' stores.

Eventually, he convinced himself he could be a stylist fulltime and started dressing friends and anyone who would hire him. Rap artists and struggling singer/actor types. Blue-blooded Park Avenue wives. Then came one or two reality TV stars and ultimately Nicole Burris – the infamous bad-girl-turned-pop-star who had her own show for three painful seasons. You may have seen the self-proclaimed "Bronx bombshell" on Dancing with Celebs or heard her latest single on the radio. Fans love her, but Bailey knows the real Nicole Burris, and she's nothing short of a living nightmare.

He spent long days and evenings piecing together outfits and jewelry for Nicole's TV appearances. He'd sort through hundreds of gowns to find the right one for her award show invites. Even choosing the right heel sometimes took days, for all of five minutes and a pose on the red carpet. The pressure had been unimaginable. It never ended, and Nicole was increasingly difficult. *Twice* she spilled wine on samples he left with her, and it was left to him to explain it away to the design shops aware of her reputation but less than sympathetic. He'd trek all over the city from design shop to design shop, armed with her blank checks, piecing together looks to land her on the best-dressed list. When the tour started for her second album, Bailey jumped ship and never looked back. He went back into fashion buying after that, but he never stayed in one place too long.

Eventually, fate intervened. It happened as he was out making a delivery – a set of women's suede ankle boots to Sylvia Klein's shop, nothing special. He hadn't expected them to move at all, but Sylvia wanted them for a runway show that night. Somehow – he can't even remember the reason now – one of the male models was a no-show. No one even realized he was missing until ten minutes before showtime.

The clothes fit Bailey, and the rest is history.

Suddenly everything he'd been doing for the past four years made sense. The stylings, the fittings, and the relationships he'd built with designers. Even his own looks made more sense, down to the tiny mole under his left eye. It's not just a *mole*, he realized. It's a beauty mark! He'd always hated it, but now it was part of his brand and signature look. It's the thing that helps get him booked.

Growing up, he'd been gangly and awkward. His younger and older brothers were the prized football jocks. Even his statuesque younger sister swam and rode horses competitively. They were all charmed, beautiful, thoroughbred products of their southern high society parents. He'd only agreed to play soccer as a way to appease his father, who was dead set on him joining the high school football team, just as he and his brothers had done years ago. Bailey couldn't have cared less about horses or football or soccer or winning or trophies. He trained with the rest of his soccer team and his brothers on weekends because, well, what else is there when you're growing up awkward and closeted in Savannah, Georgia?

Now those years of soccer and weight training were finally paying off.

He's a working model in New York City.

He met Quinn Harris during Fashion Week three years ago. Quinn was backstage with a press pass and somehow ended up lacing Bailey into an $1,800 Vincent Beau leather corset as he smoked a cigarette and told Quinn his life story.

They were instant friends.

Bailey's looking forward to seeing Quinn tonight at SKY. He can almost taste the martinis and gossip, as he struts through the door of his SoHo loft and drops his duffel on the floor with a thud.

"Lucy, I'm home!" He does his best Ricky Ricardo accent, but there's no reply. His roommate Aubrey is never home. Or at least, never at the same time. Between her flight attending and his work travel, the two often miss each other, sometimes by a matter of minutes.

Bailey just returned from the airport, after being on assignment in Mykonos for a menswear shoot for Arold Lang. It all sounds much more glamorous than it is, of course. His tan lines and the few Euros left in his wallet are the only evidence of his exotic travels.

After a fourteen-hour flight, he arrived at a posh villa set into the hilltop of Pyrgi, overlooking the sea. He was met by Jobe, the creative director. He's worked with Jobe in Mumbai, so he was happy to see him as he entered the property, standing by the infinity pool with his unruly mustache. Jobe dropped everything to give Bailey a warm hug, muttered something in Portuguese, and escorted him to the roof of the main house where lights and cameras were in place. The backdrop of the set was a collage of lights and rooftops along the breathtaking cityscape below, leading out to the coastline. Hair and makeup appeared out of thin air, like fairies, and before Bailey knew it, he was dressed in a white linen suit and being doused with a hose. His shirt was left unbuttoned, sheer, and plastered to his abs like a second skin. The black shadow along his eyelids was smudged for effect, and his hair was slicked back with grease. The entire shoot was over in minutes, as he pouted his full lips and aimed to look sexy and *Grecian*. As if he were a part of the city itself and wore two-thousand-dollar linen suits every day like it's nothing. Meanwhile, a water rig simulated rain while he stood beneath, looking picture-perfect for the camera.

Inside, it somehow felt like he was being waterboarded.

He tried not to panic.

Benson Beauvais, the photographer, yelled directions, some of which were lost in translation through his thick accent. "Beau! Tenez maintenant cette pose!"

There were two other men Bailey didn't know in similar suits on each side of him. Each did their best not to shiver or stumble off the slick roof as a storm of camera flashes blinded them.

There was a moment when Bailey temporarily left his body and got a good look at himself, soaking wet, getting his picture taken for a fashion spread in *GQ*.

Whoever would have thought, he marveled, thinking back to his childhood. His father's red, disapproving face flashed before his eyes.

The shoot wrapped, and Bailey hardly had time to enjoy the city before he was back on a flight to New York.

He stands in front of his empty fridge now, taking his phone off airplane mode.

He grimaces as five messages instantly ring through.

Two from Quinn.
 DID YOU LAND?
 DON'T FORGET WE'RE MEETING FOR DRINKS. XOX-OXO

One from his ex, *Rami*, who however handsome, is an ex for a reason, he reminds himself.
 HEY... WHAT'S UP?

There's a text from one of the models he met on set. *Admir.* The name dances on his tongue, and he's reminded of their brief tryst in the pool the night of the shoot.
 MISSING YOU ALREADY...

There's a text from Aubrey.
 AT ORD. PICKED UP AN EXTRA FLIGHT TO ATLANTA. BACK ON TUESDAY. LOVE YOU!

Finally, he sees a voicemail from his mother.
 He lets out an explosive sigh and deletes the voicemail on sight, and cracks open a half-empty jar of pickles.
 He kicks off his leather loafers and sheds his jeans, crunching loudly as he saunters back to the freezer where a bottle of vodka awaits. He enjoys having the loft to himself like this when Aubrey's away. Most times he walks around naked, blasting 90s country music, or binge-watching all the shows he knows she'll never watch with him.
 He fills a martini glass with a handful of ice, vodka, and a splash of pickle juice from the jar. They're out of orange juice.

His eyes fall to the pile of mail on the counter.

He hates mail. Nothing good ever comes in the mail, he thinks. Just junk, bills, and bad news. Occasionally, Aubrey receives a Cosmo he'll read through on the toilet. Otherwise, it's just more *stuff* to throw away.

Bailey sifts through the bills and advertisements, making a pile for Aubrey. There's three credit card offers that he tears up, a technical school brochure that goes into his pile, and an envelope with his mother's handwriting. He rips open the envelope and pulls out a crisp check for three hundred dollars.

He frowns before taking a gulp of his martini and winces at the sour kick. Without another thought, he calmly places the check back into its envelope and rips it in half.

"Not on your life!" He says to no one in particular, feeling a wave of heat color his face. This is the third check this month. He tosses the two halves of the ripped check over his shoulder, takes a deep breath to calm himself, and makes his way to the sofa.

Just as he sits down, his phone buzzes with another message from Quinn.

ON MY WAY TO SKY. YOU BETTER BE ON TIME!

What follows is a GIF of German actress Franka Potente, racing across his screen in her fiery red wig.

He glances at the time on the microwave.

Shit.

Bailey doesn't know how he always manages to be late, but he's done it again.

He takes one last gulp of his martini and wipes his chin as he makes a run for the shower. If he's quick, he can change in ten minutes, call a car, and be at SKY in twenty, assuming traffic is decent.

He's got this.

He thinks about what to wear as he rinses the airport away, sending its scent swirling down the drain. It doesn't take long to decide on the black Dolce blazer in his closet. He'll pair it with a mesh tank top and some jeans. Maybe with his new boots. Yes, perfect.

Done!

The hot water and steam feel amazing on his skin, like a renewal or a baptism. He's thankful the water's hot since this is a constant battle with the super, an older heavyset ex-boxer from Queens who blames the building's old pipes.

Bailey can't wait to see Quinn, his normal among the chaos. Quinn always knows what to say and how to make him feel at ease, especially after a long trip. Yes. This is what he needs, he thinks. To unwind and have a drink with his best friend. It's going to be the perfect ending to a long day...

Although, his mind can't help but wander back to that voicemail from his mother, the third one this week that he's received and deleted.

He can picture her, wearing her pearls and her favorite baby blue dress that falls just below her knee, sitting alone in the parlor of his family home with her legs delicately crossed at the ankles. The wallpaper is the same as he remembers. Pale green with white and pink ambrosia growing throughout the pattern. Her hair is beauty parlor fresh... bright blonde curls swept into an elegant updo. There's a mint julep in one hand and the yellow receiver of the landline in the other. Her nails are painted blood-red, clutching tightly to her drink – so tight that the glass splinters and cuts into her hand. She doesn't react. She just stares at him with a haunting look that darkens and eats into her otherwise rosy skin.

He knows what she wants… and he doesn't need to hear the words on a recording to be reminded that time is running out.

3 / APPARITION

The entrance to SKY is an unmarked, midnight-blue canopy on Madison that New Yorkers trample past without giving glance to.

Quinn eyes the entrance. He pushes his way through a large door with a silver star logo to discover a brute of a man who cards him. He smiles, as if being carded at twenty-seven isn't more of an inconvenience than flattery, and he promptly fishes his license from his wallet.

The bouncer barely looks at it.

Once inside, he gives a nod at the scene. The entire floor is polished, stark white marble with a skylight running the length of the tin ceiling with a few stars in view. He melts at the sight, realizing he's forgotten all about his old friends, the stars. He hardly looks up anymore. He's been living in New York so long, where the city lights mask their glow, he's forgotten they're still there. He's also long forgotten the crafty child who would camp in his backyard under the night sky, convincing his parents to pay for space camp.

Pendant lights hang over the bar, and soft blue lighting filters down over a row of private booths in tufted black leather. There are a few plasma screens on the walls, some with music videos and others with closed-caption evening news. He's surprised to see the foggy entrance to an ice bar tucked away in a corner.

Are ice bars *in* again?

He's eager to see the menu – likely a 4-star collage of tapas, sushi, and overpriced martinis. The stage has been set for a young, metropolitan audience, with men wall-to-wall as far as the eye can see.

There's a rift in the air, like a record skipping, as he moves through the crowd to find Bailey. He leaves a trail of intrigue behind him, like fresh blood coursing through a hoard of piranhas. He can feel eyes burning into his back, quietly sizing him up. His skin glows hot. He hates always being first to arrive. He never knows what to do with himself or what to do with his hands. The thought of striking up a conversation with strangers makes him sweaty and agitated. Why can't Bailey just be on time? The last time they'd met for Thai he even tried *out-lating* Bailey, but he still arrived first! Quinn had sat alone for fifteen minutes before Bailey roamed in without an apology.

Now, once again, he finds history repeating itself.

Having no one to converse with, he decides to find a seat at the bar, but even the bartender is too busy for banter. Quinn watches as she attends to the growing line, pouring frothy IPAs from a tap. He watches the foam spill over the side of the glass and trail down her fingers, covering her black fingernail polish. It's only once he has a beer in his hand that he relaxes his shoulders a bit and remembers he meant to keep an eye out for Tomas.

A few people dance near the DJ booth, but none of them look like Tomas. The ice bar looks deserted as far as Quinn can tell, and the line at the bar begins to dwindle. He looks into the crowd and, finally, a familiar face catches his stare.

Only it's not Tomas. It's *James Frazer*.

Their eyes connect and James heads his way with a dry smile on his full lips.

"Quinn Harris…" James sounds relieved to see Quinn. His five o'clock shadow lights Quinn's cheek on fire as they hug. He smells like chemicals. He smells like the lab. "It's been a while."

"It has," is all Quinn manages. James has always had a way of looking at him with those bottomless brown eyes, as if he's looking through him. It makes him feel warm and uneasy at the same time.

"Nice to run into you – I mean, outside of a lead or someone being brought into the morgue." James laughs, but there's something sharp below the surface.

James is tall with smooth skin the color of warm gingerbread. His hair is faded on the sides, leading up to a collage of kinks and curls tamed into orderly chaos. Today he's ditched his lab coat for a pair of navy trousers, loafers, and a crisp, white, short-sleeve button-down that barely contains his broad chest. His muscles seem to test the limits of the fabric, drawing Quinn's eye to the width of his biceps.

James is a forensic analyst for the local police stations. Scarcely in the field, he's the first to admit being in a lab all day is not the most rousing job, but it's a living. It helps he's not only good at his job, but he's easy on the eyes, which Quinn imagines must make him popular with most of the detectives he interacts with.

Apart from their professional run-ins, he and Quinn sometimes spend hours on the phone, talking until daybreak like teenagers. It might be sweet if their conversations weren't filled with death, murder, and suspicion. James is his eyes and ears in the world of law enforcement, telling Quinn nearly all the news he receives from the stations he supports... recent arrests, sightings of the DA in the hallways, and even the grim, bloody details of toxicology reports. All things only a hungry journalist could truly appreciate. Quinn lies in bed with an iron stomach and the phone to his ear, listening to James' baritone voice and the breathy, sensational details of his day.

It's almost better than phone sex.

"I shouldn't fraternize with my sources," Quinn teases.

"That's all I am, huh?" James gives a devilish grin. "A source."

It's hard not to smile around James. He has a way with people, a charm that makes him instantly likable. Quinn hasn't run a full background check on James but gathered from their talks he's very much a product of his parents. James comes from "good stock" as Bailey would say. His father is a hotshot lawyer at Gannt & Foster, one of the biggest firms in the city, known for getting celebrity clients off the hook. His mother is somewhat of a philanthropist but a true academic at heart. She was a criminology professor at Duke in her past life, before his father's law career took off and they uprooted to New York. You might say James got his wiles from his father and his smarts from his mother. They were model parents.

James and his brother, Warner, enjoyed a storybook childhood. They always ate at the dinner table like a perfect TV family. They took family vacations four times a year, and the boys were encouraged to soak in as much culture as their adolescent brains could absorb. They were allowed to backpack alone through Europe the summer of their junior year. Even in college, with the boys attending historical black universities, their parents showered them with wisdom that paved the way to an appreciation for hard work and a better life than what their own childhoods had offered. Everything was golden until a year ago.

Warner had stopped into a bodega to pick up a case of beer, but he walked right into a robbery. The distraction gave the shop owner a chance to grab his pistol from under the register. Shots rang out from both sides, catching Warner and another customer in the crossfire. Warner died at the scene, and the gunman got off on a technicality during the trial. "Juror misconduct" was the ruling that allowed him to walk free on a mistrial, giving further credence to James' belief that the judicial system is broken.

Ever since Warner's death, James vowed to transition out of the lab and work his way to becoming a detective. He knows a badge won't bring Warner back; he knows he'll never see his brother smile again, but he also knows that if you don't take direct action to make things better, you're an obstacle to change.

"You know you're not just a source." Quinn feels his face flush, as he catches a slither of James' tattoo peeking under his sleeve.

What is it about guys with tattoos? It's like kryptonite. The fact his tattoo's a tribute to Warner somehow makes it all the more sexy.

James bites his juicy lower lip as if sensing his presence is having an effect. He could play this game of cat and mouse all day but doesn't push his luck.

"How's work?"

"You can't tell?" Quinn lets out a short, bitter laugh. "My last piece was trash."

James' eyes soften.

"Don't be so hard on yourself." It's clear that he's read the social media piece now. "You're better than what comes across your desk. Anyone who knows you knows that."

"Yeah," Quinn sighs. "Just like how you don't belong in a lab."

"My time's comin'." James nods, and his face brightens. "No one lands detective overnight."

Quinn would love to have James' patience or even a fraction of his optimism. "You with a badge," he smiles. "Guess you'd really have to stop talking to me then. Cops and reporters are like oil and water."

James dares to lean in. "There's other things we could talk about, other than work..." He trails off as his gaze lands on a figure behind Quinn.

"I made it!" Bailey exclaims, as if expecting confetti to rain down. He gives Quinn a peck on the cheek that makes James swallow hard. "You just get here?"

Quinn slow-blinks. "I've been here for half an hour, Bailey."

"Babe, don't be mad," Bailey smiles, full voltage. "Let's have fun tonight!" His southern accent seeps through his words as it always does when he's been drinking. Quinn notices he sounds like a sweet southern dandy, and he wonders if Bailey stopped at another bar on the way.

Could that be why he's late?

"Hey, you remember James, right?" Quinn prompts.

They nod at one another but don't shake hands.

Quinn sips his beer and frowns. He's never understood why Bailey and James are at odds. They've only encountered each other a handful of times, each painfully awkward.

"How 'bout this place?" Bailey breaks the silence and snags the dirty martini Quinn's set aside for him.

Quinn nods. "It's nice, right? Wonder what it was before."

"A garment factory. I think." Bailey squints and carefully sips from the edge of his glass.

"Actually, they made piano benches here in the '40s. Then it became a sort of furniture showroom. Antiques and odds and ends." Of course, James knows this. He seems to know everything, which makes him a good source. His answer also explains some of the furnishings and tufted leather accents in the room.

"Hmm," is all Bailey says.

"Well, hey, welcome back!" Quinn raises his beer and changes the subject. "How was Mykonos? Bailey just got back from Greece," he adds for James' benefit.

"Gorgeous. I put some pics on the 'Gram, but they just don't do it justice. The water is so blue!"

"How was the food?"

"Amazing. Everything was so fresh. The taramasalata! Oh, my God. So good. The color's a little off-putting, but…"

"Did you do any sailing?"

"The water was a 'lil choppy."

"Damn. That's too bad."

"Hey, fellas…" James tangles his finger into his curls and inches away. "I'm gonna let you guys catch up."

"*No*, stay!" Quinn feels his stomach drop. "I never get to see you. I miss this."

"I'm here with some guys from one of the stations. We're about to go to dinner," he says with a frown. "I should go. You don't want to see these queens hangry, trust me."

Quinn sees a group of guys behind James watching and deflates a bit. He dares to meet James' brown eyes, allowing them to linger. "Call you later?"

"I'll hold you to it." He stuffs his hands in his pockets and winks, then tosses Bailey a nod and excuses himself.

Bailey doesn't miss a beat. "Feels good to be back in the states!" His voice even sounds lighter. Relieved.

Quinn decides not to address it or the fact that Bailey was late. He just wants to get drunk and have a good time. He's earned that much, he decides. "Did you bring me back a postcard?"

Bailey's face drops. "Shit. I forgot. I was rushing to catch my plane—"

"You're the worst."

"I know." He pouts and massages Quinn's shoulder with his free hand. "That's one less for your collection. I prob'ly ran past a bunch of 'em in the airport too. I'll make it up to you."

"Damn right. Drinks are on *you*." Quinn fires two fingers at him like pistols. "Pew! Pew!"

"Fine. Next round is proper martinis though. None of this swill you like to drink." He makes a face.

"This is an eight-dollar craft beer." Quinn raises his glass. "Show some goddamn respect."

"Eight dollars? Isn't it happy hour?"

"It just ended." Quinn fights the urge to point out his tardiness again. Better to just move on. "So, really, how was your trip?"

Bailey rakes his fingers through his hair, moving the blonde mop to one side. "It was good. The shoot went well. The other guys were cute," he says, breaking into a sly smile. "I made a friend."

Quinn rolls his eyes. "You're the only person I know with boyfriends on every continent."

"They're not boyfriends," Bailey says like a good southern

49

belle. "Acquaintances. Nothing more."

"Did you sleep with him?"

Bailey thinks back to Admir and can taste the saltwater from the pool on his tongue. "A lady never tells."

"You, sir, are no lady." Quinn laughs.

They toast to that and lean against the horseshoe-shaped bar.

"We should find an acquaintance for *you*," Bailey says. "This place is a fucking wasteland, though. Not the faintest glimmer of hope on the horizon." He swoons in his dramatic soap opera way and surveys the room with a defeated grimace. "Mutton dressed as lamb, wedding ring tan lines, and I can smell the bad credit from here." He doesn't mention the familiar faces from his dating app.

Quinn sees what he means. The bar is shiny and new but full of the same faces they see everywhere.

Bailey takes a healthy sip of his martini. "This is our alleged promised land, my friend." He stretches his arms out to the room like Eva Perón and sneers. "Tired New York queens, twinks with fake IDs, and the old trolls who chase after them. We should give up. Just become nuns or somethin'."

"Sister Bailey Alexander *does* have a nice ring to it."

Bailey grabs Quinn's shoulder and leans in. "We should get out now. Turn in our gay cards and join a respectable monastery with Wi-Fi before we become that old troll at the end of the bar."

Quinn looks to see a man at the corner of the bar, sitting by himself, mulling over what appears to be a half-empty rum and coke. There's something vaguely familiar about him.

Bailey gives a deep laugh, then his smile falls flat, and Quinn can tell he's dwelling on the past again. Despite his good looks,

Bailey has an impressive roster of failed relationships.

There was *Jerome*, the hockey player from Queens. They met on an app, and when the hookups turned into legitimate dates, Bailey was convinced it was meant to be – until he found him in bed with someone else. Two weeks later, he met *Isaac*, the well-built stockbroker with the gambling problem. Isaac had a deadly charm about him, a real charisma that made it hard to say no. It wasn't until $200 went missing from Bailey's wallet that he knew Isaac had a real addiction. He left him and met *Jaymin* on a shoot in Queens. It was doomed from the start. Two models should never date, he found out the hard way. *Khalil* was a blind date that he never expected to bloom into a relationship. He was a terrible flirt though, and Bailey would have ended it sooner had the sex not been so amazing. It was hard, but he broke free and met *Victor* at an industry party. Their chemistry was undeniable. He was a real southern gentleman who opened car doors and made biscuits from scratch that rivaled Bailey's mother's. Things might have been perfect if Victor hadn't struggled with his sexuality so much. He broke up with Bailey, citing the Bible, fire, and brimstone! Bailey swore off men and met *Rami* two days later. Rami was an NBA player who loved life in the fast lane. He was flashy but genuinely sweet, and they dated for four months until their conflicting travel schedules became too much. Most recently, there was *Cole*... established, romantic Cole. They were complete opposites, which is why it worked for a while. Bailey always knew Cole was too grounded for him, though. Cole wanted a husband and a house full of kids – *actual children* – running around, screaming and crying, filling the house with life. The thought terrified Bailey, and the last thing he wanted was for Cole to grow resentful of his restless heart. He knew he'd only walk all over Cole in the end. He'd change Cole's entire outlook on love and fairy tale endings. What were rainbows and bluebirds would become dungeons and dragons between them. He'd ruin him. It killed Bailey, but they parted ways, and he's been terminally single ever since.

Now he's on a mission to find Quinn a match.

"I mean, where are all the *good* men?" He insists.

"At church. At least, according to my mother."

"Good Lord." Bailey rolls his eyes.

"I'm serious. 'You should come to church with me,' she says. 'There's lots of young men – just like you – all with great jobs and very well dressed, yadda yadda…'" Quinn does his best Irish accent, which surprisingly isn't very good.

"How's she doin'?" Bailey's voice lowers.

"She has a new sponsor. She hates him."

Bailey smiles. "Sounds like her."

"Yep. She might be onto something with this church theory, though."

"Well, as much as I adore your mother, I have to disagree."

"You *are* from the south," Quinn reminds him. "Didn't you grow up in the church?"

"Exactly." He retorts. "And look at me now!"

"Are we really about to have a pity party for the model who just got back from Greece after sleeping with some random Greek Adonis?" Quinn winces, "The last time a man was in my apartment, he sprayed for roaches."

It's true. Meanwhile, Quinn's own relationship roster contains one cautionary tale after another.

Jason, his first college boyfriend, was everything that first loves and broken hearts are made of. He was gorgeous and played the guitar but was all wrong for him. Then there was *Trey*, an art major who painted countless nude paintings of Quinn before they'd have sex like animals on the floor of his shitty apartment. Afterward, they'd stay up all night debating about spirituality and trip on peyote. It was all very primal and existential. (Too bad Quinn wasn't the only painting in his collection.) Then came *Hyme*, the breath of fresh air Quinn needed. He was the sweet boy next door type with long chestnut dreadlocks and a track star's body Quinn loved to snuggle against. They dated for over a year, and he might have been the one if Quinn looked past his trust issues. After a messy breakup, he met *Ivan*, who turned out to be just like Trey, minus the peyote habit. Quinn became a serial dater after that, which led him to *Eric*, who was way too possessive, terrible in bed, and played computer games all day.

Through with boys, he swore them off in favor of older men and dated *Martin* for nearly two years. He was the first man he'd met with a legit retirement plan and who could tell him the difference between a sauvignon blanc and a pinot blanc. Martin was proudly out and visible within the community, which Quinn respected, and they had Olympic-level sex. It would have been perfect if Martin didn't suffer from wandering eye disease. They couldn't go to dinner without him checking out the waiter or the guy at the next table. They fought about it constantly until the makeup sex became redundant. Then he broke up with Quinn to date a guy half his age from the gym. Lastly, there was *Elson*, who was well-grounded and knew how to make Quinn laugh. He was smart and thoughtful – the kind of guy Quinn could picture forever with. He fell madly in love. Then Elson moved away to take a film-editing job in San Francisco, and Quinn remains convinced he'll never find anyone like him.

"Ugh. Enough about men." Bailey narrows his eyes at the room and reaches for his cigarettes. "How's work?"

A sigh escapes. No matter how much he wants to not think about it, the subject keeps coming up.

"Basically, Marcus is giving me free rein if I can pitch him an amazing story."

"Like an exclusive?"

"Beyond an exclusive." Quinn feels a knot forming in his stomach. "He wants '*something that scares me*.'"

"The hell does that mean?"

"I think he's testing me."

"You'll think of somethin'," Bailey shrugs. "Hey! You should come with me to Paris next month. I've got a runway show."

A sudden sense of déjà vu washes over Quinn.

"Paris?"

"Oui, mon ami! I'm walking the André Lefèvre show. I got the call on the way here, actually." He shimmies his shoulders and beams as Quinn's eyes narrow. "Maybe gettin' away will recharge your batteries."

"That's the second time Paris has come up today." He wonders if he should tell Bailey about the dream he's had.

"It's a sign. You should come with me." He waves a cigarette.

Quinn isn't so sure. There's something else that's bothering him, too… something to do with the man Bailey pointed out at the bar.

Bailey suddenly reaches for his lighter.

"Hey. You can't smoke in here," Quinn swats at him. "And I thought you quit, like for real this time."

Bailey makes a tortured face. "I know, I just… here, *tell you what—*" he plucks his lighter from the back pocket of his

54

jeans. "Hold this. It'll keep me honest." It's the same stainless steel lighter Quinn gifted him last year for his birthday, back when they both smoked. The initials B.L.A. are etched into the smooth finish, glistening under the bar lights.

Quinn stuffs the lighter deep into his front pocket – out of sight, out of mind. "Paris." His voice sounds a million miles away. "Yeah, I'll think about it."

"You wanna talk 'bout déjà vu?" Bailey pauses to finish off his martini, and his eyes go dark. "She called again today."

Quinn snaps out of his trance and chooses his next words carefully. "What did she say?"

"Went to voicemail. I didn't listen to it."

Quinn sets his beer on the bar and faces Bailey. "You're gonna have to talk to her eventually. Or just go."

"I'm never goin' back, and you know why." He doesn't give Quinn a chance to reply. "They kicked me out when I was sixteen. I was homeless, Quinn. Homeless. My father is one of the richest men in Savannah – and they cut me off because 'no son of his' is gonna grow up to be a sissy.'"

Quinn knows the story well. His father walked in on Bailey and the gardener's son, *Troy* – who was one year his senior and would often accompany his father on jobs. They'd worked for the Alexander family for years, so Troy and Bailey practically grew up together. His father wasn't supposed to be home, he never came home in the middle of the day, and yet there he was, standing in the doorway of Bailey's bedroom with one hand on the knob and fire in his eyes. Bailey will never forget how red his face was, the way the veins in his neck popped as he cursed and rushed Troy, threatening to throw him out the window. He might have been successful had Bailey's mother not rushed in upon hearing the ruckus, becoming a second witness.

"It's terrible," Quinn hangs his head. "No child deserves to be cast out for being gay."

"At first, I was so stunned, I mean, how was I even gonna finish high school?"

"But you did," Quinn emphasizes. "And you did it on your own. Look how far you've come, and without their money."

"You know how hard it is to pass by your own blood in the hallway and have them shun you? My own brothers and my sister wouldn't even look at me in school. Like I was some kinda leper! Like they could catch it."

"They have to see how successful you are now."

Bailey silently wonders if his brothers, Mason and Sawyer, will see his *GQ* spread when it comes out. He imagines Mason, the eldest, picking it up in the grocery store and adding it to his cart of Hostess cakes and Gatorade. He's sure Mason's let himself go by now. (He's seen his social media page.) He wishes he could see Mason's face as he fumbles through the pages, looking for grooming tips and landing on *his* face instead, staring back from Mykonos.

"My father just opened another Big Daddy's BBQ down near Times Square. You seen it?"

Quinn is familiar with the fast-food barbecue chain. How could he not be? There are more than seventy nation-wide now. He's even eaten at the new one in Times Square and it was fucking amazing, although he doesn't share this now. He just nods sympathetically, thinking about those smoky, savory ribs that fall off the bone. He should feel guiltier than he does for eating there, but he doesn't do it often. When he does, he makes a point to write a bad review afterward, finding some small flaw in the food or service. Then, as he's licking the tangy barbecue sauce off his fingers, he works in that the owner of the franchise is a homophobic fascist who kicked out his own son at the tender age of sixteen. So tender… just like those ribs.

His stomach rumbles.

"I thought about goin' down to protest the grand opening. I really did. Or call in a bomb threat." Bailey says that last part out of the side of his mouth. Never say "bomb" too loud in a crowded bar, he thinks wisely, despite the buzz that's starting to warm his chest.

Quinn doesn't know what to say. It's best to let Bailey unpack the trauma and get it all out. Besides, his thoughts have gone back to the figure sitting at the far end of the bar. There's something he can't quite put his finger on. Something familiar that he can't shake.

"If my Granddaddy Carl were alive to see what he's done with the family recipe, I swear…"

"Hey, does he look familiar to you?" He interrupts Bailey's rant. He can't help himself now.

"Who?"

"Don't look!" Quinn motions for Bailey to be discreet. "Just sneak a peek. End of the bar…"

Bailey leans to take a look, and his face takes on disgust. *"Ew. That old guy?!"*

"Shhh! Yes. Him. I can't shake this feeling that I know him." He dares to look again.

The man before them is indeed older. Quinn guesses he's in his early fifties but, despite Bailey's outburst, is still handsome in a manner that suggests he was once breathtaking. Now he's just a ghost of his former self. An apparition. His once striking features are now accented by wrinkles and extra baggage under his calm gray eyes.

There's a familiar air about him. Maybe it's his broad shoulders and the dimple in his chin that reminds Quinn of someone from TV. Maybe it's the dust of blonde hair on his arms that makes him think of his high school science teacher, who he'd had such an intense affection for. It had started as an innocent schoolyard crush. (*Everyone's had a crush on a teacher*, he assured himself.) But this was different. This was something that had become a defining moment in his life, something that ultimately awakened his feelings for men.

Before the Jasons and Elsons of the world, there was his science teacher *who had been the start of it all.*

The man before him actually looks to be the right height – a bit muscular under his black polo, which Quinn's eyes dare to dawdle on. Even the way he sits with his shoulders slightly hunched forward resonates with the memory of his high school science teacher. In fact, the more he stares… *the more he's certain*, and the words fly out of his mouth before he can catch them.

"Mr. Doyle?"

4 / CRUSH

Anderson Doyle was everyone's favorite teacher at Freeman, a small and grossly underfunded public school in Quinn's hometown of Bristol, Virginia. The reasons were obvious. One: Anderson treated the students like adults. He didn't care if they were late to class or occasionally cursed. (Shit happens, right?) Two: Anderson was also Freeman's football coach outside of class. He led the school to their first and only state championship, and who doesn't love a hero? Three: Anderson was handsome beyond belief – especially for a science teacher. Some may argue it's the occasional math teachers of the high school world who are the heartthrobs, but Anderson Doyle took the cake with his dusty blonde hair and solid build. He looked like he was cut from stone and brought to life by the gods.

Quinn found himself among the girls who lost their breath when Mr. Doyle walked into the classroom. He'd sit at his desk with bated breath, watching Anderson's backside jiggle as he wrote on the chalkboard. During lab, he'd stare into Anderson's stormy gray eyes and let his mind wander until he was flushed and squirming in his seat.

He'd never had this reaction to anyone before, and certainly not for any of the girls in his class. They all seemed silly to him in their training bras and braces, doodling cartoon hearts and arrows in their notebooks. It'd never occurred to him to approach any of them for a date or for whatever went on in the photo lab after school.

For reasons he couldn't decipher, Anderson Doyle, his teacher and Freeman's beloved football coach, consumed his thoughts. Anderson awoke something in Quinn – a fiery dragon that, once released, refused to go back into its cave or be tamed.

Quinn was a good student, in the top five percent of his class. He didn't make waves, but he soon found himself entertaining the idea of detention. It would be easy. He could speak out of turn, become disruptive in class. Maybe even drop an F-bomb at Anderson's expense that would cause the class to hoot and go wild. Anderson would have no choice but to give Quinn detention.

He imagined Anderson keeping him after class, pressing his face hard against the dusty chalkboard, his legs suggestively spread wide. Why was he suddenly acting up in class? Was he having trouble at home? Or was he just a *bad boy*? Anderson would demand to know. In his daydreams, Quinn would wet his lips and coo, "I'm just a bad boy, Mr. Doyle... I'm *so* bad." Quinn never called him Coach Doyle like the other students. He saw no real reason since he thought of Anderson as his teacher first and a coach second. "Well, you know what happens to bad boys, don't you?" He'd say into Quinn's ear, sending a tremor down his spine. "What, Mr. Doyle? What happens to... bad boys?" Anderson's smile would become a snarl as he suddenly yanked Quinn's pants down to his ankles. "They get SPANKED!"

It was only a silly fantasy, of course, but typical behavior for a teenage boy just finding himself. Quinn wasn't especially handsome in school – just ordinary – so he wasn't especially bold in seeking out Anderson's attention either. He mostly gawked along with the girls. He figured Anderson must have been aware of his good looks though. He had to know the girls ogled him and feverishly debated over how big "it" might be.

Everyone's had a crush on a teacher, but this was different. Aside from the obvious attraction, Anderson was one of Quinn's biggest supporters throughout school. He was always encouraging and gave him As on his papers. He even took time to critique papers for his other subjects and nominated Quinn for awards and scholarships that paved the way to college. A single-parent home with a pill-popping mother left much to be desired in the realm of guidance. That's where Mr. Doyle came in. He showed a real interest in his success, despite the fact Quinn had no interest in football.

Quinn might have been flattered, if this wasn't just his teacher's nature. As Teacher of the Year, Mr. Doyle was involved in nearly every school event... chaperoning dances, cheering on sports teams, acting as an adviser for student government. He challenged tradition, even protesting with the students to allow a girl to play on the varsity football team.

Mr. Doyle was many things, but to most he was a hero.

One day, Quinn found the nerve to confess his feelings. He wrote a three-page letter that spilled every longing secret he'd held within, black ink flooding the college-ruled pages. It poured out of him. It wasn't purely sexual, mind you – oh, no – this was far bigger. He addressed him as an adult confessing admiration for the other. It was a respectable letter he'd spent two days writing during study hall. He'd crafted it until it was perfect and without errors. (How would Mr. Doyle ever take him seriously with sloppy handwriting and misspellings?)

He was all dragonflies and nerves walking into class that morning, the letter tucked in the back pocket of his tight jeans. He went straight to his desk as everyone awaited Mr. Doyle's entrance. Sometimes he was later getting to class than the students, all part of the Mr. Doyle charm.

Quinn sat there chewing on his pencil, hoping it was a "corduroy day". Those were his favorite pants on Mr. Doyle because they showed nearly all of his business each time he stood from his desk. That morning, much to the class' horror, Principal Ingram strolled through the door.

In his ill-fitted suit and acid-green tie, he informed the class that Mr. Doyle was no longer with them.

Not dead.

There were sighs of relief.

Just gone.

"Let go."

Mr. Ingram refused to go into detail or answer questions. He moved on to introduce their substitute teacher, a waif of a man named Mr. Marks with thick glasses and a thin mustache. He couldn't hold a candle to Mr. Doyle.

The school was devastated.

Quinn kept in touch with a few classmates over the years. Everyone from Freeman remembers the year Mr. Doyle came and went because it was the same year Lara Barnett made the football team. The same year Travis Hall, his best friend who lived in the same neighborhood, inexplicably ran away from home. The same year some very clever person called in a bomb threat the day of final exams, and everyone got an extra day to study. It was also the year of a solar eclipse, which had everyone in town on edge and all the animals acting strangely.

Things like this didn't happen in Bristol. It was as though Mr. Doyle's absence knocked something off-kilter. The rest of the school year didn't feel the same without him, ending on a strange note that made the sweltering, aimless summer break a welcome distraction. It would take time for the school to recover, and soon after his dismissal, the rumors began to swirl.

There were rumors that he lied on his resume. No degree, they claimed. He was just a charismatic guy who knew a thing or two about science and how to throw the old pigskin. He also had a reputation for reviving school football programs and winning championships, which the school board was especially interested in. Perhaps it was all about optics and winning the championship...

There was a rumor he had an affair with a student, which Quinn was especially offended by. If anyone had gotten to Mr. Doyle first, he demanded to know who.

Then, there was the whopper. A rumor claiming Mr. Doyle was a homosexual and that the school's superintendent found out and fired him. This was a different era, long before the legalization of same-sex marriage and drag queens taking over pop culture. As scandalous as the accusation was, it was possible.

But no one knew with any certainty what caused him to disappear. The details were anyone's guess. All they knew was that Anderson Doyle was gone. Never to be seen or heard from again.

Until now.

• • •

Bailey glares between Quinn and Anderson as his brain connects the dots. "Ew. You know him?"

"He was my teacher," Quinn shrugs. "I didn't know…" Or did he? Had he believed the rumors?

"*Quinn*? Quinn Harris." Anderson leans in their direction with a curious smile that confirms any lingering doubt. Quinn would know that smile anywhere. "I thought that was you!" His face lights up, melting away the years.

Bailey rolls his eyes and takes this as his cue. "I think I need another drink," he says.

Quinn shoots him a sour look and turns to serve Anderson a bewildered smile that says, "*Wow, imagine seeing you here*!" Only he doesn't say this. He doesn't need to. The irony of this reunion isn't lost on either of them.

He rushes over and leans in for an awkward hug. The warmth of Anderson's arms encircles him, making his heart race. "*Mr. Doyle*? Wow. I had no idea you were in New York."

He shrugs his broad football shoulders and says, "I've been here for about a year now, at NY State."

"No shit. That's where I got my degree."

"No shit. And hey, call me Anderson. We're a long way from Bristol, right?"

His familiar voice reminds Quinn of home. He can almost smell their old classroom and the chalk dust.

"Right. Anderson," Quinn shakes his head in wonder. "So, NY State, that's amazing! Teaching? Coaching?"

"Assistant coaching."

"What a shame for all those science geeks."

Anderson chuckles, and Quinn sees something flash in his eyes.

"It's for the best," Anderson says. "School's changed a lot

since I taught *you*." A memory. Perhaps a memory of a younger, more awkward Quinn in his tight jeans and Chuck Taylors is coming to the surface.

"Well, I'm sure you must enjoy college more than high school," Quinn says. He fights the urge to stare into his eyes for too long. Gray, steely eyes, unlike any he's seen since Anderson disappeared. He wonders what he might discover if he falls in and dives to the bottom. "No immature kids to deal with, right?"

"You weren't immature." He recalls. "Some of your class-mates? Yes. But never you." He flexes his bushy eyebrows, clearly thinking back now.

Quinn nods and takes a sip of his beer, which has gone room temperature. He wonders what Anderson must have really thought of him back then, knowing what he knows now. *Cute jailbait? Or just a promising student?*

"You look like you're doing well for yourself." Anderson takes him in. "What are you up to these days?"

"I'm a journalist for *The Chronicle*."

Anderson's eyes go wide. "*The Chronicle*. No shit. Can't say I'm surprised though. You were always a good writer." He sounds more like a teacher again, showing his age again. "So, is this your first time here?"

Quinn had forgotten where they were. He glances around, almost embarrassed to be rediscovered at a gay bar after all this time. Somehow it feels seedy despite the expensive air in the room. He wonders if Anderson is just as surprised to find him here. Quinn wasn't especially flamboyant in high school. No one really knew... except Maggie Thompson and the Newman twins. And Jesse Reinhart. And Gretchen Perrault. One of the cafeteria ladies might have known.

"Sort of a guy's night out," Quinn says. "Bailey just got back from Greece, so we're celebrating his return."

"Ah." He tosses a look in Bailey's direction. "Nice couple. How long you guys been together?"

"Oh! We're not together," he blurts out. "Bailey's just a friend... and a bad influence." Quinn suddenly finds himself craving a cigarette. He has Bailey's lighter, but Bailey has the cigarettes.

Anderson's lips hint at a smile, allowing a bit of relief to slip between the lines. "Sorry. I just assumed you had a lover."

Quinn lets out a boyish laugh.

"A lover. Wow, I don't think I've ever heard anyone use that word in real life."

The tips of Anderson's ears glow red. He's showing his age yet again, and a few more wrinkles around the eyes now that Quinn is getting a closer look. It's like looking at one of those apps that ages you, or a funhouse version of his memory. It looks like his version of Mr. Doyle, but there's something disquieting about the reflection before him. His chiseled features have softened. His hair is thinning, with gray now coloring his temples. Even something about the way he sits looks slightly sunken. Despite this, Quinn has to admit that Anderson's aged gracefully. He reminds Quinn of a mature George Clooney, only without the Hollywood shine. Quinn can only hope for as much, picturing his father's receding hairline.

"I'm single," Quinn confesses, as if it's a plague upon him. As if it's a curse or an apology of some kind. A big scarlet "S" on his chest that keeps the locals whispering.

"I'm sure it won't be long before some lucky guy scoops you up."

It sounds like something people say when they don't know what else to say. Worse, it sounds patronizing. Quinn doesn't dwell on this though. He takes a breath and refocuses, realizing this is his chance to ask everything he's ever wanted to know.

He's not a kid anymore.

"So, what about yourself? Is there a… lover in your life?"

Anderson fidgets and says, "Can't say there is." He lets out a roguish smile before his tone slips into something more comfortable. "Guess that puts us in the same boat."

Quinn isn't surprised to learn of Anderson's scarlet "S". Queer culture can be exceptionally cruel when it comes to older men, or "trolls" as Bailey so eloquently labels them. According to queer legend – as Bailey tells it – every full moon, a gay bar possesses a few trolls lurking in their darkest corners, casually sipping on rum and cokes before luring unsuspecting twinks into their clutches to devour alive!

Quinn does the math in his head. Anderson's surely in his fifties by now.

"It gets harder when you're my age," he says, as if reading Quinn's mind. "Guys like you don't give old fogies like me the time of day anymore." He smiles halfheartedly and clears his throat.

"Guys like me?"

Anderson blushes. "You know what I mean."

"No, tell me." Quinn takes a seat on the empty stool beside him and leans in with a smile. To see his beloved teacher, the same man who was such a man's man back then, blushing like a schoolgirl makes Quinn tingly. Who would believe *Mr. Doyle* enjoys the company of men?

Anderson swats his arm playfully and looks down at his

drink. "Hell, don't make me say it…"

Quinn crosses his arms with a Cheshire grin, unflinching. He's not letting Anderson off the hook so easily, not after years of wondering *what if*.

Anderson draws a breath and says, "Fine." He leans in until they're inches apart. It seems to take forever for what comes next, as if Anderson is deliberately keeping Quinn in suspense. Then, before Quinn has a chance to crack, he calmly says, "I've had my eyes on you since you walked in."

Quinn manages a straight face but feels a rush of heat fill his chest.

"*Those green eyes…*" Anderson continues, his deep voice turning raspy, "I swear I could stare in 'em all day. I wanted to come over, but then I figured out who you were and, well…" The rest falls silent.

The DJ fades in a new song that sends a group behind them running to the dancefloor, and Quinn peers at Anderson through his eyelashes.

"I'm not that kid anymore."

Anderson swallows a small lump in his throat as his gaze falls to Quinn's lips. "You're definitely all grown up." His eyes glaze over Quinn like icing, sweet and enticing. "You could probably teach *me* a thing or two now…"

"I bet I could." Quinn winks, which might be dangerous. Has he just issued a challenge? It feels as if he's thrown down the gauntlet, and Anderson seems up for it in more ways than one. "I always thought you were so handsome," Quinn confesses.

There. The truth is out. There's no taking it back.

"You always were a sweet kid," he pats Quinn's knee.

"I'm not just saying that. I had the biggest crush on you,"

he laughs, hearing himself say the words aloud. "You have no idea." He shakes his head and has to look away now. He's sure his face has gone red. He thinks back to the letter he wrote Anderson, wishing he could remember some of the lines. Any hint of it would be better than this awkward, beer-infused confession he's pouring out in a crowded gay bar. It wasn't supposed to be like this.

Anderson's hand returns to his knee. "Careful or you might…"

"*What?*" Quinn squints.

Anderson leans into his ear, speaking over the noise in the bar. "I said, *careful, or you might get in trouble for flirting with your teacher!*" Quinn can feel Anderson's hot breath dancing along his collarbone.

"Well, I wouldn't want to get detention," he offers a smile.

Is he flirting? Is this creepy?

Bailey would surely think so. He would not approve of this, Quinn surmises.

"*This place is getting more packed by the minute!*" Anderson's nearly shouting now over the DJ.

"Christ. I can barely hear myself think."

"Well, you know… I don't live very far from here…" Anderson leans closer with sex on his breath and squeezes Quinn's thigh. "We should get out of here and catch up."

It's an obvious proposition. One that makes Quinn dizzy with its implications.

Could he accept Anderson's invitation?

It's all just so scandalous. If the girls from Freeman only knew that Mr. Doyle lives in New York, trolling gay bars, and he'd slept with him one desolate night, despite the rigid rules of gay society. He imagines the shrieks at his class reunion.

Maggie Thompson would die on the spot.

The man he's admired for so many years is right in front of him, practically melting in the palm of his hand like candy, and all he has to do is say yes.

"*'Scuse me, gentlemen.*" It's Bailey. He's appeared, as if out of thin air again, holding a shot of cheap vodka that smells like rubbing alcohol.

Quinn frowns, knowing that any time Bailey switches from martinis to shots, it signifies the beginning of the end. He's bored and will get sloppy now, and it'll be up to Quinn to babysit him for the rest of the night, making sure he gets into a car and home without puking on his new boots. The Patsy Stone of it all…

"Quinn, can I speak with you? Privately?" He gives Anderson a once-over.

Quinn contains a sigh and apologizes to Anderson with weary eyes.

"I'll be right back."

An amused smile dances along Anderson's lips. "Hurry back, lover." He gives Quinn's thigh another squeeze for good measure.

Before Quinn can react, Bailey locks arms and is pulling him into the line at the front of the bar. "You two are lookin' awfully cozy," he smooths his blazer and gives Quinn a careful look.

Quinn finishes the last of his warm beer and wipes at his mouth.

"Yeah, it's kinda crazy. He's exactly how I remember him! Just a bit older."

Bailey tosses back his shot and hisses through his teeth, swallowing the burn in the back of his throat. "A bit?!" He

70

coughs. "He's fuckin' Grampa Moses."

"He's not that old, and besides, what's wrong with talking to my old teacher?"

"Looks like yer doin' a bit more than talkin'." Bailey raises an eyebrow. "His hands were all over you."

"So what if they were?" He laughs it off. "We're both adults now."

It takes a moment. The shot has gone straight to Bailey's head, but then the gravity of what Quinn said finally hits him. He rests a hand on his chest, "Good gravy, Quinn. You can't be serious!"

"What?!" He draws his shoulders to his ears, "I didn't say I was going *home* with him, even though he... might have just asked me to..."

"Honey, listen, we all have daddy issues, but *this*..." His face hardens. "You're really entertainin' bonin' your decrepit old teacher. Come on."

Quinn folds his arms and says, "You just banged like half the models on your shoot in Greece. Did I give you any grief?"

"It was one model." He raises a finger. "One."

"Whatever. My point is, it's been five months, Bailey."

"That doesn't mean you have to fuck *Grandfather Time*."

Quinn stifles a laugh. "You're the worst."

"I mean, seriously, does the nursing home even know he's missing?"

"I hate you."

"I'm just lookin' out for you, hon," he holds his head high. "I mean, what're you trynna prove? Sleepin' with some old goat won't earn you a Boy Scout badge."

"That's out of line," Quinn frowns. "And this isn't just about sex."

Bailey drops his shoulders. "Fine. I get it. We've all had a crush on a teacher, but... no."

"This is different." Quinn glances back at Anderson. "In a way, he was kinda my *first,* you know? He's the reason I'm standing in this gay bar today. He helped me find myself – and this is probably the only chance I'll ever get to find out..." The words end on a shrug.

"Find out what?"

Quinn takes a deep breath, "To find out if there's something there. How many people get a real chance like this with their high school crush after this many years? Think about everything I've been through with Martin and Elson. What are the chances that Anderson and I would both be here tonight?" His face softens. "What if the universe just has a twisted sense of humor?"

Bailey rolls his eyes, hating how he must always be the bad guy. "You really think this is a good idea?"

Quinn's divided. Divided between escorting a very drunk Bailey home to his loft in Soho where his sofa awaits... and spending a torrid evening of passion and pillow talk with a man he might have been in love with once. Puppy love, albeit. Yet, here he is, a man now, still carrying the same questions about Anderson that plagued him at seventeen.

Where does he live?

What does his house look like?

What does his hair smell like after a shower?

What would his touch feel like on his skin?

What would his kiss taste like on his lips?

He has to know.

"I have to know."

"Fine." Bailey crosses his arms. "But don't say I didn't warn you when his dentures fall out suckin' your dick. *It could happen, and you know I'm right."*

"You're dead wrong for that." Quinn whips out his phone to request a car. "I'll get you a car."

"I'm gonna hang out for a while."

Predictable, Quinn thinks. Bailey can't just leave when he leaves, he has to stay and bag the hottest guy in the bar now. Someone half Anderson's age with a six-pack, just to prove a point.

Quinn looks to Anderson. Poor, deflated Anderson, who's had to watch all of this unfold. "Just tell me you won't do anything stupid once I leave."

"I'll be fine," Bailey says, thawing a little as he drapes an arm around Quinn's shoulders. "Do your thing, hon. Just spare me the details at brunch tomorrow."

"Are you *sure?"*

He shrugs as if he couldn't care less, "I'm sure."

"If you want me to stay—"

"Babe, just go." He kisses Quinn's cheek and shoots Anderson the side-eye. "If this is somethin' you feel you have to do…" He shrugs.

Quinn releases the breath he's been holding. "Text me when you get home?"

"Yes, mother."

Quinn makes a face and finds his way back to Anderson, who remains on his barstool, casually swirling a straw around the ice in his glass.

"Everything okay?"

Quinn smiles and closes in, close enough for Anderson to part his legs and welcome Quinn into his orbit. "You don't have to pretend," he says, wrapping his arms around

73

Anderson's neck. "I know you heard that."

Anderson's hands find Quinn's waist and their embrace tightens. "Your friend got somethin' against *goats*?" He makes a loud goat impression, loud enough to startle the people around them. "Wait. *Is that really what I sound like?*"

Quinn laughs and allows himself to become hypnotized by Anderson's wistful gaze. The raspy brass in his voice is doing something to him, something he hasn't felt in a long time. "He's really not all bad," he manages. "He's the best once you get to know him."

He feels Anderson's hands slither down his hips and slip into the back pockets of his jeans. "Let's talk about something else," His words are deliberate and soft, dripping with innuendo.

"Like what?" The words barely reach the surface as Quinn feels himself melting.

"Like…" Anderson's stare drifts to Quinn's lips, "The bottle of Chateau Laurent back at my place… you and me by the fireplace making up for lost time…" His hands take two hearty handfuls of Quinn's behind.

Quinn has no fucking clue what Chateau Laurent is, but it sounds expensive and French. Anderson dangles the words in front of him like a carrot, as if he's seventeen again and has never been allowed to taste wine.

Bailey saunters by, his stare locked and loaded. "Have a pleasant evening, *sirs*," he says out the side of his mouth.

Quinn waves goodbye but Anderson doesn't. Instead, he draws Quinn closer, close enough for a kiss, but stopping just shy. He knows how to tease him, and Quinn is enjoying every second of it.

Perhaps he just might get that spanking after all.

"Let's get out of here," Anderson says in a low growl. He

signals for his check by scribbling in the air with pinched fingers. The bartender nods in return.

Quinn looks back to find Bailey, but he's already lost in the crowd.

He suddenly has a bad feeling about leaving him and hates himself for it. Somehow, he's always the one worrying about Bailey. Somehow he's always the protector. The designated driver. The voice of reason. The one to sacrifice his night to take care of Bailey and make sure he gets home alright.

But not tonight.

The universe has spoken, and Quinn blinks to find himself led out the bar by none other than Freeman's most eligible Teacher of the Year.

5 / VANISHED

Anderson and Quinn arrive at a modest one-story brick ranch outside of the city, surrounded by what looks like two acres of manicured land. Only a few trees come into view of Anderson's headlights as they pull into a long, dirt driveway.

"This is home," Anderson squints over the steering wheel.

Not the best night driver, it turns out.

The ride was much longer than Quinn had anticipated, so he's thankful to get out of the car as Anderson kills the engine.

"It's so quiet out here," he observes.

Anderson fumbles with his keys before ushering him inside. The touch of his fingers on the small of Quinn's back makes this suddenly feel taboo; as if Quinn is sweet seventeen again, being smuggled inside the home of his teacher after school. The only thing missing is his bookbag.

Quinn steps inside and whispers, "Shoes off?"

"You can leave 'em on. Why are you whispering?"

"I don't know." Quinn makes a face. "Are we alone?"

"Of course." Anderson winces. "What, you think I still live at home with my mother? I'm not *that* big of a loser." He gives a nerdy laugh and gestures toward the living room.

It might be the energy in the room that made Quinn ask. He can feel electricity in the air as if the television is on, but it isn't.

They make their way into the living room, coming face to face with an oversized sofa and wooden coffee table that look dated. "Very retro," he approves.

Anderson's completely puzzled, oblivious to the equally bad shag carpet and wood paneling. "Retro?"

"1970's on the line," Quinn holds his pinky and thumb to his ear like a receiver, "They want their orange sofa back."

"Have a seat, smartass." Anderson snuffs out the smile forming on his lips.

"Is school in session?" Quinn sinks between the cushions and steadies himself as Anderson plops beside him.

"School's out," he says wearily. "And thank God. It's a thankless, underpaid job."

"Damn. How do you really feel?"

Anderson backpedals and says, "I'm just glad to be on the field again."

"Around all those hot football jocks," Quinn teases.

"They're hopeless." Anderson tosses his head back in anguish. "Some of these kids are hell-bent on goin' pro. I hate to think where they'll end up when they don't get drafted. I'm glad you never played for me." He adds.

"You are?"

"With *those* chicken legs?!" He hoots, "Damn right, I am."

Quinn elbows his ribs.

"These chicken legs are fast! I ran cross country, remember? I could have been your secret weapon."

"Right," Anderson's laugh fades as he catches his breath. "Seriously though, I'm glad you didn't try out. You were such a talent – my *best* student. I knew you had your whole life ahead of you. You had it all figured out. You didn't belong on that field."

Quinn quietly regards him, seeing more of the old Mr. Doyle seeping through.

"I didn't go into the field of science or land a spot in the space program." He says this slowly, testing to see if Anderson might be disappointed.

Anderson nudges him. "You're doing what you love. That's what matters."

Quinn doesn't go into the latest saga at work, how he needs a big story, or he's doomed to write fluff pieces forever. He'd love to have Anderson's advice but he's careful not to ruin the mood.

"I do like your house," he says, to make up for his earlier reaction. "I'd need like five roommates to afford this much space in the city."

"It's nuthin' fancy, but I like it." Anderson lets his stare fall to Quinn's lips once more. "It's quiet."

Not for long, Quinn thinks, taking a look around. The living room is positioned in the center of the house. There's a hallway to his right that he guesses leads to the bedroom and bathroom. The entrance to the kitchen is to his left, with a breakfast bar that reveals dated white appliances, yellow floral wallpaper, and a pantry door on the other side. Quinn can hear the faint hum of the kitchen's fluorescent lights from where he sits.

"Where's all your stuff?"

Anderson furrows his brows. "What do you mean?"

"Did you just move in? There's just like a clock on the wall. No photos, no books…" Not even knickknacks or odds and ends thrown about. None of his football trophies are on display either. What little there is seems to have its strict place.

"You should see my apartment. I've got laundry all over my bedroom floor and shit everywhere. This place looks like a museum in comparison."

"How about I start a fire?" Anderson half-smiles. It reminds Quinn of the way Tomas smiled at him earlier.

"Fine." There's a playful sparkle in Quinn's green eyes. "Change the subject."

Anderson hops up and tosses a smirk over his shoulder.

He watches as Anderson squats in front of the fireplace. The white waistband of his briefs peeks back as he removes the fireplace screen to assess the situation.

"Hey, I've been meaning to ask!" Quinn jolts. "What the hell happened to you?"

Anderson fiddles around at the brick mantelpiece. "What do you mean?"

"Why did you leave Freeman?"

Anderson sucks in air between his teeth. "Long story," he says as he restacks logs on the fire grate. "Basically, I was at the wrong place at the wrong time."

"Meaning?"

"Drag brunch." He shakes his head as if the words alone spell doom. "I went with a friend, and there was this really loud group of women, a bachelorette party or some shit. Bunch of ol' cackling hyenas," he positions some kindling into place and strikes a match. "Luck would have it, Larry Ingram's wife was there. Part of that group."

Quinn frowns, thinking back to Principal Ingram and his acid-green tie.

Anderson's face glows by the mounting fire. "The old witch must have told him she saw me at a gay bar and that was that. Back then, it was more common for teachers to be purged out of public schools for being gay or lesbian. I suppose I should have known my days were numbered."

Discovered at a gay bar. Quinn knows the feeling. "A lot of us wondered what happened. You just kinda vanished." He hears sizzling pops as the thick, intoxicating smell of musky oak fills his nostrils.

"Vanished?" Anderson brushes the soot off his hands and faces Quinn. "I'm right here." A comforting smile spreads across his face like peanut butter, and Quinn feels his heart flutter. Yes. Here he is. Weathered by the years that have passed between them, but back in his life all the same. "I'll pour us some wine."

"Sounds perfect." Quinn folds his hands in his lap and watches Anderson walk off to the kitchen. He wonders what Bailey is doing. Certainly not being entertained by a gentleman the likes of Anderson Doyle, he thinks. The romantic glow of the fire mixed with wine is a recipe for an incredible night. He feels giddy like a new bride on her wedding night, minus the cherry of course; *that* had long been obliterated by Jason Payne, a tall, sandy-haired psych major he'd met during freshman year at NY State.

Quinn jumps at the sound of music blaring from the kitchen. The volume sharply drops, followed by static and voices cutting in and out. Finally, a hauntingly beautiful voice calls out, crooning a love ballad from the 1960s. If he needed a reminder of Anderson's age, this radio station – or the fact that Anderson even owns a radio – would surely be it. Quinn's heard the song playing before, but there's something eerie about hearing it again in 2019. It gives him a chill.

Anderson emerges from the kitchen with two crystal glasses of wine and a winning smile. Quinn suddenly can't help but wonder how many students he's banged over the years, and if this is a thing. Is this what men battling a midlife crisis do in lieu of buying a convertible?

Anderson hands him a glass and plops down, closer this time. Quinn catches the rich air of the wine, warm and lingering in the space between them. He leans in, foreheads almost touching, to clink Quinn's glass.

Quinn cracks a smile and watches Anderson take a slow sip, savoring the expensive wine on his tongue. He doesn't know much about wine except that it goes straight to his head and makes him sluggish. He can still feel his body buzzing from his last beer and really wants to enjoy what comes next, not be too drunk to remember it the next morning. That's Bailey's M.O., not his.

He sets his glass neatly on the coffee table, surprised to not find a coaster. "I'll have some in a bit." He inches closer, their legs now touching.

Anderson tries not to look disappointed at Quinn's full glass, but his eyes betray him. He's opened a new bottle just for the occasion, only for Quinn to turn his nose up at it.

Fucking Millennials.

He recovers quickly and wraps an arm around Quinn's waist, drawing him in. "Cut to the chase then, shall we?"

Their lips connect and Quinn's entire world collapses onto itself. He tastes the spicy warmth of red wine on Anderson's tongue as it wrestles with his own.

So this is what it feels like, he thinks.

Anderson moans and pulls Quinn onto his lap.

Quinn straddles him on the sofa as the fire between them grows. Flames and classroom memories flash behind closed eyelids as their kiss deepens. Quinn's fingers find their way into Anderson's hair, craving more of him.

Anderson's hands expertly find their way under Quinn's shirt, and in one quick

Motion, Quinn's T-shirt is over his head. Thank God he's done yoga earlier, he thinks. Still, he feels like a fat seven out of ten as Anderson takes it all in.

No six-pack to be found here, sir. Just a spare tire and hints at pectorals.

Anderson doesn't seem to care. He takes one of Quinn's nipples into his mouth, and Quinn arches his back in ecstasy.

Is this really happening?

His kisses trail up Quinn's chest to his neck, making him lightheaded.

Quinn cups Anderson's face and kisses him with everything he has. He can't tell how long the kiss lasts. Minutes? Lifetimes?

Finally, Anderson's mouth breaks away, just as Quinn feels something stirring beneath him. Anderson's manhood presses hard against his jeans, aching to be released. Anderson pushes himself off the sofa with a free hand as Quinn wraps his legs around his waist. He cradles Quinn's ass as he spins them around; gravity gives away as they fall back in space, back in time, and onto the couch cushion. Anderson is on top of him now; the two make out like teenagers after the prom.

They grind until Quinn feels a twinge of pain behind him.

"What's wrong?" Anderson's out of breath, dazed and drunk from their kisses.

Quinn pushes him away with a free hand. "My phone." It must have slipped out of his back pocket in all the chaos, digging into his back. He fishes it from between the cushions, and the two take in the moment, sharing a hearty laugh. "Well, out of all my teachers, you're certainly the best kisser." Quinn quirks.

"There've been others?"

Quinn's eyes dance with mischief. "I might have had a crush on your replacement at Freeman."

"Liar."

Quinn chuckles and moves his phone to the coffee table. "Nothing happened."

"Better not have," Anderson growls. "This ass is mine..."

They claw at each other, grasping handfuls of flesh as their tongues do battle. Anderson's fingers fumble at Quinn's belt buckle. "You have no idea what you do to me," he moans. "What you've always done to me."

Quinn slithers out of his jeans, thankful he's worn one of his sexier pairs of boxer briefs.

Anderson smirks with approval. "*Oh, you're in trouble now, boy...*"

Quinn laughs, "What, you gonna tie me up and *punish me*, Daddy?"

Anderson lunges back at the words, breaking the current between them. His eyes go empty and Quinn watches the color leave his face.

"What? What's wrong?"

Anderson removes himself and rakes his eyes over Quinn's body as if seeing him for the first time. "No. No, I'm not gonna punish you," he mumbles. "You need to leave."

"What?"

"You, you shouldn't be here," he stammers. "You need to go."

Quinn huffs, "You're shitting me, right?"

"You need to go!" Anderson's voice booms as he grabs handfuls of his own hair. "You need to go. Now! You need to go…"

Quinn watches Anderson come undone, spewing words like a broken robot. He grabs his jeans to cover his lap and asks, "Did I do something wrong?"

Anderson's shaking his head now, rubbing the back of his neck and shaking his head wildly. "You can't be here. You need to go."

"Mr. Doyle—"

"DON'T CALL ME THAT!"

"Fine! Jesus. What the fuck is wrong with you?" Quinn steps into his jeans. "You invited me here."

"You shouldn't be here."

"Yeah, I got that part." Quinn looks for his shirt. "Wow. You're kicking me out, after all that."

"You need to just… do as you're told!" Anderson's twitchy and pacing now.

Quinn no longer recognizes him. "Is this some sort of bad trip? Are you on something?" He reaches out, but Anderson snatches his hand back. "Do I need to call someone?"

Anderson finds Quinn's shirt and tosses it at him. "I'm begging you, Quinn. Please, just go." His voice cracks and his eyes have a glassy sheen to them.

"I don't get it, but fine." Quinn gets dressed, exasperated. "Let me use your bathroom real quick, I'll call a car and be out of your fucking hair."

"No." He shakes his head. "No. You should go."

"Seriously? I gotta take a piss, Anderson." The name is sour on his tongue now. It's turned, like spoiled milk. All the sweetness is gone and only a bitter aftertaste remains. "Can you just be a fucking gentleman and show me where the bathroom is?"

Anderson glances down the hallway, then down to the floor. His mouth moves but Quinn can't make out the words.

"Hello?"

"*Fine.*" He grunts and points. "Make it fast. Then go!"

Quinn storms past him. Before he finds the door to the bathroom, he feels the heat rushing to his cheeks and hot tears taking over. He closes the door and rests his back against it. His reflection stares back from the mirror over the sink, in disbelief.

He rushes to the sink, turns the faucet, and splashes water on his face, the sound drowning out his tears.

His mind races...

What did he do wrong? Granted, there's no guidebook for hooking up with a long-lost teacher, but he thought he'd handled himself pretty well, all things considered.

Maybe Anderson's ashamed. They were all over each other, and suddenly, like a switch being flipped, Anderson wouldn't let Quinn even touch him! Is this some kind of ex-gay relapse? Had he been recruited after Freeman? Had Quinn knocked him off the wagon and is this the blowback?

Maybe it's a bad trip. Anderson mixed some molly – or what he thought was Molly – with his Viagra and now he's out of his mind, Quinn imagines. Plus, who knows how many rum and cokes he downed before Quinn arrived? He could be hallucinating.

Maybe there's a Mrs. Doyle. Quinn can see it now. Her business trip got cut short, and she's about to walk in any minute. Perhaps Anderson heard her car pull into the driveway. She's been gone, but now she's back! That would explain the house being so clean. What if she's about to come bursting through the door, exhausted from her trip and eager to kick off her kitten heels and down a glass of Chardonnay? She's probably an academic type. A professor at NY State. Yes. They met on campus. She was off at some fancy conference he bowed out of to stay in town and cruise the bars. She's probably oblivious about her husband's sexuality. They probably haven't had sex in months, but that all feels perfectly normal now. Or maybe she secretly knows. Finding Quinn here would settle it. Even if she'd walked in earlier, back when he gave Quinn the wine and they were clothed and only chatting, their intentions would have been obvious. Quinn would have *exuded* guilt. He doesn't have a steel poker face like Bailey. He would have said the wrong thing, and her worst fears would have been confirmed instantaneously.

Quinn's imagination runs wild, but none of his theories feel right.

He wipes at his eyes and catches a glimpse of the shower curtain in the mirror. He turns to discover that everything in the room is blue. Blue shower curtain. Blue bath mats. Blue toothbrush. The white linoleum flooring with small, pale blue flowers is peeling in a few areas. The dim smell of bleach lingers in the air.

He turns off the faucet and dries his hands on one of two matching blue hand towels. They feel new and unused.

It strikes him that he'll have to tell Bailey how this night has spectacularly gone down in flames. *Rejected by an old goat*, Bailey will declare and shake his head. Then the pity will follow. The curse of the scarlet "S" strikes again, and Quinn knows he's in for a long car ride home.

He puts the towel back and it slips off the bar to the floor. "Fuck."

He has a good mind to leave it, to disrupt order and leave

86

one piece of rebellion behind; a sign that he was here.

Bailey would leave it. Then he'd piss all over the bathroom and tell Anderson to fuck off on his way out. He'd give zero fucks about Anderson's apparent OCD and odd need for order.

But alas, Quinn isn't Bailey.

He relieves himself, then leans to pick up the towel off the floor – and that's when it catches his eye.

There, under the heat grate in the floor... something lies at the bottom, the edge of it barely in view.

Quinn freezes as the air in the room thickens. He slowly kneels, tracing his fingers along the edge of the grate.

Warm air passes through.

It looks loose.

He peers closer and tests it.

It's loose.

He throws a glance over his shoulder, although the door is closed, then carefully lifts one edge of the grate. It gets stuck for a moment as he lifts it high enough to get a hand inside.

Holding the grate up, he pulls out a hidden stack of *Polaroids* bound together by an old rubber band.

The face staring back is young. Maybe sixteen or seventeen. Brown hair and bright green eyes like his own. He smiles back at Quinn in the photo, wearing a green and burgundy striped tee. A date, 2/23/2007, is scribbled at the bottom of the Polaroid in black marker.

He flips to the next photo and his stomach plummets.

It's the same boy. Mutilated. His eyes are vacant and glazed over. He's bruised and his throat has been cut. Deep gashes tear through the same green and burgundy tee, covered in dried blood. The date at the bottom of the Polaroid reads

2/24/2007.

Is this real? Why would Anderson have these?

With a trembling hand, Quinn spreads the photos on the floor like playing cards and a small cry escapes him.

One photo after another, it's more of the same carnage. Smiling faces followed by portraits of death. Before and after. Living, then dead. Alive, then carved and bloody. There's so much blood. He covers his mouth to keep from screaming.

Quinn has seen crime photos before, images that James had been bold enough to text him once, but he's never seen anything like this. All of their throats have been cut, that's the constant – but there are so many other angry gashes. There's no pattern to the knife wounds, just pure anger unleashed. They'd been slaughtered like cattle.

There's something else he notices despite his frazzled state. *They all look similar.* In a way. Same features. Same hair color with green eyes… only the dates written on the photos change, and the boy in each photo ages.

He scans a finger over them. 2007… 2008… and then his finger stops at a familiar face.

Travis Hall.

His best friend, who ran away from home their junior year of high school. Only… *Travis never ran away*. He never even made it out of Bristol apparently.

Quinn tears up as he stares at the lifeless photo. Travis' throat has been cut. He's shirtless on a plastic sheet, a white glimmer of his collarbone peeking beneath threads of flesh. He looks frozen in time, the same age Quinn last saw him…

This was the same kid who used to eat alone in the cafeteria before they met. The same kid half the football team bullied until Quinn reported it to Principal Ingram. They became fast friends after that. Sneaking into R-rated movies together. Hanging out at the mall after school. Even camping out in Quinn's backyard.

The same kid… butchered before him.

Quinn swallows the lump in his throat as tears sting his eyes. He clears his throat and presses on. 2010… 2011… the boy in each photo continues to age… 2016… 2017… 2018… until he finally flips to the last photo. There's no date, but the man looks to be Quinn's age. A trimmed beard. Same build. Same brown hair and green eyes.

Flipping through the stack of photos is like watching the same person age and be murdered, again and again.

There's a loud knock at the door and Quinn shutters, dropping the grate. Before he can recover and catch it, it bangs shut!

He feels the air in the room go still and his mouth goes dry as he realizes…

Anderson knows.

6 / DADDY

Quinn pushes the lock on the door a second before the knob rattles!

He scurries away from the door until his back hits the cabinet under the sink. Hugging his knees into his chest, he watches the doorknob rattle and shake.

His heart bangs around in his ribcage like a frightened bird trying to escape, as Anderson bangs against the door, trying to barge his way in.

Is this really happening?

Suddenly the rattling stops.

Has he left? Has he gone to get something to force his way in with?

"I didn't want to do this." Anderson's voice is calm on the other side of the door. Too calm. There's a matter-of-factness in his words that rattles Quinn more than his outburst earlier. "You've forced my hand, Quinn."

Quinn scrambles to his feet and braces for the door to fly open. "I'm calling the police, you sick fuck!" He reaches for his phone but comes up empty.

Where the hell is his...

The coffee table. He pictures it sitting next to his full glass of wine.

"Not likely," Anderson says. "The only thing you're gonna do is scream."

Scream. Yes! Quinn tilts his head back and screams for help. Blood-curdling cries for the neighbors to hear!

"That's right, *scream for Daddy!*" Anderson chuckles. "Don't you think the last one might have tried that?"

He's right. As Quinn's predicament sinks in, he realizes Anderson has probably prepared for that. For *this*. For everything he's doing now. He looks around the bathroom... No window. No way out. He checks the cabinet under the sink... Toilet cleaner, bleach, plastic gloves, a few old cans of bathroom cleaner, and one roll of toilet paper. Nothing useful. There's also nothing sharp in the room. There's nothing he can use as a weapon; and if there were, Anderson has removed it.

"I have to say I'm a little disappointed," Anderson sighs. "Turns out you're no different than the rest."

Quinn feels like a lab rat in a controlled environment. The bathroom has clearly been staged, perhaps after "the last one" got trapped here.

"You can't stay in there forever, Quinn," Anderson says. "Although all this *foreplay* is making me *so* fuckin' hard right now—"

"People will look for me! They'll know I'm gone."

"They'll look for a while." There's a dullness to his voice. "Then they'll stop. That's how it works."

"I have family."

"What, your *mother*?" He laughs wildly. "Your junkie mother... Right. I remember her."

Quinn's hands become fists.

"Let me guess, she's gonna make missing posters and put

91

your photo on milk cartons. Remember when they did that?" Another chuckle. "Do you know why they stopped?"

Quinn doesn't answer.

"You'd think too many missing people, right?"

He doesn't answer, but yes. That seems logical.

"Think bigger." Anderson's tone slips back into teacher mode. "It was the pediatricians. Too many complaints by pediatricians that the photos frightened young children. Adults weren't really paying attention to the images on the milk cartons anymore. All the photos started to look the same, and the only ones paying attention were young kids trying to enjoy their cereal."

"My DNA's all over this place, asshole."

"Rewards are pretty rare these days too for info on missing people," Anderson goes on. "I don't suppose your mother could offer one. No. Now Travis Hall! *You remember your friend, Travis, right?* His father went all out. A $10,000 reward. They searched those woods near the school for months, but they never found him... and they never will."

Quinn looks around the bathroom. Maybe he's overlooked something.

"How long do you think she'll look for you?" Anderson asks. "Until she starts itchin' for her next fix?"

"People at the bar saw us leave together. Lots of people. *Bailey!*" As soon as he says his name, he regrets it. Would Anderson go after Bailey to tie up loose ends?

"How much you wanna bet that creampuff couldn't describe me? Describe me to the police, I mean. A detailed description."

Quinn quietly considers this.

"What would he say? 'He left with some old guy?' Know how many of us old goats were there tonight?"

Quinn keeps his eyes on the doorknob.

"Here's a hint. More than me."

"Surveillance cameras!"

"Ah, good! But not installed yet." There's a dance in his voice. "Now you're thinkin', Quinn. But, as you can see, I've done my homework."

Quinn thinks he sees the knob move ever so slightly.

"Has it crossed your mind yet?"

Quinn turns to look under the sink again.

"Was it just a coincidence, running into each other tonight? Or were you just at the wrong place at the wrong time?"

It hadn't crossed his mind, but now it's all he can think about. Did Anderson track him down after all these years?

Is he the one who got away?

"I don't think I'll tell you," Anderson decides with a giggle. "I'll let you wonder as I'm opening your fucking throat." The words sound orgasmic as they leave him. Quinn imagines Anderson's eyes rolling back in his head, dizzy with bloodlust.

The doorknob turns. Quinn's sure of it this time. He faces the door, ready for what may come. "I'm not like them," his voice quivers. "I'm nothing like them..."

"Think so, huh?" Anderson laughs from the other side. "Let's find out!"

There's a click, the knob turns, and the door whips open.

Quinn extends an arm to flick open Bailey's lighter. Anderson's eyes widen as Quinn's other hand wheels forward with the aerosol can of bath cleaner.

There's a burst of light and a loud whoosh of fire as Anderson's arm goes up to shield his face, a beat too late. Burnt fumes and heat fill the doorway as Quinn drops the can and rushes forward, ramming his weight past Anderson. He only looks back once to see Anderson flailing, grabbing at his face and trying to put out the flames traveling the length of his arm.

Quinn's amazed the makeshift torch worked since he's only seen this in movies. He'd forgotten Bailey had given him his lighter at the bar until he bent down at the sink and felt it press into his thigh. Anderson must not have seen Bailey hand it to him; otherwise, he might have found a way to confiscate it. Hearing Anderson wail behind him is a small victory as Quinn runs and crashes into the front door, fumbling with the knob. He flips the deadbolt and pulls. The door rattles but refuses to open. He tries again, looking for another lock he might have missed.

"You think I was gonna let you go?!" Anderson's voice booms behind him.

That's when Quinn sees it. The doorknob has a keyhole instead of a tab lock. It's an odd configuration, something he naturally wouldn't have noticed coming in. If he had, he might have just mentally filed it as another oddity of the house, like its dated wood paneling and shag carpet.

The reality that he's locked inside starts to sink in. Anderson must have done it when he was cornered in the bathroom.

Suddenly, like an optical illusion, the front door slides out of reach as Quinn grasps at the air wildly. Anderson has him by the collar, yanking him down to the floor with a thud that knocks the wind out of him. Quinn kicks as Anderson drags him back into the living room, like a caveman dragging a wild animal into his lair to slaughter.

Quinn feels himself being pulled until he's sitting on the floor between Anderson's legs. He suddenly feels the warmth of Anderson's chest on his back. He kicks to break free as

Anderson wraps an arm around his neck and leans back. The smell of burnt fabric and singed flesh fill his nostrils.

Anderson grunts, pulling his arm tighter across Quinn's throat.

Quinn scratches at Anderson's arm until he's released. He gasps for air and jolts forward. The front door comes into view again, looking miles away now.

Something yanks against Quinn's neck, and he flies back into Anderson's deadly embrace. His eyes land on the ceiling, the yellow glow from the kitchen off to his left. There's another tight pull and he feels his throat closing. Between ragged gasps, he reaches for Anderson's hands, but they're no longer at his neck...

Quinn's eyes go wide with terror as he feels the cold metal of his necklace press into him, cutting his air short. He kicks and wriggles to get free, feeling the pressure on his throat intensify. There's a loud grunt behind him, and Quinn can picture Anderson sweating and grinding his teeth as he pulls on the chain around his neck. Quinn's eyes begin to water and the ceiling starts to lose focus.

"That's right... just go to sleep, lover. It'll be over soon," Anderson grunts between clenched teeth.

Quinn swings an arm back, reaching, but comes up empty. He feels Anderson's knee wedged into his back, pushing him forward as Anderson leans *back* with all of his weight! The chain is wrapped tight in his fingers.

He's not letting go.

Dark spots flash in front of Quinn's eyes as he feels his lungs start to burn. He tries to capture a breath but can't. It feels like he's drowning.

Think, Quinn, think!

He tilts his head back, as much as Anderson's grip will allow and leans *into* him, clawing weakly at Anderson's grip on the chain.

Anderson rests his chin on Quinn's shoulder, almost intimately, as he tightens his hold.

He feels Anderson's lips brush his earlobe and realizes Anderson's also holding his breath, waiting for him to fizzle out before he'll release his death grip.

Quinn blinks hard and moves his hands down to his waist, unfastening his belt as quickly as he can.

Anderson yanks on the chain!

Quinn tries to cry out but can't. With all the strength he can muster, he lifts his hips and yanks on the buckle.

"Hey, stop that. Hey!" Anderson's words are loud and wet in Quinn's ear, but there's nothing he can do without letting go.

Quinn hears the buckle hit the floor and feels around until he has the opposite end. The smooth leather strap feels heavy in the palm of his hand.

Anderson leans back and dodges as Quinn swings the belt wildly. Their bodies rock on the carpet as he ducks another swing!

Quinn swings again. Then once more, harder this time. He plants his feet, lifting his hips, and swings until he feels the buckle connect with something hard.

Skull.

Anderson cries out sharply and his grip slips.

Quinn sucks in as much air as his burning lungs can soak in. He kicks free and rolls onto his stomach. He gasps and coughs while Anderson writhes on the floor, holding the side of his head.

Quinn pushes himself onto his knees, coughing and grasping at his neck. He peers back into the living room but doesn't see his phone on the coffee table.

Anderson groans and starts to crawl in his direction.

Quinn flings himself backward, kicking until he's managed to get onto his feet. He makes it to the front door and steadies himself. He can't help but try the doorknob again… a mere reflex at this point as he fights for survival. He rattles the door and grunts before giving up.

Anderson is slowly recovering, willing himself onto his feet.

Quinn stumbles into the kitchen and scans the room for another way out.

The kitchen is just as orderly as the rest of the house. A small, white vintage stove that looked unused. Faux granite laminate countertops. Dated appliances. A toaster. No dishes or silverware in sight. Just an open bottle of wine and a radio sitting by the sink playing ballads from the past.

He turns to face the pantry and finds a deadbolt at eye level.

Who locks their pantry?

Perhaps he's locked up the knives.

No.

Think, Quinn.

It's not a pantry…

He quickly undoes the sliding deadbolt and opens the door. He catches a fleeting glimpse of stairs leading down into darkness before Anderson slams into him, sending him flying into the stove.

Anderson grabs a handful of Quinn's hair and yanks his head back. "Youuuu… are making this very difficult!"

Quinn struggles as Anderson forces him facedown over the stove. He can feel Anderson's hips pushing against him.

He prays Anderson doesn't think to turn on the burners.

God, if you're listening, don't let him turn on the burners!

Quinn pushes back and drives an elbow into his stomach.

Anderson grabs Quinn's wrist to spin him around, and the back of his knuckles come at full speed! With one swipe, his fist crashes into Quinn's jaw and sends him reeling.

Quinn slams into the sink, bracing himself on the counter as blood floods his mouth.

"You should have left when you had the chance," Anderson says, out of breath.

Quinn spits into the sink and cringes, dizzy at the sight of his own blood. Part of him is in denial. *Is any of this really happening? Did he doze off in yoga class? Is this all just a terrifying nightmare?*

He feels a set of hands grab his shoulders. Quinn reaches for the closest thing, the open bottle of Chateau Laurent, and swings! He watches a wave of red wine and glass wash over Anderson as it shatters against his head. A wild thought runs through his mind then. Did Anderson lace the wine? Was he meant to pass out?

Did Travis drink the wine?

Quinn makes a move for the basement door – but slips, landing hard on his wrists.

Anderson seizes the moment. He drives his foot back as if he's about to punt a football and delivers an earth-shattering blow to Quinn's ribs. Quinn screams and curls into a ball as the kicks beat into him.

He lunges and crawls to evade Anderson, one elbow before the other, feeling shards of littered glass bite his arms as his elbows beat into the floor. Anderson's hands claw into the fabric of his shirt. There's a hard tug that lifts Quinn off the floor. The room tilts, like a tripod being knocked over, as Quinn's flung onto his back. Anderson's face comes into view, hovering above him, wild and cut up with glimmers of dark glass sparkling under fluorescent light. The kitchen smells like a bitter mixture of wine and blood.

Anderson murmurs something before straddling Quinn with his full weight, both hands latched around Quinn's sore, angry throat.

Quinn fights back for what feels like hours. His gurgled screams and useless kicks echo off the kitchen walls.

Anderson presses his weight into his hands and an ungodly noise escapes, "Ahhughhh!" He strains, red in the face, as a trail of spit dangles from his mouth.

Quinn feels a tear trail down into his ear. The room starts to go dark and the rhythm of his heels hitting the floor grow sluggish.

Anderson is silent above him now... *focused*, with a concentration in his eyes that resembles the man he adored so many years ago. It feels abysmally ironic that behind the murder on Anderson's breath is the same man who kissed him less than an hour ago. Beneath the blood and fury on Anderson's face is the man of Quinn's teenage dreams.

Suddenly, Anderson's shoulders spasm – a quick jerking motion that makes his eyes go wide.

Then again.

He gasps and his grip loosens as he arches his back.

Quinn wheezes, trying to fill his mouth with air, only to discover fresh blood spilling in. The taste is thick and heavy on his tongue like metal.

There's so much blood...

Spattering his face.

In his eyes.

In his mouth.

Rolling down his cheek.

Collecting in the hollow of Quinn's neck.

Anderson's shoulders jerk and Quinn sees a faint glimmer behind them. A light rising and falling.

Anderson's grip releases as he gives a deep, gurgled cry. Blood sprays from his lips.

Quinn blinks hard, and a knife behind Anderson comes into focus. Everything in his body tells him to scream. His stomach tightens and the muscles in his throat act on memory, but there's no sound. Just a raw, burning rattle.

The light appears again, dancing along the edge of the knife. Quinn watches as it dives between Anderson's shoulders, and the weight of Anderson's body collapses onto him.

A pair of green eyes glare down at their tangled limbs as the knife continues to rain down.

Pinned to the floor, Quinn feels faint huffs of breath on his neck with each blow. He watches the light fade from Anderson's eyes as he stares back, paralyzed with fear. Blood pools around them, warm and sticky on Quinn's arms. He feels the pressure of Anderson's body being pierced, the knife threatening to pierce through and skewer both of them as loud sobs fill the air – crazed sobs that have lost count and all sense of time.

Quinn fears the stabbing will never stop. He cries out weakly enough to signify that he's there.

The knocks against the now vacant body on top of him slowly come to a halt. Quinn uses a free arm to shift Anderson's weight off him, and the figure above them snaps into focus.

He's tall and lanky with sunken, thinning features. His face is badly beaten, one eye nearly closed shut. His collarbone seems to jut from his bare chest, the white of the bone nearly visible under translucent skin. He clenches onto the knife, oblivious to the gore that covers his arm. The extent of his wounds is hard to decipher beneath the dirt and splotches of blood that have aged and turned black. Tortured eyes the color of emeralds stare back, dazed but brilliant as they project from dark circles. He's barefoot, and Quinn can smell him, a rank combination of piss, blood, and suffering.

He faces Quinn with the knife in his trembling hand.

Behind him, the basement door stands wide open.

Quinn scrambles away from Anderson's body, adrenaline kicking in now. "It's okay!" He extends a hand and a soft nod to indicate he means no harm. "It's over."

A sigh leaves the bloody figure as he sinks to his knees, sobs filling him once again; sobs so heavy and thick that they shake his entire core. He winces at Anderson's body as the reality of what he's done sinks in.

"What's your name?" Quinn asks as he assesses the skin under his blood-soaked T-shirt with one hand. *Had his stabs reached through?* "You must have people looking for you, yeah?"

The bloody stranger glances back at the basement door, then returns his gaze to Quinn with a shudder. "What day is it?"

Quinn has to think for a moment. He remembers he went to yoga earlier. "It's a Friday. July 19th."

He deflates a little.

The resemblance dawns on Quinn that he recognizes him from the last photo in Anderson's sick collection. What's worse, minus the carnage and matted beard, he could easily be mistaken for Quinn. The resemblance is chilling.

This could have been Quinn in Anderson's basement.

Quinn stands slowly. "Is anyone else down there? Are you alone?"

He nods faintly. "Just me."

"I'm gonna call for help. I need to find my phone."

"Did you unlock the door?" There's a sprightly tone to his words; something that plucks at the bloody puzzle pieces between them, trying to gauge Quinn's role in all this. "I tried, I kept trying to escape before, before he came back to—" he tears up as the words become helpless sobs.

"It's okay," Quinn nods, wanting to hold him. He's seen the photos, but can't imagine the torture that transpired just beneath where they stand.

"Thought I was gonna rot away down there."

"He can't hurt anyone anymore. He can't hurt you." Quinn wipes at the blood on his own face and kicks Anderson's hand near his foot; a test, really. If this was a horror movie, Anderson might have jumped up by now in that way monsters and villains are so good at, when you least expect it. But Anderson Doyle wasn't invincible or made of steel. He was just a man. Flesh and blood hiding a twisted monster who had everyone fooled.

"I blacked out," he goes dreamlike, trying to recall. "He must have drugged me," he rubs at the chill on his arms, smearing fresh blood on them. "What about you? How'd you get here?"

"First date gone wrong," Quinn says wryly as he bends to search Anderson's pockets. "This fuck was my science teacher if you can believe that."

His glare hardens as he shifts his weight off his knees and

slumps to one side on the floor.

"It was a long time ago," Quinn explains, sensing his confusion. "I haven't seen him in years. Until tonight." He doesn't find a phone in Anderson's pockets. Or a wallet. But he does find a few bloody bills and a small key. "Ha!" He holds up the key to the front door triumphantly, although it doesn't mean much to his dazed companion at the moment. "Did you have a phone when he brought you here? *Of course, you did,*" Quinn sighs. "He must have hidden them. That's okay!" He forces himself to sound positive and consoling, although he has no plan at all for what should come next. He does know he should call the police. This is a crime scene now. There's been a murder.

He wishes he could call James right now. James would surely know what to do – but that would look suspicious when the authorities pull phone records later. He's seen enough crime TV to know that. Why didn't he call the police first, they'd demand to know? "We'll walk to a neighbor's for help," he decides impatiently. "Who knows where the hell our phones could be?"

The sound of violins slice through his thoughts as another love ballad begins to play from the radio. Quinn winces and reaches turn it off. His fingers leave blood on the dial as the song fades into silence.

"Allen Denney." The words fill the air like a curse.

Quinn looks back to the bloody figure sitting on the floor, "Is that your name?"

"*No...*" He extends a blood-covered arm and points at Anderson as if it's obvious. "Coach Denney."

Quinn feels the blood drain from his face. "No, that's Anderson *Doyle* from Bristol, Virginia. Science teacher... got fired my freshman year, trust me," he laughs dryly. "I know this psycho."

He shakes his head firmly and a tear streams down his face. "No. *No*... We met on campus. We work together in the athletics department. He's the assistant coach. He, he took me to dinner that night," his eyes dart around wildly. "I, uh, I remember I ordered lamb chops! They were chewy. He ordered the ribeye. He kept sayin' I reminded him of someone," he recalls. "Someone he used to know. That's Coach Denney. Hundred percent."

"That guy." Quinn aims a finger at the body, face down, bleeding out. "That's the guy who did this to you? You're sure you don't mean Coach *Doyle*?" He insists. "I think you're in shock."

"And I think I'd recognize the sick fuck who cut pieces out of me night-after-fucking-night! That's Coach Denney," he spits and starts to rock back and forth.

A cold silence falls over the room as they lock eyes. Identical, green eyes with the same gleam of wonder and horror.

Quinn crosses his arms and swallows hard to find his next set of words.

"Something tells me we're both wrong."

7 / SUGAR

The police precinct smells like burnt coffee.

Quinn has been treated for his wounds and allowed to take a shower, but only after being examined by a medical technician, who took a DNA swab and scraped under his nails. Only after that, and being passed around a hoard of detectives who all asked the same questions, was he escorted to a grimy shower that smelt of mildew and soap – the kind of pink, stringent soap full of chemicals you find in rest stop bathrooms. It took close to an hour to wash down all the blood and get his nerves together.

He sits in a cold interrogation room with his hair still damp, wrapped in a red flannel blanket that faintly smells of perfume. He wonders who the last trauma victim was who found herself wrapped in this blanket. Had she gone through anything nearly as terrifying as what he endured?

He can only guess that the clothes he wears were dropped off by Bailey after the call he made upon arrival. He wears a pair of riding boots, camouflage-green joggers with suspenders and a large, floral print Lacroix sweatshirt – which look ridiculous paired together in real life, off the runway. People don't dress like this outside of magazines, he must remember to tell Bailey. A T-shirt and jeans, to replace his bloody ones being held in evidence, would have sufficed.

The room he's in looks remarkably like something off television, with its gray cinder block walls and stainless steel furnishings. One table, two chairs facing one another. There's a camera in the far corner of the room, and of course, no interrogation room is complete without a two-sided mirror running one length of a wall.

He hasn't been arrested, though. If anything, he deducts, they're looking to see if his story changes, if what he's told the 911 responder on the phone aligns with what he says next. They'll also cross-check it against what he's told the detectives at the station. It's a game of telephone.

They'll likely bring in the "big guns" next, he thinks glumly. It's akin to facing the big boss in the last level of a video game. If he can just get through this last round, he wins and can go home. He craves his own bed, a greasy cheeseburger, and a cigarette before sleeping the rest of this evening away. It's been months since his last cigarette, something he's prided himself on, but he figures he's earned it. He's just survived a monster. One cigarette won't kill him now.

The door opens and in walks Detective Denise Bradshaw. She's petite with pretty brown skin and natural locks that she's swept into a clumsy bun. She wears a white top under a black blazer with a colorful necklace that might have come from an art market, handmade by some local artisan. Her nails are painted a distracting bubblegum pink, and her right ear is lined with silver piercings and hoops. Quinn spies a tattoo on her wrist with a name he can't quite read upside-down, surrounded by flames. The name of a past boyfriend or girlfriend?

She doesn't look like a cop. He likes her immediately. He

wishes they could just skip all this nasty interrogation business and hang out at Tarrant's for brunch. In another life they might be friends, but these are the cards they've been dealt.

"Quinn Harris?" She doesn't wait for confirmation. "Detective Denise Bradshaw." She presses her lips tightly together as they shake hands, and her hazel eyes soften at the sight of him. "How you doin' by now, hon? Sounds like you've had one helluva night."

"I'm hangin' in there," he says with a shiver. "Would love some coffee and a cigarette to tell you the truth."

"I think we can make that happen," she says, cracking a wide smile. "I can use a cup myself. I've been here all damn night. Two more hours, then I get to go home to my babies." Her face glows.

He imagines two little ones rushing her at the door when she gets home, dangling off her neck as she hugs and showers them with the kind of kisses only a mother can create.

She leans in with a hushed voice, "We'll have to sneak in the cigarette – *public health regulations an' all that shit* – but tell me how you like your coffee, hon."

"Black. Please."

"Sugar?"

"No, thanks. Actually…" he backtracks, "I'll take some cream if you have it?"

"We can do that." She turns in her chair to face the mirror, "Two coffees. One black, one with a splash of cream." She points between Quinn and herself at the table.

"That's some service," Quinn blinks. "Do we drive forward to pay at the next window?"

Her lips fall just short of a smile. "You're funny. Nice to see you still have a sense of humor after what you've been

107

through." It reads more like an observation than admiration.

"If only you knew my luck with men," he muses, touching the bandage at his neck. "Look, Detective Bradshaw—"

"Denise, *please.*"

He takes a sharp breath. "Denise. *Look*, unless I'm under arrest for something, I prefer to move this along so I can get some rest and a jumpstart on therapy. Someone just died on top of metonight." He hears his voice crack. "I've given my statement – more than once – so please, if we can just get on with this?"

She nods like a talk show host, eager to show that she's hearing him. "I hear what you're saying, Quinn. It's tragic what's happened. It's fucked up, is what it is," she levels with him. "It's a miracle you were able to escape, from what I understand." She opens the manila folder she's brought in and flips to the second page. "Says here you rigged some kinda flamethrower?" Her eyebrows shoot up. "Pretty badass."

"Have you been able to ID him?"

"You said in your statement he was your teacher, right?"

She knows this already. How many times has he mentioned it to the other detectives?

"Right, but apparently who I thought he is, isn't who he really is," he explains. "We're pretty sure he's been using an alias, maybe all along."

"By 'we' you mean yourself and the other victim?"

"You never answered my question." Quinn crosses his arms. "And that other 'victim' has a name."

"Well, of course," she stammers, "Of course he does."

Henry Collins. It wasn't until a police cruiser arrived that Quinn recalled hearing the name on the news. He hadn't even recognized Henry through all the bloodshed. His hair was dirty and matted, he was missing a few of his front teeth, and his face was so badly beaten it was difficult to look at him for long. He'd been missing for nine days. Before help arrived, Henry confided that he works for NY State's athletic department as a trainer, which is how he met Anderson. He'd been charmed by Anderson's interest in him, which sounded painfully familiar – no doubt history repeating itself, Quinn surmised.

Henry's family donates a shit-ton of money to the university. Most notably, his notoriously conservative father, Ted Collins, is campaigning for Lieutenant Governor. Had it not been for that, Henry's disappearance might not have received the coverage it did. The photos of Henry that flashed across the news portrayed him as a handsome and wholesome all-American guy next door who disappeared without a trace after the team's football practice one evening. The broadcasted photos look nothing like the broken shell who'd staggered out of Anderson's basement. There were photos of Henry smiling in his team uniform, opening gifts with the Collins family at Christmas. There were even photos of Henry and his girlfriend, Kendall – a pretty brunette with former debutante written all over her. As Quinn watched an EMT check Henry's vitals and shine a small flashlight into his eyes, he wondered what pretty lies Anderson spun to seduce him. He also wondered if anyone knew of Henry's attraction to men. *It certainly didn't seem like public knowledge.*

Quinn is surprised that the resemblance between himself and Henry has yet to come up. Perhaps Denise hasn't clocked it.

"How is he?" Quinn thinks to ask. They'd been separated after leaving the crime scene, put into different cars and, he suspects, different rooms at the station – unless they took Henry to the hospital first, which is likely. Once the police arrived, Henry went into shock and was barely coherent. He even overhead the EMTs say something about a blood transfusion. While Quinn has been running the gauntlet after being treated at the scene, Henry's probably somewhere being tended to in a hospital bed.

"I'd say he's blessed to be alive," Denise's eyes go wide. "Considering what we found in the basement... power tools, rusty pliers... a drill..." she shakes her head.

Quinn wonders if they also found a camera, but before he can broach the subject of the photos, Denise moves on.

"He's out of ICU, last I heard." She drums her fingernails on the table. "Nothing since then, but hey, no news is good news, right? Although, I'm sure you'd disagree," she adds with a smirk, looking as though she wants to say more but doesn't.

"What do you mean, I'd disagree?"

They're interrupted by a quick knock before a uniformed officer strides in with their coffees, a lighter, and an open pack of cigarettes. He's a few years Denise's senior with a bushy mustache and salt and pepper hair. Denise doesn't acknowledge him even as he leaves, letting the door slam behind him. Her eyes stay on Quinn. "You know you saved him tonight, right?" She gently nods her head. "If you hadn't been there, if you hadn't unlocked that door to the basement—"

"He's the one who saved me. And what he did was self-defense. I've included that in my statement, and I'm willing to testify if need be."

"We're not there yet." Her voice levels out. "First, I want to hear from you, in your own words, what happened tonight."

He wants to rip his hair out and scream but he fights the urge. This is what they want, Denise and whoever's watching from behind the mirror, but he mustn't get riled up. He has to stay calm and simply tell her what happened. Again.

He takes the lighter of the two coffees with a cautious sip. It's piping hot and stale on his tongue.

Denise has produced a pen and looks ready to write in her file.

What the hell's in that file anyway?

Quinn's never been good at reading upside-down. He still hasn't made out the name on her wrist. It looks like… Deandre? Or *Dierdra*?

He gives up and takes another sip.

"No detail is too small," she primes him. "Your history with the deceased could be key to understanding what's happened tonight."

Quinn's no longer sure of anything having to do with Anderson Doyle, or whoever he was. He's been trying to take inventory of what he knows to be true from their time together at Freeman, but the lines are now blurred. He swallows and sets his cup aside. "What do you want to know?"

"How did you meet?"

"High school. Like I said, he was my science teacher, but he was also the football coach. I guess more people would remember him for that. He was sort of a big deal."

"What does that mean?"

"In the year he was there, he groomed a losing team to win the state championship. He was a fucking hero."

"Did you play?"

"With *these* chicken legs?" He stops, shocked by how easily he's just quoted Anderson.

111

Denise smirks, amused by his response. "My oldest plays," she offers. "He's good. Wants to play in the NFL one day."

"Good luck with that," Quinn says. "Only about 0.09% of high school senior players get drafted by an NFL team. That's nine in 10,000."

Her face falls. She's less amused by his cynicism and curtly turns back to the interview. "What was your relationship with him like in high school?"

It's a loaded question. He reaches for his coffee and uses the opportunity to organize his thoughts. He feels it's safe to leave out his sugar-sweet schoolyard crush on Anderson. He'll tell her Anderson was supportive as his teacher and helped him earn scholarships and so on, but that's all. What's most relevant is what transpired tonight. Their reconnection tonight is really where the story begins, he decides. He might have to divulge that he went home with Anderson intending to have sex with him. He wonders if she'll judge him for this, the way the last detective looked at him with a disparaging glare.

His eyes dart around the room as he sips, trying to reconcile how the day took such a wild turn. Life seemed so simple just a few hours ago, laced with a warm buzz and first-world problems. Now a missing person has been found along with a dead body, and Quinn's at the center of the investigation.

He feels nauseated.

Denise notices his posture change. "Everything okay?" She slides the pack of cigarettes across the table.

"Fine. Yes." He perks up and reaches for the pack although he no longer has a taste for them.

She smiles anyway as he sets the cigarettes aside. Her demeanor is almost gracious, like a host at a tea party whose guest just declined helping themselves to another finger sandwich.

There's something not right.

He can feel it.

There must be a reason she's so accommodating; the patronizing gleam to her eyes, the coffee, and cigarettes – it's more than a good cop act.

Suddenly, something she said earlier leaps to the top of his mind: *No news is good news, right?*

There was something in her expression that doesn't sit right. *How much does she know about him?*

"You were saying?" She arches her manicured brows and motions for him to continue.

Could she know that he's a journalist? She must have run a background check on him by now.

Quinn leans back in his seat and throws a glance at his reflection in the mirror. "Who's watching?"

"It's just you and me, Quinn." She narrows her eyes. "Focus on me."

"Are they watching to see how much I know?"

"Is there something you'd like to share?"

"I'm aware that Henry Collins and Anderson Doyle were having a *romantic* relationship before Henry killed him tonight – something I'm sure his father, the 'future Lieutenant Governor', wouldn't want me to know or *write* about."

Her eyes go weary as she releases a long sigh.

"Well. I'm glad you brought that up." She closes the folder and crosses her arms. Now that Quinn has laid his cards on the table, there's a pause before she speaks again, but when she finally does the words come out carefully measured. "Your occupation makes this a sensitive matter, certainly."

"For who? Ted Collins?"

"This is an open investigation."

"And your main witness happens to be a journalist. I imagine that's rather inconvenient."

She glowers and asks, "Is this the part where you 'give' me an opportunity to 'control the narrative'?"

"Something like that. Trauma victims aren't the most reliable sources, I'm sure you're aware. They confuse things, sequences of events... details... I'd hate to write an *emotional* account of what's happened tonight. Filling in the blanks could get interesting. Unless you care to help with the facts?"

She stifles a laugh and glances at the mirror. It's as if she's looking for guidance but there's no reply.

"I have questions too," Quinn says. "Questions about the man Henry *killed* tonight." He's sure to emphasize the word. He wants whoever's watching to know he has leverage in case he needs it. He won't be railroaded. "An equal exchange of information," he offers. "A real conversation. I'll show you mine if you show me yours."

"This isn't a negotiation."

"Collins' campaign team already has a PR circus on their hands," he counters. "Who knows how they'll try to spin the gory details. But if it comes out that Henry actually had a romantic relationship with the man he murdered, that's a very different can of worms. His conservative base won't look past that. That can't be good for poll numbers, and that's what this is all about, right?" He waves about the room. "Damage control? Seeing how much I pieced together at the scene? I've already given my statement."

"I think you're in shock," Denise says flatly.

"I think I'm pretty fucking aware of what's happening here."

Denise's jaw tightens as she glances between Quinn and the mirror. It's obvious now that Quinn's a loose cannon. Who knows what he might write if given the chance? She sighs and gets up from the table, the folder firmly gripped in her hand. "Wait here."

She slams the door behind her and Quinn sighs, in awe of his own misfortune.

He looks back to the two-way mirror and he's sure of it now. Someone from Ted Collins' campaign team is behind the glass, if not Ted himself. He wonders how tight the Collins family is with the police commissioner – they must be fairly cozy if Collins' team can have the police intervene like this. Quinn's not entirely surprised though. He's heard rumblings of this sort of thing happening, and James has whispered rumors to him full of corrupt cops in the shadows and shady deals formed under tables. *One hand washes the other… quid pro quo…*

A few minutes pass and Denise reenters, her face more relaxed. "Change your mind about the cigarette?" She's left the folder behind this time.

"Yeah, I quit," he says.

She tosses him an odd look as she sits. "Well. Your cooperation in this investigation is important – to all parties involved. We just want to understand what's happened." She draws a deep breath before continuing, "We have questions, and if there are certain questions you have *that I'm able to answer*, I don't see the harm in that. Off the record, of course."

"His name." Quinn leans forward intently. "I need to know his real name."

She purses her lips together, already regretting this. "The deceased has been identified as *Andrew Dunn*. His prints

115

pulled a match from a case in Tennessee where he was under investigation."

"For similar behavior? Involving a student?"

"The murder of his wife."

Quinn can hardly believe it. He can't imagine a past life where Anderson, or *Andrew* as it turns out, was happily married with a wife – or perhaps *not so happily* if he murdered her.

"The case was dropped. Lack of evidence, small-town politics…" she shakes her head. "That was years ago. Would have been nice to put this psycho away before it reached this point."

"So he gets away with murder in Tennessee, then what?"

"Funny enough," Denise eyes the cigarettes on the table, "there's no legal paper trail for an 'Andrew Dunn' after the murder of his wife. He changed his name."

"But he coached high school football, he was a teacher!" Quinn points out, "He seemed to live a normal life."

"There's nothing 'normal' about the house you were in tonight."

Quinn holds his breath, knowing he's not going to like what comes next.

"He didn't live there, Quinn," she says, almost apologetically, as if she feels for how naive he must be feeling at the moment. "It was a kill house. He bought it under an alias, but there's no evidence to suggest he ever even slept there. The basement was designed to be a torture den. You can tell he put a lot of money and effort there. Upstairs was just…" She searches for the right word.

"Staged?"

It fits. It explains why Quinn didn't see any personal

116

belongings in the house.

"He went through great lengths to appear normal."

Quinn feels his throat tighten and fresh tears well in his eyes. "How could he do it?"

She deflates some and her shoulders drop with a sudden sense of gloom. "You never know what people are capable of." There's a sadness in her voice. "I've seen a case where a nanny – with no history of violence, mind you – suffocated a newborn 'because it wouldn't stop crying'. A newborn."

He's speechless. He can't fathom how anyone could be so evil. He's been trying to imagine his version of Andrew filleting and torturing Henry with knives and power drills, and he can't. Even after seeing Henry's mutilated body... even after scarcely surviving Andrew's death grip around his own throat, his mind can't make sense of it.

"Unlocking what makes people like Andrew Dunn tick is not an easy job. That's why we need your help," she says. "And your discretion. This is a very sensitive time for the Collins family and Henry still has a long road to recovery." She wets her lips and carefully adds, "This is an occasion to be celebrated. Henry has been found – thanks to you – and *that* is what the press needs to focus on. Hell. Andrew Dunn is *dead*," she shrugs. "It's case closed as far as I'm concerned. Henry being at Andrew's tonight doesn't have to cloud the fact that he's been found, and he gets to go home to his family."

"Are you suggesting—"

"Henry's sexuality is also not of importance," she cuts in. "The last thing he needs is the press sensationalizing it."

"I would *never* write anything that would out Henry or endanger him," Quinn clarifies. "That was never my intention here and that's not something my community does. Coming out is personal. No one deserves to be thrown out the closet."

No. He could never out Henry. Henry's been through enough.

"That's good," Denise nods slowly. "I'm glad to hear you say that. I'm sure the family appreciates your cooperation, and, in fact, someone should be in touch soon regarding the reward."

"Reward?"

She clasps her hands on the table and leans in, saying, "When Henry first went missing, the family issued a $50,000 reward to anyone with information that led to his safe return. *With your cooperation*," there's a spike in her tone, "I'm sure the family would be willing to increase that."

His mouth goes dry. He doesn't recall hearing anything about a reward. He also doesn't like what she implied about *not* placing Henry at Andrew's house.

"The details can be sorted out later," Denise's voice returns to normal. "Meanwhile, I've got two teams trying to locate Andrew's home, his actual one, where he might have planned the abduction. We're thinking it's politically motivated. Out of all the people on that campus, what are the odds that Ted Collins' son was taken? Perhaps there was a ransom in the works," she shrugs. "There's enough evidence at the kill house for a conviction, if he were alive. The case is practically closed, but we can't leave any stone unturned."

Quinn finds himself nodding. He's listening to Denise, but her words are fuzzy along the edges. Nothing is as sharp as it was before mention of the "reward".

This is what it's all been leading to.

"I've answered your questions," he hears Denise say. "Now I have to know if you recall anything Andrew might have said that could help, anything that seemed off at the time or struck

118

a chord. No detail is too small."

No detail is too small.

He mulls over what she's said, wondering how much to tell her.

He toys with the idea of telling her he'd been enamored with Andrew, and yes, he'd gone home with him to fulfill some silly fantasy. Why not at this point?

He considers telling her that her notion of what's happened tonight couldn't be further from the cold dark truth. Denise thinks this is an isolated incident. She thinks Andrew kidnapped and tortured Henry out of some insane grudge against Ted Collins for political reasons or for ransom.

He bites his lip... and nearly tells her about the photos he found, the stack of Andrew's victims who would disagree with her grand theory.

But he doesn't.

8 / YOUNGBLOOD

The fluorescent lights in the office are giving Quinn a headache. He swears he can hear the soft hum of the bulbs, crackling and buzzing under their electric glow.

He's had only a few hours of sleep before coming into work, so it's very possible that delirium has set in. He'd been completely disoriented after leaving the police station. Denise had offered to have an officer take him home, but he declined. He didn't completely trust her, and the idea of getting into a car with someone he didn't know terrified him. Even alongside a police officer, who's sworn to protect and serve, something in the darkest corner of his mind tugged at the notion of his body being later discovered in a landfill.

Despite what some might call a rescue, he was still a witness to a murder and a horrific crime scene. He doesn't know the depths of Denise's investigation or the full scope of the parties involved. Also, let's not forget that getting into Andrew's car was a hard lesson learned. So when Denise asked, with her warm hazel eyes, if he'd like a police escort home, he said, "Pass," without missing a beat.

Once free from interrogation, he found Bailey, who greeted him in the lobby with hugs and a million burning questions.

"Sweet Jesus, I've been so fuckin' worried!" He snatched

Quinn into a tight embrace. "How *are* you? I can't believe that asshole tried to *murder* you!"

"Yeah. That surprised me, too," Quinn mumbled cynically.

"Holy shit!" Bailey pulled back to inspect Quinn's bruised eye and the bandages on his arms. "He did this to you?"

"Think this is bad? You should see the other guy."

"Wow." Bailey rolled his eyes. "Too soon, babe. Too soon. Let's get the hell outta here."

Quinn gave him the abridged version of events on the ride home to his apartment, although he didn't feel like talking about it anymore, least of all discussing what a mistake it'd been to leave with Andrew in the first place.

Bailey didn't dare say, "I told you so," after watching Quinn slump through his apartment door and collapse into an armchair half-covered with laundry. Instead, he promptly raided Quinn's fridge, making him a quick turkey sandwich with a beer to wash it down. "Here, babe. You've gotta be starvin'."

Quinn ate silently, trying to block out the image of Andrew strangling him from above as blood rained down.

Once Bailey fell asleep on the couch, Quinn made his way to the shower. He peeled off the clothes Bailey lent him and folded them carefully before stepping under the scalding hot water. It felt good to use his own soap. It felt good to let the water wash away the smells and memories of the past few hours.

He slept awful in Bailey's bed, and it showed when he arrived at work. The office is buzzing with rumors and uncomfortable glances at the bandages on his arms. The bruise on his eye has also turned a particularly foul shade of purple by now, and his neck is still bruised and angry from

Andrew's grasp.

You'd think that in a room full of journalists someone would march to his desk and pry for details. *Was he mugged? Was he in a car crash? Was it a bar brawl?* Any other time, his coworkers are neck-deep in his business, even daring to tread into the murky waters of his love life or lack thereof. There are constant attempts to play matchmaker, matching him with any gay man that comes to mind, as if sexuality alone is enough for a successful, meaningful relationship. Lavandra, one of the proofreaders, is especially hellbent on playing Cupid: "I was at a wedding in Chelsea this weekend and *guess what…*" This is the part where she swings her braids to one side and blinks her long fake lashes. "The bride's cousin has a friend who's gay. I'm not sure what he does or if he lives in the city. I'm not sure how old he is, but she said he's super nice. You guys should meet. I gave her your number to give him. *No need to thank me, boo. You know I be lookin' out!*"

With this kind of help, it's no wonder the most action he's received lately is from a serial killer.

Lavandra only shoots him a solemn look this morning, as Ren slides his chair over to Quinn's desk. He's wearing a deadpan expression and leans in with bass in his voice, saying, "Hey man, tell me who did it. Just say the fuckin' word, man, and I will FUCK THEM UP for real."

Quinn chuckles for a number of reasons. One: Ren's too late to fuck anyone up. Andrew's body is cold in the morgue by now. Two: Despite Ren's size, the thought of him in a fight is laughable. He's a gentle giant who watches bloopers and cat videos half the day when he doesn't think anyone's watching.

"My knight in shining armor." Quinn's grateful for the laugh, though his ribs still hurt from where Andrew kicked him. It's a miracle nothing's broken.

"You know you're my boy," Ren says, his face serious now. "So if you got, like, gay-bashed or somethin'—"

"Oh. No, it's not... that." Quinn's touched though. He wants to reach out and rest a hand on Ren's arm to reassure him, but he doesn't. "Let's just say I had a rough night."

"Fair enough," Ren gives a nod and his afro sways in tow.

"So, I'm guessing the whole office thinks I've been bashed?" Quinn cringes.

"Pretty much."

"Great. That's just great," he groans inwardly.

"Don't worry 'bout them, man," Ren makes a fist. "I'm here if you need anything, alright?"

"Just kiss the wife and the twins for me when you see them," he gives Ren a fist bump and frowns. "Life is short."

· · ·

Marcus has been waiting for Quinn to knock on his door. A handful of staff writers have texted to ask if he's seen Quinn. There's little real concern in the messages that ping his phone. They largely want to know if Marcus knows anything, which he doesn't.

The placement of Quinn's bandages concerns him, but he's ruled out a suicide attempt. Marcus can point to a few people in the office who might off themselves one day, but Quinn's not on that list. He's not the type. Mary in HR? She's the type. Last summer, an intern walked into a stall and caught her on the toilet, cutting the inside of her thigh with a razor. Mary denied it, almost convincingly, and ever since Marcus makes it a point to stop by her office on his way in and say good

123

morning, fearing he might find her chair empty one of these days.

His thoughts return to Quinn. If anything, he decides, a boyfriend has roughed him up. He doesn't know anything about the men Quinn dates, nor does he have an interest. He just hopes Quinn is smart enough to leave the abusive bastard. He read somewhere that LGBTQ members fall victim to domestic violence at equal if not higher rates compared to their heterosexual counterparts. Regardless of who you love, no one deserves this kind of treatment. It's not his place, but Marcus thinks he might say just as much when he sees Quinn.

"Got a sec?" Quinn asks with his head through the door.

Marcus waves a hand for him to come in. His eyes are strained on one of four mounted TVs facing his desk running the news. "What can I do for you, youngblood?"

Quinn walks over, holding a yellow legal envelope. The look on his face is unreadable as he undoes the metal fastener and dumps its contents onto Marcus' desk. He takes an ink pen and carefully spreads the Polaroids of Andrew's victims across Marcus' desk like a magician doing a card trick, daring Marcus to pick from the pile of mutilated bodies.

He watches Marcus' face go cold and says in a leaden voice, "I found something that scares me."

• • •

Marcus insists that Quinn start at the beginning but first he dials his receptionist, Dory, telling her to clear the rest of his day. "No one gets through. No one comes in."

He entertains the idea of leaving the office altogether, maybe taking Quinn somewhere more private to walk through what's happened, but he realizes that might look suspicious to the rest of the staff considering Quinn's injuries. Instead, he turns up the volume on one of the TVs, and they move to a round conference table in his office. He rarely uses it, except for eating breakfast, so he wipes off the crumbs of granola and breakfast cereal and allows Quinn to carefully arrange the photos in order of the dates written on them. Before and after. Alive, then dead. To do this, Marcus lends Quinn a pair of latex gloves he fishes out of his desk. Quinn doesn't question why he has latex gloves in his desk. He's heard stories about Marcus' glory days in the field. He was quite the renegade back then and old habits die hard.

Once Quinn has brought him up to speed, Marcus pushes his glasses back onto his nose and leans back in his chair with a heavy breath. Considering what Quinn's been through, it's amazing he survived the night, let alone came into work today.

"Who else knows about this?"

"The photos?"

Marcus nods emphatically.

"No one." It feels dangerous to say this. The significance of this isn't lost on Quinn, either. He realizes the weight of what he's done. It had been a ballsy move to take the photos in the first place, and at the time, he didn't know why he did it. Perhaps if Travis hadn't been in the pile, he might have been thinking more clearly. He might have told the officers who responded to the 911 call where to find the photos – or later mentioned the photos to Denise. But *Travis* was in the pile. As much as he wanted to look at this objectively as a journalist, he knew the killer intimately and one of his victims personally. This isn't a normal case.

"How'd you keep these from the police? They didn't find

them on you?"

"Henry and I were both covered in blood, so I figured there'd be some kind of medical exam," Quinn shrugs. "I knew the cops would lock the crime scene down, so I doubled back to the bathroom for the photos after I called 911 from a neighbor's house. I hid them in the neighbor's backyard, under their deck. Then I took a cab back early this morning to get them before work. I just... couldn't leave them behind in that house."

"You could face some serious time for this. I don't have to tell you that." Marcus scowls and lines crinkle across his forehead. "For now, if anyone asks, I have to deny ever seeing these."

"I get it," Quinn nods. "In a way, it's good that I have them, right? I can't trust

that detective with them apparently... I thought about bringing them to the feds instead, but who knows if Ted Collins has someone on payroll there?"

"Potentially his brother, to start with," Marcus says. "He's got a brother who's a crime analyst in the Albany office. Hell. The whole family's either in politics or law enforcement. His father – you're probably too young to remember this – his father, George, ran for city council back in the '80s. He's a war vet. Loaded. Would've won if that scandal with that girl didn't come out."

Quinn makes a face. He doesn't want to know the coarse details. "What else do you know about Collins?"

"Typical politician." Marcus shrugs. "His wife comes from money. This is his third wife. They seem to get younger and younger..."

"What else?"

"Collins has friends in high places. You were right not to take these to the feds just yet. Plus, walkin' in headquarters with photos of murdered boys might've been a hard sell."

"Without proof they were Andrew's, they might put *me* under investigation," Quinn says. "I can't let them fall into the wrong hands."

"Then what's your next play? This is your show now," Marcus says, careful not to sound too much like a proud papa. He hadn't expected Quinn to come to him with something this heavy, this soon. It was only yesterday that he'd thrown down the challenge, and somehow the universe had answered. "With this smoking gun you absolutely have to play this right. There can be no missteps."

"I don't know how they'll spin Henry being found, but what's clear is that they don't want to connect Henry with Anderson – I mean *Andrew*. From what I gathered, they think the abduction was politically motivated, and they'd rather sweep this whole thing under the rug. But Henry killed Andrew. I was there. I saw it firsthand. He did it to save me, to make Andrew stop." He pauses, seeing Andrew's face flash before him, bloody and twisted. "But if Henry's implicated in Andrew's murder – *orin any murder* – his fathers' campaign is sunk."

"Obviously." Marcus has been following Ted Collins' smear campaign closely. His extremist thirty-second campaign spots air every few hours to take aim at his opponent, Stacey Marek, the city's first female African American candidate for Lieutenant Governor. "He'll never allow his son to be investigated for murder, even if it was self-defense. He won't let it get that far."

"Right. And, sure, Andrew's dead now. They could argue

Henry did the world a favor, that he's a fucking hero, right?" The words taste ironic on his tongue. "But the larger problem is this... if they sweep everything under the rug – *if what Andrew did doesn't come to light* – then, even in death, Andrew gets away with these other murders. That's twelve murders!" He points to the photos. "Twelve unsolved disappearances. Twelve victims who will never get justice. Think of all the parents who will never know what happened to their boys..."

"Are you sure you want to take on Collins?" It's not really a question. It sounds more like a warning from Marcus. He's thinking about Quinn's safety, but he's also thinking about the magazine if a legal fight ensues.

"If I can't use Henry, I have to prove that Andrew was tied to one of the other victims." Quinn feels his phone vibrate in his pocket. He knows it must be James, who has left him a string of voicemails.

"If they know you have these photos..." Marcus shakes his head warily. "If they find out Andrew had other victims..."

Quinn runs a hand through his hair. "That's a nasty can of worms they won't want to open. Not during an election. Hell, it changes the whole narrative." He chews at his lower lip. "If they find out what Andrew actually was, who knows what they won't do to cover it up?"

Marcus huffs and gives Quinn a long look. "Quite the quandary you're in. It's almost impressive."

"Thanks," Quinn takes a little bow. "I wouldn't have brought this to you if I didn't have a plan though."

"Then let's hear it." Marcus adjusts his glasses and folds his arms. "Where do you start?"

Quinn points to the first photo, dated 2/23/2007. "I start with him."

"Got a name?"

Quinn picks up the photo in his gloved hand. The boy in the Polaroid gleams back, his smile frozen in time, unaware of the fate about to befall him. "Shouldn't be too hard to ID, assuming there was a missing person's report filed in 2007. I'm guessing they never found a body, for any of them."

"Why do you say that?"

"Because I know how he thinks. I mean, *thought*." Quinn grimaces. "He was neat, concise. He was a man of science. He would have accounted for any number of outcomes – maybe even going as far as dissolving the bodies in acid! Who the hell knows what he had access to?"

Marcus' face goes dark. "If there are no bodies—"

"I know. No bodies, no evidence."

It's a shame he can't ask Andrew what the hell he did with their bodies. It's now a secret he'll take to his grave.

"Your connection to that son of a bitch is what makes this work as a story," Marcus says. "Don't forget that."

"Yet another reason this detective and Collins don't want me writing about this."

"Exactly. Who better to tell the story than a survivor? And the fact that they tried to pay you off… Classic." Marcus kills the smile pulling at his lips, knowing that this story has the ability to be explosive. He stands and laces his fingers behind his head. "That Collins is as slippery as they come. I don't doubt he's got a few cops on payroll."

"I wouldn't be surprised if I get a visit soon, circling back on the 'reward'."

"You don't have a lot of time then." Marcus strolls back to his desk. "You have my support on this but you need to move fast. We can cover flights, but just keep track of your other expenses." He reaches into his desk and brings out a tape recorder. He points it in Quinn's direction. "You also need a failsafe."

Quinn chews at his bottom lip. "A failsafe?" He's hoping Marcus doesn't mean what he thinks he means.

"In case anything happens to you." The words come out more casually than he intended. "Not that it will – but you never know." He drops his head. "I mean, if Collins wasn't involved in this. Jesus, if that kid in the basement had been anyone other than Ted Collins' son…"

"I really hit the lottery, huh?"

Marcus approaches with the recorder, "I've seen some pretty dirty campaigns in my day. Some of these guys will stop at nothing to control the narrative, and if you get in their way, well…" He's trying his best not to scare Quinn, but he sees he's already failed. "Look," he levels with him, "I'm not gonna sugarcoat this shit, Quinn. Like you said, you can handle the hard stuff, right?"

Quinn tightens his jaw and gives a steadfast nod.

"Right. So when you do this, you have to divulge everything – where you've hidden the photos, what you know about Andrew, how Collins is involved in this… everything. It's insurance. You have to give this to someone you trust." He holds out the tape recorder. "But it can't be me."

Quinn shakes his head to show that he understands, then takes the recorder. It feels heavy in his hand, like a loaded pistol.

"Is there someone you trust? Someone not associated with the media?"

"There's my friend, Bail—"

"Don't tell me their name!" Marcus puts up a hand. "Just

make the arrangements." He goes back to his desk and sits. He glances at the time on his monitor and realizes they've been in his office for over two hours. "You should get back out there."

Quinn glares down at the tape recorder in his hands.

"Quinn?"

He jerks his head up. Marcus is standing now to escort him out. "Right. I'll keep you posted." He gathers the Polaroids.

"Start looking into the victims, and let's keep a pulse on this thing. I want to hear if that detective or any of Collins' people reach out."

Quinn clears his throat and pulls his shoulders back. "Will do. I'll find a way to connect Andrew and locate the bodies. The boys in these photos deserve justice."

"Which damn sure won't happen if Collins has anything to do with it. Those photos would never see the light of day if you hadn't found them first."

So why does Quinn feel a knot in his stomach?

He gives Marcus a confident nod on his way out. "Thanks for the chat, boss. I feel much better," he says, loudly enough for anyone listening to hear.

"Don't mention it, youngblood." Marcus pats his shoulder. "My door's always open."

Quinn walks the floor of the newsroom. He walks past rows of cubicles that fall silent as he passes. He walks past his peers, who give him a sympathetic tilt of their head. He quickens his pace, feeling their eyes burn into his skin. He's practically running now, past HR, past his desk, and Ren who stands to ask if he's okay. He bursts through the door of the men's room, locks himself inside a stall, and sinks to the floor just before the tears spill over.

9 / GOOD TREE, BAD APPLE

Quinn knocks twice before Bailey answers the door.

"You made it!" Bailey's smile is laced with worry. He's wearing a navy striped apron over his gray tank top and ripped jeans. He looks like a model off-duty, casual but somehow still photoshoot-ready should the occasion arise.

Quinn will never understand how he pulls this off. He leans in for a hug, careful of his bandages.

"Make yourself at home, babe. I've got hors d'oeuvres and your favorite beer." Bailey points to the kitchen counter that's covered with craft beer and platters that have been delivered by the caterer.

Quinn eyes a cheeseboard, some mini ham biscuits, deviled eggs, mini crab cakes, a casserole, and a fruit plate with piles of brightly colored watermelon, berries, and cantaloupe. "Why so much food?" He's mortified. "Looks like a funeral spread."

Bailey looks at him with wide doe eyes, as though it's obvious. "We're celebrating! We're celebrating you not being murdered."

Quinn cracks open a beer and takes a long swig. "You know I hate surprise parties."

"Look!" Bailey beams. "I even got you some of Big Daddy's Country Fried Ribs! I'm heating 'em up in the oven."

"How'd you know I like those?"

Perhaps Quinn hasn't been as careful about his guilty pleasure as he thought.

Bailey places one hand on his hip and balances a cocktail in the other. "I'm your best friend. It's my fucking job to know these things."

Suddenly Aubrey emerges, dressed in her tight flight uniform with a roller bag dragging behind her. She swipes her blonde bangs from her eyes and gives Quinn a bubbly smile. "Hey, Quinn. Congrats on not dying!"

"Uh, thanks?"

She gives him a quick hug. She smells like expensive French perfume and hairspray. "Sorry to miss your party, but I've got a flight to Cabo to catch and the pilot is cute. Mama can*not* be late."

"Bring me back a postcard?"

"Don't I always?" She winks and blows Bailey a kiss on her way out.

"She's been trying to fuck this pilot for months now," Bailey says, rolling his eyes once she's gone.

"More power to her."

A thick silence fills the air.

Bailey scowls, and his eyes gloss over. "I never should have let you leave with him. It's all I keep thinkin'." He fights back tears. "I really am the worst."

"Don't." Quinn puts down his beer and rushes forward. "This is not your fault. You couldn't have known. Don't blame yourself." He cups Bailey's face and kisses his forehead.

Bailey closes his eyes on impact and smiles weakly. "If somethin' were to happen to you," he swears, "I don't know what I'd do."

"I'm fine. Really." Quinn pushes back and goes for another sip. "I lived to tell the tale." He pauses to savor the bitter pilsner in his mouth before swallowing. "And that's what I intend to do."

"What about that detective, Bradshaw?" Bailey folds his arms.

"Don't worry about her. I have a plan. I spent yesterday doing some research—"

"So *that's* why you didn't call me back yesterday." Bailey flexes his eyebrows. "You were at the library all day, weren't you?"

Quinn freezes, guilty as charged. "Marcus let me take some time from the office. I'm on assignment. I just needed time to unplug and figure things out." He swallows, realizing he's drinking his beer too fast. He'll never get through the evening and keep his composure if he doesn't slow down. The last thing he needs is another meltdown.

"You know how you get when you investigate a story," Bailey says dryly. "It's not healthy. You definitely need to eat. I bet you're starvin'." He nods and marches into the kitchen.

Food is the last thing on Quinn's mind. He takes off his jacket, feeling comfortable in a pair of dark jeans and a gray baseball tee with his old, scuffed Chuck Taylor's. His hair is still slightly damp from the shower, the ends curling and wild as he tosses his hair out of his face.

It's dusk outside. Bailey's drafty floor-to-ceiling windows give a breathtaking view of the city lights and traffic on its way home.

There are only a few pieces of furniture in the living area to lounge on: an old gray sectional, two mismatched armchairs from Aubrey's last apartment, and a dark wood coffee table with metal finishes. The kitchen faces the opposite end of the space where exposed brick walls map out the bedrooms and a shared bath with an old clawfoot tub. Things are constantly needing to be fixed, but neither Bailey nor Aubrey are there long enough to be inconvenienced for long. At the moment, Bailey has clothes and fashion magazines strewn about the Oriental rug in the living area. There's a television on a console with a record player beside it. Rows of records line a metal shelving unit in the corner, and three large industrial glass shades hang over the space, creating a warm glow that draws Quinn over.

He parks himself on one end of the sectional and removes his shoes, pulling his knees into his chest. "It's actually a good thing you got so much food. I invited a plus one," he says, hugging his knees.

"Who? That hottie from your yoga class?"

He wishes. "No. I invited James. It'll be better if I talk to you both at the same time."

Bailey instantly rolls his eyes. He can't imagine why Quinn has invited James or what he could possibly want to talk to *both* of them about. Bailey and Quinn tell each other everything. What does James have to do with any of it? He can't make a guess. Eventually, he realizes the delay in his reply is stretching on and wills himself to say, "Great," in an upbeat, Mary Poppins octave. "The more the merrier!" He delivers the cheese board to the coffee table. "Maybe I'll see what the super or the drug dealer who lives next door are doin'. Invite 'em over too…"

"Why do you dislike James *so much*?"

"I never said I didn't like him." Bailey wipes his hands on his apron.

"It's what you don't say." Quinn looks at him earnestly. "He's a good guy. I wish you'd get to know him. He's actually—" There's a quick knock at the door that cuts him short. "*Here*. That must be him. He's early."

Bailey raises an eyebrow. "I'll get it. You just sit there and look pretty."

"Play nice," Quinn pleads.

Bailey struts toward the door, tossing his apron aside. He takes a quick breath before snatching the door open.

James gives an awkward smile and hands over a bottle in a paper bag. "I guess this is for you. I never show up anywhere empty-handed."

Bailey eyes the bottle, a mid-range cabernet, and stuffs it back in its paper bag. "He's inside," he manages with a small smile. It's the absolute least he can do since James, nonetheless, is now a guest in his home. People may accuse Bailey of a lot of things, but they'll never accuse him of being a bad host.

James shuffles past Bailey and catches a whiff of the ribs in the oven. "Is that Big Daddy's BBQ I smell?"

"I didn't know you were coming." Bailey holds out a hand to take James' blazer. "I only got enough for Quinn since I don't eat that garbage. *It's not even real Southern BBQ, you know*. Who puts tomato sauce in their BBQ? Any respectable sauce is vinegar-based. Everyone knows this."

"Right…" James nods slowly, then asks the question he's been dying to ask since Quinn introduced them months ago at a day party in Brooklyn. "Is it true your father is 'Big Daddy'?" He's read somewhere that Big Daddy is a bible-thumpin' southern aristocrat of the fiercest kind. He takes in Bailey with his torn jeans and bad boy chip on his shoulder as if the rumors can't be true.

"Oh, it's true," Bailey smirks, reading his face. "What can I say? Good tree, bad apple."

Quinn stands to intercept James.

"That's some spread." James eyes the food in the kitchen.

"We're having a party," Quinn informs him, "It's my 'congrats-for-not-dying-at-the-hands-of-a-psychopath' party."

James makes a face. "Congrats?"

"Thank you."

"It's a celebration of life!" Bailey shouts from the kitchen with his head in the oven, checking the ribs.

James closes the distance between himself and Quinn, pulling Quinn into his strong arms. He smells like the lab and aftershave. Quinn can feel his heart beating through his dress shirt – a pale plum color that looks perfect against his golden-brown skin. For the first time in days, he feels safe, locked within James' solid embrace.

Quinn smiles and closes his eyes for a moment. "Thanks for coming."

"I should have brought a gift."

"You are the gift."

James tenses, and Quinn silently kicks himself.

Way to go, Quinn, he thinks. *You're a fucking poet.*

They slowly pull apart and James stares into Quinn's technicolor-green eyes, wincing at his bruised eyelid and bandages. "You okay?"

"I'm okay. Really."

"One of my buddies at the station saw you being brought in and texted me. He's one of the guys I was with at SKY the other night – he recognized you – but I never got to really introduce you since we had to leave for dinner..."

"That's okay," Quinn shakes his head. He's only met a handful of James' cop friends. Even then, it seemed like James didn't know exactly how or what to introduce Quinn as. *A friend? An associate? Someone he flirted with but had yet to make a move on?*

"He told me Bradshaw's leading the investigation. I've heard things about her." There's a weight to James' words. "Some people think she's mixed up in some kinda…" he hunches his wide shoulders, searching for the right word.

"You mean she's *corrupt*."

"Sort of," James frowns, "I mean, sure, there are dirty cops out there, but I hear she rubs elbows with some heavyweight *politicians* – the kind who pay good money for some influence on the force. She's in a league of her own."

"It definitely felt more like damage control when she was questioning me."

James makes a tortured face. "I hate that you're wrapped up in all this."

"And it keeps getting worse," Quinn adds with a cynical smile. He can't help feeling like everything keeps unraveling. Each step forward is like pulling a thread on a sweater. "The fact that Bradshaw's looped in with Ted Collins is definitely not good."

"What are you gonna do about the 'reward' offer?"

Quinn scoffs. "I'd tell her to shove it up Ted Collins' tight ass if political warfare wasn't on the table."

"He runs a nasty campaign." James' face sours. "Remember the TV spots when he ran for mayor? I can't imagine what went on *behind* the scenes."

"Did you see the news on Henry? They're only reporting that he's been 'found' and is safe at home. No mention of me or that monster who took him."

They share a daunting look as Bailey saunters over, his lips breaking into a wide smile. He's holding a platter and a cold beer for James. "Let's eat, shall we? There's plenty of nibbles and I think I have a quiche in the fridge if this isn't enough."

James takes it all in, shooting Quinn a bewildered smile. "Are more people joining the party?"

"Hope not!" Bailey's smile is sharp like a double-edged sword.

"I guess let's eat." Quinn surrenders to Bailey's southern charm. He's clearly trying to help the only way he knows how.

If there's one thing Bailey's mother has taught him – aside from how to make a perfect mint julep – it's that people need to eat in times of crisis. Food is healing.

Bailey turns on some jazz, which he figures is a safe choice, and dishes out plates as they settle into the living area. He runs back into the kitchen for silverware, quietly cursing himself for not thinking to bring them out sooner. He should have just asked the caterer to leave a small staff behind to serve, that's what his mother would have done. But he's not sure what Quinn has to discuss with them. It might be sensitive, too sensitive for the help to overhear. He sighs to himself and decides to focus on being a good host. That much he can manage. He'll keep everyone's drink full, replenish their plates, and pray for the best.

As he reaches for a serving spoon his phone pings with a text message from his mother. It's as if he's thought her up.

He stares at the message that reads, "IT'S NOT TOO LATE," then sighs loud enough for Quinn and James to hear and turns off his phone.

• • •

Soon enough, everyone is grazing from the platters Bailey has brought out and politely sipping their drinks. It feels forced and trivial since no one truly has an appetite. Everyone's mind is on what's brought them together and what new horrors Quinn may have to share.

James eyes Quinn between bites, trying to read his expression. The fact that he can't is unnerving – but he's also distracted by Bailey who's telling them about the caterer he uses, as if anyone gives a damn. He's never understood the friendship Quinn and Bailey have. In fact, he would never pair them as best friends in a lineup. Quinn's intelligent and tenacious, and Bailey's so... *Bailey*. His father's a franchise millionaire and his mother's a well-known socialite among Savannah's most elite circles. How Bailey has landed himself in this rundown loft, trying to survive off his looks as a model is beyond him.

"Mayonnaise. They put mayonnaise in their chocolate cake batter! Sounds disgusting but it makes all the difference," Bailey swears.

James stands to start clearing the table, directing his gaze to Quinn.

Quinn takes the note and gathers himself as James and Bailey collect empty plates. Bailey offers them coffee or tea, as if they're on an airplane or at a country club social. Quinn holds tight to the beer he's been nursing, and Bailey ultimately makes himself another gin martini before plopping back on the sofa next to James.

All eyes are on Quinn now as his heart takes a dive, realizing it's time to tell them the worst part of his ordeal. Here goes nothing...

"So, by now, you're both aware that I was attacked the other night."

A chill frosts James' muscular arms. By now, he knows all about the harrowing encounter from the police report he's read four times, incredulously. Imagining Quinn fighting for his life makes his stomach churn. He's also read Quinn's formal statement, which does a piss-poor job of explaining why he was with Andrew Dunn in the first place, although he can guess. It's certainly a blow to his confidence. He would have loved to be the one to take Quinn home that night. Perhaps if Bailey hadn't shown up and if he wasn't with friends that night, things might have gone differently.

After reviewing Quinn's statement and the crime scene photos, James couldn't help but call in a favor to see the scene himself. He knows he shouldn't be assigned to work the case or testify in court about any findings because of his relationship to Quinn. He also knows Quinn would be upset to learn he's been inside the house and seen the evidence firsthand... the two wine glasses on the coffee table... the dried blood on the kitchen floor...

"It turned out that Anderson—" Quinn stops to correct himself. It's been hard to think of Anderson Doyle as Andrew Dunn, but he must get used to it now. Anderson Doyle is long gone, or more accurately never existed. Apparently, he was merely a character Andrew Dunn created to fulfill his bloodlust. Quinn must learn to separate the two now. "*Andrew Dunn* had someone in his basement he was torturing and planning to kill."

"The son of this Ted Collins guy who's running for office." Bailey jumps in to show he'd been listening the night he picked

Quinn up from the police station.

Quinn stands and gets his jacket. "I didn't know Henry was in the house when I arrived. Things went from zero to crazy pretty fast." He fishes an envelope from the inside pocket of his jacket that Bailey and James eye suspiciously. It's the moment of truth. He stands as if he's about to announce an Oscar winner from the envelope, only there are no winners here. "Remember how I said that things keep getting worse?" He almost has to laugh at this point to keep from crying. It's amazing how one decision has changed his life forever. "Not only did I find Henry at the home of Andrew Dunn, but I also found these…" He produces the photos from the envelope and the temperature in the room plummets.

Bailey and James glare at the photos, stunned, as he places them on the table, one by one. By now, even if the stack wasn't in chronological order, Quinn could place the photos in order without looking at the dates. He knows them by face now.

"Jesus Christ!" Bailey places a hand to his throat and gasps, trying to comprehend what he's seeing. "A little warning would have been nice," he sputters and shoots Quinn an incredulous look.

Meanwhile, it doesn't take James long to digest the photos. He's seen his share of gore and dead bodies, but what makes the color drain from his face is what Quinn has done. "These came from the house? You took evidence from a crime scene?!"

"They're safer with me," Quinn says.

James shakes his head and says, "Quinn, you're one of the smartest people I know. I know you know the ramifications – you could get jail time for this. Obstruction of justice. Tampering with evidence… They could slap you with all sorts of charges."

Bailey reaches to inspect the closest photo.

"Don't touch it!" James barks and shoots Quinn a pointed look. "Although it's prob'ly contaminated already."

"I've been careful," Quinn promises.

"And Bradshaw knows nothin' about this?"

"No clue."

"Who else knows?" James presses.

"Just you and Bailey. And one other person."

"Who?"

"I can't say." Quinn desperately wants to tell him it's Marcus but knows with time James will figure it out. He's smart. Too smart for his own good at times.

"You *can't say?*" James scoffs in disbelief and rubs the lines forming on his forehead, as if fighting a migraine. "I, I don't know if I can even fix this, Quinn," he stammers. "Even if I can get these into evidence somehow, this isn't the kind of thing that goes unnoticed. There'd be red flags. Questions. It's too risky."

"I'm not asking you to fix this." Quinn keeps his tone neutral. "I'm just asking you to listen. I need you and Bailey to know what's occurred and what I've uncovered –in the event something happens to me."

"What do you mean?" Bailey panics. "Are you in danger?"

"Here's the thing," Quinn levels with them. "Collins likely has a few cops on payroll. I think we've established that. Now think about it. If they had found these photos first, they would have buried them. They do *not* want a fucking serial killer tied to the disappearance of his son or his campaign, trust me. It's all about optics. They want to tidy this mess up as fast as they can – and if they had these photos there's a chance *not*

143

one of the boys in these photos would receive justice! At least, with the photos in my possession, I can try to give them that."

"Justice." James looks bleak. "How do you intend on doing that?"

"By telling their story. As of now, they're still 'missing persons'. There are people and families who still think some of these boys just *ran away*! But I know the truth. They were murdered and I know who did it. I have to prove what really happened to them – what almost happened to *me*."

James can barely believe what he's hearing. "You're gonna write a story about this?"

"James, that could have been me in these photos – *twice* I've dodged becoming one of his victims. It could have been me instead of Travis back in 2009." He points to Travis' brutalized photo. "I knew him, James. Travis Hall. We were best friends. God only knows why he chose Travis and not me. Now, years later, I run into this maniac at a bar and nearly die at his hands again. Henry and I walked away from this. These other boys weren't so lucky. They deserve – and their families deserve – to have their stories told. Let's not forget that I knew this monster personally and lived to tell the tale. Who better to tell this story than me?"

"He has a point." Bailey nods.

James shoots him an exasperated look. "Not helpful."

"It's not just about the story, James." He can see how this might be an obvious conclusion, given his profession. "It's about closure. I need to know why this happened to Travis. I need to know *why*. Also, people aren't born serial killers. There must have been something that drove Andrew to cross that line."

James inhales. It's a lot to take in. He lets out a long sigh as

144

his eyes start to soften. "I get that you want closure. You've been through something very traumatic. I just don't want you to get hurt again." He sounds more like the James that Quinn knows now. Endearing and practical. "Andrew Dunn is dead. When does this end?"

"Every story has a *beginning*," Quinn says. "And this isn't a normal case, James." Quinn points to the rows of photos. "Look at them. What do you notice?"

James doesn't want to say it, but Bailey doesn't mind. He perks up in his seat and points with his martini glass. "They sorta look like you, especially the last few."

"Exactly! Same hair color, same features, same eye color. But they start young, right?" He points to the boy in 2007, the first photo in the series. "Now look at the next photo... and the next one. The years go on and it's like looking at *the same boy* grow up, only he's killing him. There's a pattern. Every year, there's a new boy who looks the same as the last, only older. It's like they're all the same person."

James leans in, studying the photos as he counts. "Twelve victims. What would possess him to do this twelve times?"

"What would drive him to want to kill someone *again and again*? That's the real question. That's the story!" Quinn can't help the smile that finds its way to his lips. It's so obvious in his mind. *How can they not see that he needs to write about this?* "Don't you see? It's not about *them* necessarily. To Andrew, they were all the same. This was all about *one* person."

"Well, who?" Bailey blinks.

"I'm glad you asked." Quinn has been waiting for this. "I thought the answer might be here, within these photos, right? So I spent most of yesterday ID'ing each of them."

"All twelve?" Bailey winces. "Where do you even start?"

"It was actually easier than I thought it'd be," he's happy to report. "I already had a timeline thanks to the dates written on the photos, so once I found their missing person reports and matched them with their school or college records it wasn't hard to place Andrew Dunn with each of them. Sometimes he was their coach. Sometimes he was their science teacher, like in my case." He pauses at the memory of Mr. Doyle smiling from the front of the classroom, chalk dust caking his fingertips. "Most of the yearbook photos I found even had either a science club or a staff photo or a *football team* photo with Andrew and the victim in it. It was all just a matter of matching dates."

"So you've ID'd the victims and placed Andrew at their schools. You can prove he at least knew them." James looks pensive, but he finally gives an impressed nod. "I'd say that's some good detective work."

"But that doesn't answer why he was doing this – and there's something that doesn't add up in the sequence." Quinn frowns. He realizes he's mostly talking to James at this point. This sort of investigating is outside of Bailey's wheelhouse, although he hasn't counted out any insights Bailey can bring to the table. Sometimes a fresh set of eyes can see what people too close to an investigation can't. "I spent a lot of time looking for similarities between his victims. Sure, the physical similarities are there. Some kids in school even thought Travis and I were brothers because we sorta looked alike, I guess." *Did they?* It hadn't occurred to him at the time, but looking back now, he can see the similarities. He pictures Travis's smile, recalling how Travis had approached him the day after the bullying stopped to thank him. Somehow he'd known it was Quinn who helped put a stop to it. "Anyway, Andrew clearly had a

146

type." He clears his throat.

"But what about their backgrounds?" James offers.

"Yes. Exactly." Quinn smiles faintly, happy to see James put on his detective hat and jump on board. "They were mostly from small towns, especially his first few kills. I looked at their transcripts and they all thrived academically. They were basically wiz kids."

"Like you," Bailey says.

"I wasn't top of my class or anything, but I did well in school." Quinn tries his best to sound modest. "I *enjoyed* school – a lot like these guys as far as I can tell. They were very bright, active students – or players in some cases. About half played football." He slides closer to the table. "This one, *Garret Johnson*," he says, pointing to a photo in the second row. "He was student body president." Garret's throat is slashed open in the photo. The pupils of his emerald eyes are dilated, the light sucked out of them. "This one, *Ryan Wilks*, was a quarterback, prom king, and volunteered at a homeless shelter on weekends. Golden boy." He moves on to the last row. "*Dennis Ford* – his classmates called him Denny – he was taking college-level calculus classes his sophomore year."

"You've done your homework," James says, further impressed.

"There's something else I noticed. Even though they all had pretty spotless records there seemed to always be… something off, like something big they were dealing with outside of school. Life at school looked perfect, but life at home was a horror show."

"What do you mean?" James finishes off his beer, wishing for something stronger.

"Well, take this one, *Sean White*. He was president of the

science club, president of the Young Democrats club, on the yearbook staff, and ran the student radio station, all while holding a 4.0 GPA! Meanwhile, his father's a drunk who beat the living shit out of him until child protective services intervened." He pauses for effect. "I think he joined all those clubs to spend as much time as possible at school and away from home."

Sean's throat looks as if it's been ripped open.

"Jesus." Bailey looks as if he's about to lose the contents of his stomach.

"What about *you*?" James asks. "I mean, does it fit? How were things at home?"

Quinn and Bailey share a look.

Finally, Quinn explains, "My mother's a recovering addict. She was in a car accident my sophomore year. Nothing too major, but her doctor gave her pain meds for her back."

In an instant, James sees where this is going and regrets asking.

"Next thing I know she's pawning my video games for money to buy prescription drugs from the kid down the street."

Bailey knows the story well, and it hurts to see Quinn relive it.

"Pretty soon after that, my dad left us – they divorced, and um, things got pretty bad after he abandoned us. There were some nights we didn't eat. I remember getting called to the principal's office because she'd been arrested. She shoplifted a bunch of shit from Radio Hut. I guess to sell, for pills..." He gazes off, remembering the court hearing and how she'd cried her way out of it, only to wind up back in court three weeks later for stealing cheap jewelry from Harold's to sell off. "She'd even steal from me. *All my college savings?* Gone. I will die twice over before I pay off these damn student loans." He smiles, aiming to crack a joke, but James and Bailey only stare back, destroyed.

"I'm sorry, Quinn." James' deep voice is a whisper now. "I had no idea."

Quinn hunches his shoulders to his ears. "Tough break. But, yeah, to answer your question, things weren't great at home. I'd say I fit the pattern. Travis too. His dad was a drunk, used to beat on his mom. A real cliché I guess." He clears his throat again and moves on. "Back to our golden boy, *Ryan Wilks?*" He aims a finger at Ryan's disfigured portrait. "He was a foster child! Actually, four of these boys were. Four out of twelve. And another one was adopted. What are the odds of that?"

James scowls. "Doesn't feel like a coincidence."

"No, it doesn't. And it would make them easy targets if Andrew gave them even half the attention he gave me in school," Quinn adds bitterly. "This later one, *Lewis Spencer*, was in college. This is once Andrew stopped teaching high school apparently – Lewis swam, did mission work in Nairobi, and just proposed to his girlfriend before he went missing."

"So they weren't all gay," Bailey notes.

It's the kind of observation Quinn had hoped he'd make. "No. Not conclusively. It's not clear what Andrew's relationship was like with them outside of being their teacher or coach or *colleague* like in Henry's case, but what's clear is that they all appealed to him. They all fit the profile. *Except...*" he directs their attention to the very first photo in the timeline from 2007. "*Damon Porter.*"

"How do you mean?"

"If he was Andrew's first kill, it stands to reason he'd be like

149

the rest to follow, right? But, aside from his looks, what I found indicates he was the polar opposite!"

"Huh." James makes a face. "That's weird. I mean, I'm not a licensed psychologist but don't most serial killers stick to a pattern?"

"I'd think so too. But, like I said, Damon was the polar opposite of the profile." He runs down the list in his head, "Not a remarkable student by any means… got into a lot of fights… spent most of his time in detention, even got arrested for vandalism – and guess what? His parents were like something from an after-school special. His father was a doctor. His mother was a lawyer. They lived in an affluent neighborhood. Hell, if anything they had a hard time keeping *him* out of trouble. I found a court receipt where they bailed him out for God knows what." He shakes his head. "Bottom line? He doesn't fit the profile."

"Then why is he here?" Bailey motions at the photos. He's munching on the remaining fruit, with the platter in his lap, determined to not let it go to waste. "Why would this sick fuck choose *him*?"

"Good question." Quinn leans forward with a quick sip of his beer. "I think he was a fluke."

"A fluke?"

"Like me."

It's clear that he's losing them now.

James narrows his eyes. "A fluke. You mean like, what, a bonus kill?"

"Do serial killers do that?" Bailey asks, wishing he'd made his martini a double.

"We'd have to consult with a specialist, but I guess it's possible," James offers. There's a glint in his eyes that suggests he's enjoying this intellectual sparring with Quinn. He may not like the turn of events, but he can't deny the excitement building between them. "So you think Andrew took you as some kind of 'bonus kill'?"

"Well, think about it. If he already took Travis as his 2009 kill in the timeline, and since he already had Henry in the basement for this year's kill, then why go after me?" Quinn poses the question to the room. "Sure. Maybe he just got greedy. Or maybe I was 'the one who got away' – maybe he actually wanted *me* instead of Travis back then and he saw a second chance. Either way, if I was meant to be a bonus, it got me wondering if there were *other* bonus kills, right? *What if there are victims who aren't included in the photos...?*"

"Oh, God," Bailey doesn't like where this is headed. Not one bit. His head's already spinning from the number of corpses on his coffee table. He can't imagine there being *more* victims in this twisted saga. He's thankful Aubrey isn't home to witness any of this.

James is instantly intrigued by Quinn's theory. He has questions, but knowing Quinn he's already done the research. "What did you find?"

"It wasn't easy without a photo," he grimaces. "I started with a search for missing persons who fit our description and would have been the right age to fit the timeline. They had to be one year younger than Damon and fit the profile. Broken family, academic rock stars, all that. Right?"

James and Bailey nod. They're with him so far.

"I got a bunch of hits. Way too many." He frowns, "So I took a different route and looked into *Andrew.*"

"Clever boy." James winks.

"Well, despite the fact that he changed his name every few

years, one thing stayed the same – he loved football and he loved to win. So I started following the trail of state championships, cross-referenced it with my list and *boom*! I got a hit. Just *one* boy from a small town in Tennessee called Sweet Ridge, and that fit! The year he went missing, his school's team won the state championship for the first time ever, and guess who was the fuckin' coach?"

"Andrew-mutha-fuckin'-Dunn." James would jump up and give Quinn a fist bump if it were appropriate, but it's not, so he doesn't. Instead, he simply nods from his seat with a wry smile of approval. "So he fits the profile and the timeline."

"He fits it *perfectly*," Quinn beams. "I pulled his yearbook photo and the resemblance is…" Disturbing. But he doesn't say this. "It's crazy how much we look alike," he says instead. "He went to John Morgan High School. They were the Panthers. I put our yearbook photos side by side and we could have been twins at that age or at least brothers. He grew up on a small farm that looks sort of rundown from the photos. He was extremely bright. He excelled in all of his AP classes and French. Andrew was his science teacher, just like in my case, and Andrew coached the year this kid disappeared. Not only that…" He takes a breath. "There was a lot of suspicion around his disappearance. It was like this big scandal in town. There's *so much* here compared to Damon Porter's case – and there's no other case like it prior to this. This could have been what started it all!"

"So… what does all this mean?" Bailey cuts in, waving his empty martini glass.

Quinn holds his breath, then gives them an anxious half-smile. "I think this kid *Adam Walker* was his first kill," he says confidently. "I think I found the original."

10 / THE ORIGINAL

A scream tears out of Adam's throat as his eyes snap open. He struggles to catch his breath as he examines both sides of his hands, then curls them over to check his fingernails.

No blood.

It was just another dream.

His heart hammers in his chest and it takes a moment for his surroundings to sink in, to realize he's safe.

The flight from Paris Charles de Gaulle Airport to London had been quick, but he felt wiped out. It'd taken everything within him to hail a cab and navigate his way through check-in at The St. Langham. The bellman, Aarul, a lanky middle-aged man with a thick Bengali accent, insisted on carrying his luggage to his room. Normally, Adam would never allow this. Not only because bellmen insist on asking a barrage of annoying and intrusive questions – *Where are you from? What brings you to London?* – but because they can possibly ID him if it ever comes to that. They're good with names, which is of no consequence since he always travels under an alias – but, more damaging, they're good with faces. He bets Aarul never forgets a face.

Adam lies in bed and stares at the ceiling, mulling this over. He should have been more adamant, he thinks, but he was too tired from his travels to fight Aarul off.

He glances at the clock as a yawn escapes. As much as he'd love to sleep in, there's work to be done. He kicks off the sheets and makes his way across the sprawling hotel suite to open the drapes. London's crisp gray sky and iconic cityscape come into focus along the River Thames. There a few boats sprinkled throughout the river taking in the brisk morning air and calm water. The London Eye stares back at him; something he's only seen on television. Back in Sweet Ridge, the closest thing they had was a rickety Ferris wheel that made an appearance once a year during the country fair.

The phone in the sitting area rings, slicing through the memory like a warm knife through butter.

Adam tears himself from the window and marches over to answer. He sinks into a cream-colored sofa and a woman's mellifluous voice comes over the line, "Good Morning, Mr. Morgan?" Her accent reminds him of an English nanny. Hearing her address him by his new alias gives him a strange sense of reassurance. It's also a reminder that he's playing a role. He's now *Jonathan Morgan* for his duration in London. "Your breakfast has just been delivered. As instructed, we've left it outside your door, but are you sure we can't deliver it personally? Perhaps you'd like to dine on your balcony this morning?"

"No. Outside is fine." He's decided against having an accent himself. He knows he could never carry it for any real length of time. He's never been good at accents.

"Very well. Is there something your private concierge can arrange? Perhaps a car for the day or a massage?"

Adam's never had a massage. The idea of lying facedown and vulnerable with someone hovering over him doesn't sound relaxing at all, so the car takes precedence. "A car for six-thirty would be fine." He does his best to sound unimpressed, as if he's enjoyed this type of treatment his whole life.

His black car service is promptly confirmed and Adam hangs up to retrieve his breakfast. He peers through the peephole first, leering at the empty hall, then rolls the dining cart into his suite.

He positions the cart in front of the large, ornate fireplace and takes inventory. There's strong black coffee, Earl Grey with milk and sugar on the side, a basket of dry toast and breakfast biscuits, a savory lobster omelet with truffle hollandaise, pan-fried tomatoes, sausages, fresh fruit, and champagne, which he sips from the bottle as he scours the newspaper. He wears a pair of briefs with one of the room's plush, white bathrobes draped over him loosely.

He flips past pages of editorials, crosswords, and mattress advertisements until

finally, there on the front of the business section, he finds what he's looking for.

WESTMINSTER WELCOMES THE CITY'S FIRST 5 DIA-MOND LUXURY HOTEL

There's a photo of a man in a bright yellow hardhat, standing with his arms folded before a towering structure that glitters in the background. He's handsome, in a rugged billionaire playboy way, with copper skin and deep-set eyes the color of water. The caption reads, *HOTEL MOGUL LEVI CHANDLER DEBUTS NEWEST PROPERTY, THE CHANDLER, WITH WEEKLONG CELEBRATION.*

A smile makes its way to Adam's face, as he circles the article with a pen, and takes a bite of his toast.

155

• • •

The Chandler doesn't disappoint. From street level, its height and architectural detail make it a true marvel among the inner borough's hardened landscape. It's a dizzying wonder of glass, concrete, and steel with a rooftop infinity pool as its crown jewel.

Adam's driver brakes and his door is instantly opened by the valet staff, who don crisp black uniforms with gold lapel pins of the Chandler's iconic C logo. "Good evening, sir. Welcome to the Chandler!"

He glances toward the rooftop as he exits the car in his tuxedo, a purchase he made in Paris and barely had time to have tailored. He's freshly shaved, with his dark hair slicked and tamed by an obscene amount of hair gel. He looks more like a *high society gentleman* than the skinny country boy in overalls who used to catch frogs on his family's farm in Sweet Ridge. He's come a long way, literally miles and continents away from his modest origins. He's also changed physically. He's stronger now, bulkier from hours clocked at the gym. He's also traded in his dirty overalls for a more refined wardrobe. Spending money on fashion labels is not only part of the job but a necessity to blend in. As he's aged his face has changed, his jaw becoming more chiseled, his nose broadening. Over time, even his accent faded away, as if it never existed. And if, God forbid, he should run into one of his old schoolmates, which he's confident will never happen, he'd surely walk by them undetected. He's no longer Adam Walker, the boy who escaped Sweet Ridge and cheated death. He's *Jonathan Morgan*, who is very much alive and has an invitation to the city's most exclusive party.

"I'm here for the reception," is all he has to say before he's whisked away to the lobby. The lobby is opulent but modern, with polished Calacatta Gold Marble floors and high ceilings that display thousands of crystals hanging among glass bulbs, like a deconstructed chandelier covering the entire ceiling.

Adam gravitates toward a string quartet performing near the bar at the opposite end of the lobby and takes a seat.

"Welcome!" The bartender raises his eyebrows. He has a brawny build and skin like midnight with a full beard that's groomed to perfection. "The name's Dupree, what can I get ya, mate?"

"A vodka with St-Germain on the rocks."

"Ah, the man has good taste." He flashes a beautiful smile with teeth so white Adam wonders if they're veneers. "So what brings you to The Chandler?" Dupree extends a hand.

This couldn't be more perfect, Adam thinks. It's always good to establish a relationship with the hotel bartender. Next to the front desk, they're the eyes and ears of the operation.

Adam wants to be memorable so he shakes Dupree's hand enthusiastically, "Jonathan Morgan. I'm a writer with the *London Herald*, covering the big grand opening."

"Ah, nice." Dupree holds his smile and continues mixing.

"I'll be interviewing Mr. Chandler himself." Adam grins like a teenage fan.

"Good luck with that. I've only met him once, but he seems nice enough."

Adam's counting on it. They chat for a while before Adam pays his tab and makes his way to the front desk. A tall, elegant blonde in a black off-the-shoulder gown greets him. She holds a paper-thin tablet in her hand and beams a red, toothy smile worthy of a lipstick commercial. "Welcome to our grand opening. May I check you in, sir?"

"I'm here for the reception."

Her eyes light up like a pinball machine. "Even better!" She refers to her tablet and the screen casts a white glow on her face, washing out her makeup. "What's your name, love?"

"Jonathan Morgan, with the *London Herald*."

"Ah," her eyes grow larger. "Fantastic. Let me just find you on the list here…"

Adam instantly breaks into a sweat, although he has no reason to be worried. He made arrangements months ago to be on the list and even has a fake ID and press pass, should she ask for it.

She scrolls and punches the screen with a finger. Her eyes are growing frantic, although she's holding the same candy apple-red smile.

"I have my credentials." He reaches for his press pass.

"No… well, I can't seem to find…" Her smile collapses as she scrolls. "No, sorry. Oh, wait! *Morgan*." She beams. "There you are. Sorry 'bout that!"

"No worries." They both share a laugh, although his nerves are rattled.

Thankfully a server waltzes by with a glass of champagne. She plucks one of the stems from the tray for Adam and escorts him toward a set of elevators. "So, as I'm sure you're aware, tonight's reception is on the rooftop level with access to the pool. It's only accessible by this private elevator," she says, pointing to a red carpet leading to a set of gold elevator doors. "Tomorrow we'll host high tea on the terrace at 3pm, followed by a champagne tour of the hotel for VIPs and press."

"Sounds lovely." He makes a point to not seem overly impressed though. Instead, he makes an effort to look bored, as if he'd rather be home watching the game, but must attend this stupid party he's been assigned to cover for his job at the *London Herald*.

"You're just in time for the boss' big speech." She winks and inserts a gold card into a panel next to the elevator. The doors chime open, revealing a lift attendant in a black uniform and matching cap. He's handsome in a boy-next-door way, with tousled brown curls peeking from under his bellhop cap and a square, clean-shaven face.

"I should be scheduled for an interview with Mr. Chandler on Monday?"

She squints. "I'll have to check. I'll have our communications director call your mobile."

He nods and steps onto the elevator. She bids him adieu and moments later he's soaring toward the rooftop to meet his new destiny. It's a longer, more awkward ride than he expected. Having the attendant mutely gawking at him doesn't help, and Adam has to wonder how much Levi Chandler is paying him to push elevator buttons and look handsome.

The doors chime open and a rush of warm air and daylight flood the elevator. The attendant welcomes Adam with a grand gesture as the doors part to reveal a rooftop terrace with a glossy infinity pool in view. The sun sets on its edge, reflecting the sky's fiery colors and clouds, melting together like scoops of orange sherbet and lemon sorbet. There's an impressive bar to the right with a team of mixologists in black leather aprons, crafting potent cocktails. To the left is a small white stage that's been set up for the occasion with a jazz ensemble performing. Surrounding the pool is a row of white loungers and seating, occupied by the city's most elite guest list.

Adam makes his best attempt to blend in, and it isn't long before he's approached by a server with a tray of hors d'oeuvres. "May I offer you a bite?" He's blonde with a flirtatious smile and muscles that threaten to rip through his vest with one false move.

Levi Chandler certainly has a talent for hiring handsome bellmen and servers, Adam notes. He trains his eyes on the colorful array of small bites but, to his dismay, nothing looks recognizable. Most of it looks raw, and he's never been a fan of sushi – something he suffered through with Vaughn, who once insisted on taking him to the "best" sushi restaurant in Paris. What he wouldn't give for some of his mother's buttermilk fried chicken at this point...

Adam takes a chance on a delicate pastry cup that has a dollop of red caviar. He's had caviar before, so it seems like a safe bet. The server watches for his approval as he pops the entire pastry cup into his mouth. It tastes briny like the ocean and the texture is creamy on his tongue, which he wasn't expecting. There's also something slimy registering on his palate. He makes an educated guess that it's sea urchin and his mouth is tempted to reject it back onto the tray. Instead, he wills himself to give a tight-lipped smile and a nod to the server, who seems satisfied now.

He swallows hard and chases down the flavor with a long sip of champagne. He decides he'll order room service as soon as he gets back to the hotel – or maybe stop for a burger on the way.

There's a wave of applause for the musicians who are now standing to bow. There's some shuffling and buzzing among the crowd and it's clear that something is about to happen.

Adam looks to find Levi Chandler standing behind the stage,

talking to his publicist – a curvy woman with caramel skin, oversized glasses and braids. Levi looks like his photo in the paper, which is a good start. He's surprisingly quite a bit taller than Adam imagined, which is also a good start. His dark hair is cut low and wavy, and his copper skin is a reflection of his Trinidadian mother and his English father, which also explains his accent and cool blue eyes.

His father, *Peter Chandler*, is a prominent plastic surgeon who's built an empire on celebrity surgeries and costly skin creams that promise to reverse the hands of time. He has various spa clinics sprinkled throughout London and along the west coast of the states, with a new clinic opening in New York next year. Levi, "the golden child", was born into the family dynasty, but ultimately doesn't have the stomach to "carve into women and pump them full of silicone." Those are Levi's words from an interview in *Enterprise* two years ago. Legend has it, during his sophomore year at UCL, Levi spent the summer yachting in the Med and went off the radar for four months. He never returned to med school or to shadow his father's surgeries that would bequeath him the keys to the Chandler beauty empire.

His parents were furious. At first, they assumed the worst – that he was dead – when he didn't return home to dock.

Levi had gone into hiding in a small boutique hotel on the Amalfi Coast – a three-and-a-half-star property at best on Praiano's rocky cliffside. Despite its beautiful sea views, Casa Helena was rough around the edges and in desperate need of a remodel. The pool needed retiling, the AC only worked half of the time, and there were watermarks throughout the ceiling of the lobby where the rainy season had taken its toll. These were all repairs the family who owned the property hoped to get to one day, but ultimately didn't have the resources to fix. It certainly wasn't The Ritz, but Levi had succeeded in his version of running away from home and was grateful for the seclusion.

Adam can appreciate this. If anyone knows what it feels like to disappear, it's him. He's done so spectacularly and has no intentions of returning to Sweet Ridge.

After months of speculation and failed "rescue" attempts by his parents, Levi returned to London as the new owner of Casa Helena. He purchased the modest twenty-two room property in cash and, after months of remodeling, it stands as the original installation in what has become a global luxury hotel and resort brand.

His parents were beside themselves.

Who leaves school and runs away to buy a dilapidated hotel in Italy?

Levi also didn't return home alone. He returned with a fiancée – an American who was on vacation in Campania with her sorority sisters.

Lauren Holmes, now Lauren Holmes-Chandler, of the London Chandlers.

She now stands at the opposite end of the stage with a cigarette in hand, blankly watching Levi converse with his publicist and tossing occasional glances at the rooftop crowd. She comes to all of his hotel openings, so it's no surprise that she's here for the opening of The Chandler, despite the boredom on her pretty face. She wears a fitted, pale tangerine dress with a vintage designer shawl draped over her tan shoulders. Her shapely legs suggest that she was an athlete of some kind during her university days. She runs a hand through her bottle-blonde shoulder-length curls, and the light catches the eight-carat cushion-cut diamond on her wedding band.

Everything about her looks expensive, down to the gold finish on her heels as she stamps out the cigarette she's been smoking.

She looks up and her eyes land on Adam in the crowd congregating in front of the stage. There's a brief moment of recognition, a tiny dance in her eyes and a nod that Adam hopes no one else has noticed.

At no point should they be seen together, or people would suspect they're acquainted. Not if the job is to go as planned.

She's being reckless.

Adam wants to wipe that smirk off her face, but he settles on tearing his eyes away sharply, hoping she'll get the hint.

There's a tap on the mic, and a man who introduces himself as the hotel's general manager thanks everyone for coming. He has a hint of a Cockney accent. He stands behind a podium that's been brought out with the Chandler logo in gold.

Adam can barely concentrate on what he's saying after Lauren's little stunt. He must remember to mention it the next time he calls her on the burner phone.

There's a fresh round of applause as Levi is introduced. He walks toward the podium with a warm smile that burns bright, as he spots a few familiar faces in the crowd. His navy suit looks impeccably tailored, though his tie has been long since forgotten, revealing hints of chest hair under his starch white shirt. There's an easiness about him, a playfulness that people in the crowd seem drawn to as he does a little dance on his way to the podium. He beams a handsome smile and one of his hands absentmindedly rubs the back of his neck.

Adam notices that, just for a fleeting moment, he almost

looks nervous. But then, any tell is quickly overshadowed by that big toothy smile.

"Good evening, friends." The sound of Levi's accent is almost musical as he speaks. There are strong notes from his mother's Trinidadian heritage with hints of his Londoner upbringing, and yet he doesn't sound like he's from one place or the other... just strangely somewhere in between. Somewhere with its own language. Somewhere with its own dialect, native only to him. "Thank you for being here this evening for what is most certainly a very exciting occasion in Westminster's history. I'd like to thank Mayor Livingston and Councilors Mather and Boles for joining us." There's polite applause. "I'd also like to thank..."

As cameras flash around him, Levi goes on to give a laundry list of city officials and individuals who have been instrumental in The Chandler's birth and construction. Lauren looks more bored than ever as Levi completes his acknowledgments and goes on with his speech.

"Chandler Hotels and Resorts has become synonymous with uncompromising quality and forward-thinking luxury. To be bestowed a five-diamond rating is not only *very difficult*," he says with a chuckle that the audience joins in on, "but it's the ultimate honor. It's a symbol of exceptional accomplishment that signifies many of the principles this company was founded on... attention to detail, innovation, next-level comfort, and of course, creating transformative guest experiences. I consider it my greatest blessing and accomplishment to bring this award home to London, the city I was born in."

There's thunderous applause and cheers from the crowd as he holds up the plaque honoring his five-diamond achievement for all to see. Cameras flash and strike like lightning to capture the money shot of Levi with the glittering award. He allows them their moment, widening his smile for photos he knows will be plastered on front pages the next morning.

Then, Levi takes a breath and leans into the podium. There's a shift in his expression as something dark colors his eyes. "It doesn't seem that long ago that I started this company," he says. "Those of you who know me understand that a career in the hotel and hospitality industry is the furthest thing from the life I was bound for." There's a taut silence hanging over the crowd now. It seems that most are aware of who Levi's father is and the story behind the Chandler empire. "I was on a course to become an entirely different person than who I am today," he says bitterly. "And who knows, perhaps I would have excelled and done fine things in another field – but the life that I've *chosen*... The life I've chosen for myself is proof that we are all captains of our own destiny. Anything is possible if you believe in what you're capable of over what *others* believe you're capable of. You can have the life you want. You can live the dreams people tell you are mere fantasies, if you just believe in yourself. Never allow people to convince you that your wildest dreams aren't within reach." He smiles sweetly, and there's a luster in his eyes as he aims a finger toward his shoes. "We're standing on seventeen stories, eight years, and five diamonds in the making." There's wild applause as he smiles proudly. "Thank you for being a part of this journey with me. Thank you for your support. Enjoy the rest of the evening. Grab a drink from the bar – and remember to never stop dreaming."

It's a good speech, likely written by someone on his staff... except for that last bit. There was something intensely personal in the way he spoke. Something surprisingly vulnerable in how he looked into the crowd with those penetrating blue eyes of his; it was as if he was seeking out the person who needed to hear his message the most.

A DJ starts to play an upbeat deep house track and it's clear that the formalities of the evening are now over.

It's time to party.

Adam finds the handsome blonde server from earlier and requests a vodka with St-Germain on the rocks. It's returned with a wink and some scribbling on a napkin the glass is served on. Adam peers at the four digits written in blue ink and deducts it must be a room number, perhaps to some sort of hospitality suite within the hotel. He won't risk sneaking off and blowing his cover over something as trivial as a fling, but it's just the shot of confidence he needs to carry out what happens next.

He spies Levi standing near the pool, talking to a couple who look like his ideal target demographic. They're young, likely early thirties, and are dressed flashy but stylishly. They look well-traveled and excited to have a hip, new hotel as part of the city's offerings.

Levi has lost his jacket and the sleeves of his dress shirt are rolled up to his elbows. He's smiling at the young woman who's using her hands as she speaks, likely gushing over the sky infinity pool that's directly at Levi's back. He's holding a large glass of rosé in one hand, his other hand tucked neatly in the front pocket of his trousers.

Adam makes a beeline for them.

In a moment that's over nearly as quickly as it begins, Adam cuts through the trio and throws up a hand, as if waving to someone at the other end of the rooftop – his elbow sharply bumps into Levi. Adam looks back with wide, apologetic eyes and watches as Levi balances his glass of rosé, juggling the contents from spilling onto his shirt. He comes within inches of stepping back into the pool, but miraculously manages not to lose his balance and fall in.

It's a surprise to both of them as their eyes meet, lost for words. Adam was sure he'd used enough force to knock him into the pool, or at least knock his wine onto his shirt, but Levi had done some fast maneuvering to avoid disaster.

The plan had been to jump in after him and feign some sort of awkward "rescue", something memorable that would make a good *how-we-met* story in Levi's mind. But so much for that...

"Sorry," Adam finally manages. "So sorry! I'm such a klutz."

"Uh, *no*. No worries." Levi shrugs it off and turns his attention back to the couple, who are still holding their breath having witnessed his near spill into the pool.

They continue their conversation as Adam casually walks away.

One Mississippi.

Adam makes his way toward the bar.

Two Mississippi.

Adam doesn't look back.

Three Mississippi.

He refuses to look back, although it's *so* tempting.

Four Mississippi.

This will be the real test, the test to see if he's made the impression he's hoped for.

Five Mississippi.

Finally, Adam tosses a glance over his shoulder, a simple careless glance that's void of any anticipation, and he finds

Levi staring after him.

Their eyes meet again, and a tiny smile forms on the edge of Levi Chandler's lips.

11 / HOMECOMING

Sweet Ridge is home to half-empty strip malls, pageant queens, and pie-eating contests. It's a wasteland of quaint general stores, farmland, and houses that mostly look the same. There's what you might call a town center, where everything is peculiarly – however conveniently – located within a circle. Enter and you'll first come to the post office, then city hall, then a grocery store across the street, then a small gas station, a few small boutiques, a diner, the hardware store, and finally The Dell on your way out. The Dell is where the locals gather to drink, talk shit, and play darts on Saturday nights. Meanwhile, the town's teenagers either gather to drink cheap beer behind the slaughterhouse on the outskirts of town or take over the local roller rink – where the girls skate circles around the boys in their cut off jean shorts and knee-high socks.

Sweet Ridge is home to bar fights, cornfields, and drag races along uneven dirt roads at night. It's home to town gossip, murky politics, and a myriad of secrets that housewives keep tucked under their bonnets like dark, untreated roots.

It's many things, with the exception of no longer being home to Adam Walker, the boy who mysteriously vanished before the homecoming game of 2006.

Occasionally, someone will whisper his name, like an urban legend – conjuring up memories of a strained police investigation and surrounding news stations storming the small town. There are parents who still insist their children come home from playing well before the street lamps turn on. The teachers who have remained at John Morgan High School since Adam's disappearance are careful not to speak his name or entertain stories their students spin, claiming to see Adam's ghost roaming the science wing after school.

They'd love to wring their hands clean of this dark era in the town's history. They'd love to forget and move on with their dairy pageants and country fairs, but time won't allow them.

Homecoming always comes back around and what should be a time of celebration turns into a season of dread. Like the return of a curse, the town's once-a-year 8pm curfew ensues and mothers and fathers are compelled to keep a white-knuckle grip on their children's whereabouts. The elementary and middle schools eliminate recess and high school students are banned from eating lunch outside. Even the seniors, who customarily enjoy a few liberties, feel caged during Homecoming – and any absence from class raises red flags and panic among the faculty. Eventually, the big game arrives and everyone smiles and cheers on the home team to get through it, masking their fear bubbling just below the surface.

The newest generation argues it's puerile and superstitious to think that it could happen again, that a student could go missing or be taken – but the wild theories surrounding Adam Walker only add fuel to the fire.

"Some people think it was the janitor," Quinn says. "That

170

he killed Adam and ate the body."

"People can't actually think that," Bailey scowls from the passenger seat of their rented jeep. The rolling farmland surrounding Sweet Ridge zips past him in the background as he lazily dangles an arm out the window.

"After Adam disappeared it came out the janitor had a record. Then he was 'dismissed'. It turned into the Salem witch trials around here. Everyone was under a microscope."

"No one was charged with anything?"

"No body, no evidence." Quinn peers over the steering wheel in response to the GPS and takes a left onto a dirt road, passing by the stench and squeals from what he deducts is the local slaughterhouse. "Seems like people suspected foul play but no one fingered Andrew Dunn."

"Wonder why. He looks like a creep if *I* ever saw one." Bailey says without thinking, then shoots Quinn a sideways glance, recalling their encounter at SKY. He rolls up the sleeves of his pale pink sweatshirt and fumbles with the band of leather bracelets on his wrist.

"Andrew put this town on the map as coach when they won the state championship. He's a hero in their eyes. There's even a conference room at the library named after him."

Bailey inwardly rolls his eyes.

Quinn suppresses a smile and glances at the GPS. "We should be getting close."

"Are you nervous?"

"A little." Quinn takes a breath. "I just can't believe we're really here and I'm about to meet with her face to face."

"Did she seem reluctant?"

"At first, definitely. Then I explained that I work for *The Chronicle* and that got her attention."

"Hmm." Bailey tosses a glance out the window and runs a hand through his hair.

"This won't exactly be fun, but I'm curious to see what she can tell me about our pal Andrew. No one at the school returned my calls."

"Should be interesting," Bailey says with a faraway gaze.

"Hey, thanks for coming." Quinn offers a small smile, breaking the trance.

"Sure. You know, I'm excited to see the farm. Makes me think of home," he glances out the window again, just in time to see a lush green field flash by, dotted with steer.

"You miss it?"

Bailey narrows his eyes and says, "No..." but his high-pitched response doesn't sound convincing to either of them.

Quinn slows the jeep as the road changes to gravel and they approach a gated entrance. Beyond the gates, a winding paved driveway is visible, lined with trees blooming with crimson-red cherries.

The gates are open, but Quinn finds himself slowing the jeep to a complete stop at the mouth of the entrance. Although he's expected, there's something foreboding about finding the gates wide open. There's something menacing in the way the cast iron bars stretch open, inviting him into the unknown.

Bailey shrugs and Quinn can't help but bite his lip as he eases on the gas, slowly passing through the gates.

What's on the other side isn't nearly as stark as Quinn's own imagination. He removes his sunglasses to take in the picturesque landscape, divided with white wooden fences and trees so perfectly green and full that they look as if they've been drawn with crayons along the blue horizon. He hasn't spent any real time in the country. He only has antiquated references from movies and postcards to mentally put together what a proper farm should look like – but this doesn't disappoint.

There are goats and chickens and hay bales galore. There's even a small cornfield with a scarecrow nailed to a wooden cross structure. The expression on his burlap face looks more annoyed than menacing, causing Quinn to smile as they drive by.

Bailey perks up at the sight of five large horses, galloping within a ring. "Wow. American quarter horses!"

Quinn isn't sure what this means but the fact that Bailey is impressed (by anything) speaks volumes. They drive by a barn and a stable complex until a large white farmhouse, complete with a wraparound porch, comes into view. There's a flurry of activity outside, including farmhands scurrying around with buckets, workers painting one side of an old shed, and a gang of men unloading a tractor.

"That's a Steiner 500!" Bailey's eyes go wild with boyish glee.

"What's a Steiner 500?"

"Only one of the best tractors on the market," he gushes and snaps a finger. "Trust. I know my tractors."

"You can take the boy out the country…"

Bailey leans out the window for a closer look. "Quinn, that tractor costs a fortune. It's *gorgeous*."

Quinn prepares to park and glares at the heavy-duty red and black tractor being unloaded from a flatbed. "This place looks a hell of a lot different from the rundown photo I found online…"

"I had sex on a tractor once." Bailey suddenly recalls with a smug smile.

Quinn sighs and feigns disbelief, "*You*? Having sex *on a tractor*? I don't believe it."

"It's not as hot as it sounds. Gets way too loud after a while."

"You had sex on a *moving* tractor?" Quinn gives him an insufferable look and turns off the ignition. "We're here. Let me do the talking, and leave that damn tractor alone." He hops out the jeep and takes a look at the three corn-fed farmhands huddled around the flatbed. "Leave the men alone, too."

Bailey slams his door with a huff and inhales, giving a nostalgic smile. "Wow. Never thought I'd miss the smell of hay and horse shit."

"Is that what that is?"

"Fresh country air!" He grins. "You get used to it. My father used to make us clean the barn as punishment. Let's just say I spent a lot of time in the barn."

"Shocking."

"Are you sure you don't want me to stay?" It sounds like an innocent enough question, although Bailey's quietly sizing up their surroundings and the men who have now directed their gaze at them. He knows that sleepy towns like Sweet Ridge don't always welcome outsiders and that every farmhouse has a rifle tucked away in a corner somewhere, loaded and waiting for the first sign of trouble.

"No, why don't you get us checked in the motel – and maybe find a place for dinner in town?" Quinn notes from Bailey's silence that he isn't in love with this idea, and adds, "Besides, she's only expecting me. I won't be able to explain what you're doing here."

Bailey nods once slowly, knowing there's no changing Quinn's mind.

"Can I help you?" The tallest of the men approach. He's

wearing muddy cowboy boots, jeans and a white Henley shirt with the sleeves rolled up. He looks like he's been rolling around in the dirt all day, but somehow... it works. Brown curls escape the back of his faded baseball cap and his scruffy beard reminds Quinn of his ex, Eric.

"I'm, uh, here to see Vera. I'm Quinn Harris from *The Chronicle*. She's expecting me."

"She's inside," he says around a mouthful of tobacco and gestures toward the house. "I'll take ya." He eyes the jeep suddenly as Bailey turns the ignition.

"I'll call you when I'm done," Quinn shouts over the engine, dismissing Bailey before more questions arise. They wave goodbye, and Bailey is soon driving toward the other side of the beyond, eyes in the rearview.

"I'm Gus. I help Miss Vera out 'round here," he introduces himself. A twangy country accent registers as thick as barbecue sauce. There's something charming about it, Quinn decides, and he feels his face flush as he appraises the rugged farmhand before him. Gus is tall but solid – with muscles that can only come from hard labor on the farm. He glares at Quinn, his brown eyes brimming with suspicion. He looks as if he wants to say something but doesn't.

"Nice to meet you," Quinn shakes Gus' hard, callused hand. A wild thought crosses his mind involving a tractor and the feel of Gus' rough hands caressing his skin. He shakes it off as Gus yells something to the other men, then follows Gus up the porch steps.

The screen door creaks open as he's ushered inside.

The house smells like cornbread, fried chicken, and an antique store all at the same time. Quinn senses some activity in the kitchen straight ahead of his view; the sound of bubbling pots and someone singing under their breath. To his right is a formal dining room. He spies a stack of newspapers and a thin layer of dust on the plates and platters that clutter the lengthy mahogany farm table. To his left is a parlor with a large stone fireplace, two oversized cornflower-blue sofas and a white coffee table with fresh flowers. There's a rocking chair in one corner, and framed photos sprinkling walls covered in faded floral wallpaper.

"You can wait in here." Gus points toward the parlor and gives him a long look. "I'll fetch her."

Quinn does as he's told and waits until Gus is out of view to peruse the photos. Strange, unfamiliar faces stare back. Some in black and white. Some in color. They could be anyone. Distant cousins fishing... sisters-in-law in sundresses at a family reunion... memory upon memory, frozen in time. Quinn searches until he discovers a familiar face on the wall.

If he didn't know better, Quinn might mistake it for his own sixth-grade photo. He vaguely recalls having a similar red-striped polo back then... the smile and the nose are the same... and then there are those same intense green eyes... He marvels at the picture in its wooden frame and bets his own mother might mistake Adam Walker for her own son in this photo.

He takes a step back and realizes now that photos of Adam are everywhere. There's a baby photo, taken just days after Adam was born. There's a photo of Adam at the playful age of five by a lake, holding up a fish half his size. There's a photo of Adam at ten straddling a horse. Then Quinn's eyes land on what appears to be a family photo at the center of the fireplace mantel. Adam is in the middle, looking no more than seven and wearing a black suit with a crooked bow tie. His face is expressionless except for a hardened, stormy look in his eyes. The woman smiling to the left of Adam can only be Vera Walker, the woman Quinn's traveled nearly 800 miles to look in the eyes and explain what he's discovered regarding her son's disappearance. The man on Adam's right with a hand on his shoulder must be Adam's father, Tom. He's tall and broad with dark features, pitch-black eyes and a tense smile that looks rehearsed.

There's something disconcerting about the photo. It might be the unspoken tension captured in that split second by the camera. It might be Tom's firm hand on Adam's shoulder. It might be the look in Adam's eyes...

Quinn leans in, glancing between Adam and his father. He recognizes the look glittering at the bottom of Adam's gaze. He knows it well from his time with Andrew Dunn, wrestling on the floor as Andrew strangled him from above. He knows the look all too well...

It's fear.

"He was eight in that photo," a voice calls out behind him.

Quinn turns to find Vera Walker in the doorway of the parlor. She's petite in a long, flowing blue skirt and white blouse that look as if they might swallow her whole. A delicate embroidered scarf and a herd of silver necklaces and charms hangs around her neck. Her steel-gray hair is rounded up into an untidy updo and her sad eyes are a familiar green. They go wide at the sight of Quinn, as if seeing a ghost.

He should have anticipated this reaction but he didn't. "I'm Quinn Harris—"

"I know who you are," she balks, taking a step back as she says this. Logic tells her one thing, but her eyes can't help but be momentarily tricked by the sight before her. She rests a hand on the doorframe to steady herself.

"You okay, Miss Vera?" It's Gus, who's stopped on his way back out to the yard. The resemblance has also registered with him. At first, he'd shaken off the nagging feeling that Quinn seemed familiar, but now the hair on the back of his neck is standing on end.

She mumbles a reply, but she can't tear her eyes away from the man in her parlor who looks so much like her son.

The screen door creaks open and closes with a bang, and Quinn and Vera are left alone, gaping at one another.

It takes Vera a moment to remember her manners.

"Can I, uh, offer you some tea?" She suddenly wishes for something stronger, like a nip from the bottle of moonshine her neighbors, the Belchers, gave her last Christmas.

"No, thank you." Quinn declines and the two take a seat, facing each other awkwardly. "Thank you for agreeing to see me."

"Yeah, well… it's been a while since anyone came 'round here askin' about Adam." Her words are drenched with suspicion.

"I'm sure you must miss him very much."

Her eyes go shiny as she shifts in her seat. "There's not a day that goes by I don't think about him."

Quinn nods sympathetically and reaches for his recorder. "I promise not to take too much of your time. I hope you don't mind if I record?"

"What's all this about?" She wrings her hands and shifts back and forth in her seat, already overwhelmed. "You said on the phone you have information about Adam?"

Quinn presses record. "I'm investigating a rather…" He searches for the right word. "It's a *unique* missing person case in New York. There are some similarities that I believe are tied to Adam's case."

"Similarities?" Vera shakes her head, at a loss. "What similarities?"

"Namely, Andrew Dunn." He watches for her reaction.

She squints her green eyes in confusion. She can't imagine what Andrew Dunn and Adam have to do with some case in New York City – which she's only seen on TV, by the way, while watching the Macy's Christmas parade. The math isn't adding up.

"I'm hoping you can tell me more about Andrew Dunn. I've made a few inquiries but, I have to say, people seem to clam up when I mention his name."

She shrugs uneasily and tucks a stray gray hair behind an ear. "What do you wanna know? He, uh, coached the boys on the team but that was a long time ago."

Quinn is silent. He knows if he lets her keep talking she'll eventually tell him something useful.

"Well, he was *real nice.* I mean, he taught the kids, he was a real good football coach an' all." She nods, hoping this answers the question, but Quinn's silence pushes her to keep thinking. "He lost his wife, Sara…" She trails off and rubs a chill on her arms.

"What can you tell me about that?"

"Oh, that poor man." Her face turns grave. "People actually accused that man of murdering his own wife." She whispers, "But I don't believe that!"

"Why not?" The words slip out faster than he can catch them.

Vera shakes her head adamantly, saying, "You just had to know him. Coach Dunn was hard on the boys, but he wouldn't hurt a fly."

179

Her words sting on multiple levels. Quinn suddenly wants more than anything to prove her wrong with the Polaroids he's now cataloged into his phone. What would she think of Andrew's bloodthirsty appetite for butchering boys like pigs?

"What does all this have to do with Adam?"

Quinn takes a deep breath and dives in, telling Vera everything but the goriest details. She listens in shock, wishing once again for that nip of moonshine. Hell, she thinks, she could have snuck a healthy drop in her tea without Quinn being any the wiser.

"I know this is a lot to take in," Quinn says, pausing to gauge her disposition. She looks a bit woozy. "But looking back on Adam's missing person's report and having encountered Andrew myself, I think it's very possible that Andrew Dunn was involved in the disappearance of your son."

"That's not possible." Vera shakes her head in clear protest.

"What was the relationship like between Coach Dunn and Adam?"

She shrugs and makes a big effort to think back. "Adam had him for science... he seemed to do good in class."

"Did they spend time together outside of class?"

"Noooo," she squints. "Don't think so. I know some of the kids had extra tutorin', but not Adam." She breaks into a wide smile. "Adam was so smart. I don' know where he got it from – but he always got A's when it came to his schoolin'. He'd get mad if he got a B!"

Quinn smiles politely and presses on. "Is it possible that he took a liking to Adam *because* he was such a good student?"

Again, she shrugs.

"Were there ever any rumors or signs of a..." He wants to tread lightly here, but doesn't know how else to say it.

180

"*Inappropriate* relationship with Adam – or any of the other students?"

She clutches one of her necklaces. "Of course not!" For a second, her wide eyes race to the photos on the fireplace mantel.

"Did Adam have a girlfriend?"

"No." But there's something in her tone that reads between the lines, confirming what Quinn has suspected.

"Did Coach Dunn ever come here to the house, or…"

"Mr. Harris," she holds out a hand to stop him and stands. "Listen, I don't know if I understand all this 'bout missin' boys in New York or what-have-you." She waves a hand and the bangles on her wrist sing like wind chimes, "What I *can* tell you is that Coach Dunn did *not* kill my son. It's not possible."

"How can you be so sure?" Quinn realizes how desperate he sounds, but he doesn't care. Everything in his gut screams that there's a connection between Andrew and Adam; a connection that holds the answer to what led to years of killing and twelve dead bodies. Sitting in the house that Adam grew up in only amplifies the feeling. He can't fathom how Vera can't sense it too.

She sighs and her face softens, as if feeling sorry for this strange man from New York who's blown through her door, slightly jetlagged and tortured with so many questions.

"There's somethin' you should see, hon." She finally nods. "Wait here." She goes, who knows where, and reappears a moment later with an old cigar box cradled in both hands, as if it contained something sacred. "I never told my husband, Tom, about this." Her eyes shoot back to the pictures on the mantel, to the family photo glaring back. "He died last July."

Quinn accepts the box and can't help but ask, "How did he

181

pass?"

Vera slowly takes a seat beside him and watches him lift the lid of the cigar box. "There was a, uh, tractor accident." She nods, like a wife who's finally accepted the loss. She nods as if the memory of Tom's mangled, crushed body is any less vivid than the day Gus came tearing into the house with the news and blood on his boots. She'd never seen Gus' eyes so wild before. "He didn't go quickly," she says then. There's a sudden bitterness and sadness. "Might say it's sorta fittin' after what he done."

Quinn's mind scrambles to understand what she means as he thumbs through the contents of the box.

"I should have protected him." Vera's voice suddenly cracks, her eyes fixed on the family photo on the mantel. "He was my baby..."

Quinn's eyes dart between the box and Vera. He follows her gaze to the photo over the fireplace. He measures the fear in Adam's eyes and grimaces at the image of Tom's hand on Adam's shoulder.

A tear rolls down Vera's cheek as Quinn fishes a stack of postcards from the cigar box. He flips through more than a dozen exotic locations and distant cities, a collection of travels and memories that have somehow found their way to this small box in Sweet Ridge. Greetings from Italy... Greetings from Dubai... His mouth goes dry as he skims the handwriting scribbled on the back.

Having a great time in Italy. Ciao! – Adam

It's rained almost every day! Seattle's the worst. J Missing you! – Adam

182

It's official. I hate skiing. Sending love from Aspen. – Adam

Quinn traces his finger over Adam's handwriting on the smooth cardstock, feeling strangely more distant and somehow closer to him than ever before. He imagines Adam writing each postcard with its corresponding city glittering in the backdrop.

Vera's kept them preserved like artifacts and in the order of Adam's travels. "That one came just last week." She clears her throat and points to the top of the stack.

Quinn's breath catches as he holds up the most recent postcard with a photo of the Eiffel Tower in all its glory splashed across the front.

"*Paris*," he mouths, awestruck. "We meet again."

• • •

"Adam Walker is alive," Quinn says, as if it's a miracle. "All this time, I've been assuming he was dead because he fit the pattern, but... he's alive!"

"Dead people don't send postcards," Bailey concurs and scowls over his menu.

They've retreated to a small diner – the only diner – in Sweet Ridge, for an early dinner and to regroup. It looks like a typical roadside diner stuck in the '50s with its checkered floor and booths made of cracked red leather and chrome. A few locals are perched on barstools, sipping coffee between bites of pie.

"What if he *escaped*?"

"From Andrew?" Bailey's having a tough time with the menu. Everything's either deep-fried or loaded with gravy.

183

"Is it possible he just ran away? I mean, that's what I would do – especially if his dad was all handsy."

"I wonder how many people on the farm knew Adam was being abused?" Quinn removes his shades and pinches the bridge of his nose. "Still, there's something not right. I can't imagine Andrew not gunning for Adam. There's got to be more to the story."

"Hi there! Can I get you guys started with sumthin' ta drink?" A tall brunette, complete with a '50s waitress uniform and matching hat has joined them. Her eyeliner is smudged, and Bailey can't help but be enamored with the classic hue of blue eyeshadow that tints her eyes. Her yellow and pale pink uniform is stained from the waist down and there's fresh ketchup on her white bobby socks. She holds a notepad and an eager smile as her eyes dart between them, like one of those black and white cat clocks from the '50s.

"A sweet tea for me." Bailey scans her from head to toe. "With a twist of lemon."

"I'll just have a water, please. No lemon."

She pops her gum and leans in suddenly, asking, "Y'all ain't from around here, are ya?"

It might be Bailey's outfit that tipped her off. In addition to his pink sweatshirt with holes in it, he's wearing tight jeans, a Gucci fanny pack, and combat boots. He looks ready for anything. "We're from New York," he shrugs.

"New York?! Oh wow…" She hugs her notepad to her chest. "I got a cousin who went there once. Flew on an airplane for the first time and everything!"

"Wow." Quinn gets a read on her name tag. "I take it you're from Sweet Ridge, Jenna?"

"Born and raised."

"So you went to John Morgan then?"

She nods and smooths a hand over her ponytail. "Almost finished. I had my baby girl my junior year and had to leave. I'm gon' get my GED though," she adds, trying to weigh the expression on Quinn's face. "Hey, how 'bout I bring you guys a slice of cherry pie on the house? You can't leave Sweet Ridge without a bite of our famous cherry pie!"

And just like that, she's gone.

"Charming." Bailey flicks a wrist and turns his attention to his phone. There haven't been any cryptic text messages from his mother today. Just a text from Aubrey, who just landed in Chicago. He turns on a dating app, just for shits and giggles to see what the locals look like. (It's slim pickings. Not *nearly* the amount of horny Midwestern country boys he expected logging on. Pity.)

"I bet she knew Adam," Quinn says, biting his lip. "If she went to John Morgan, she must have heard of Adam Walker."

Bailey doesn't look up from his screen. "Who, the waitress?"

"Yeah. She looks like she might be around his age now." Quinn does the math in his head. The bags under Jenna's eyes outweigh her youthful facade. "Besides, how many Adam Walkers could there be in this town?"

"Voila!" Jenna is back with two generous portions of pie. "You hafta take a bite an' lemme know what you think," she says, smiling proudly as if she just finished baking the pie herself.

Quinn and Bailey share a look as they pick up their forks.

Bailey's the first to take a heaping bite. "Mmmph," he licks a spot of whipped cream from his lips. "Damn, not bad. Reminds me of my Aunt Peg's cherry pie. She's the baker in my family," he explains nostalgically. "Everyone else bakes for shit."

Quinn's not a big cherry pie fan but he finds himself taking a second bite. "It's good. Kinda tart. I like that." He licks his fork.

Jenna beams as if she's just been crowned Miss Sweet Cherry Pie. "Everyone loves our pie. The cherries are local – or 'organic' I guess you'd say," she says and fancily waves a hand. "The cherries come from the Walker Farm down the road."

"As in Vera Walker?"

She nods and Quinn's appetite sours.

"Interesting." Bailey shoots Quinn a rueful smile and takes another bite.

"Y'all ready to order?"

They pick up their menus and make game-time decisions. Meatloaf for Quinn and chicken-fried steak for Bailey.

Jenna jots it down, then suddenly leans in with her hands resting on the edge of their table. Her voice becomes hushed. "Hey, sorry, did I hear you guys say somethin' about Adam Walker earlier?" Her face looks strained.

"Uh, yes!" Quinn replies. "Did you know him?"

"Know him?" She gives a witty laugh and says, "He was my best friend. Hell, we went back to preschool."

"That so?" Quinn smiles. "I hear he's somewhat of an urban legend around here."

Jenna rolls her eyes and wipes her hands on her apron. "You could say Sweet Ridge's got somewhat of a dark past. Adam just found himself at the center of it, I guess."

"What was he like?"

"*Smart*," she laughs. "He was a force to be reckoned with, trust me on that, but he was also so... brave. I mean, *nothin'* scared Adam. Well, nuthin' 'cept for Tom – his daddy." She

186

pauses to catch her breath. "That man was the devil incarnate. Adam though, he did things I could never do. Just the way he carried himself… almost like he's been here before, you know? Like he had it all figured out."

Bailey rests his fork on his clean plate. "Sounds like you two were close."

"Oh, yeah. I'd cover for him all the time. He'd tell Miss Vera he was at my house when he was really with his boyfriend," she smirks.

"Adam had a boyfriend?"

She grins like the cat that ate the canary. "You could say that."

"Sounds like you have the inside scoop."

"I'm not one to gossip," she says. Then, her eyes dart around the room to see if anyone's listening before spilling the tea. "He was seein' a married man." She raises a hand, as if testifying before God. "Not only that, but he was a teacher at our school!" She squeals and leans back with wide eyes, waiting for their reaction.

Quinn's not surprised though. He knows exactly who she's referring to. "By any chance, did this man also coach football?"

"Coach Dunn!" She nods. "What a creeper. He was real sweet on Adam though, always favored him in class."

"But you're saying they had a romantic relationship." Quinn needs to hear her say it. He needs to be sure.

"Oh, yeah."

"How do you know?"

"Adam told me," she shrugs. "He told me everything, like uh, how they'd meet up out of town and how Coach Dunn used to buy him things all the time. It was real hush-hush though, 'cause of, well, you know…"

"No one else knew?"

She chomps on her gum and frowns. "Don't think so. Adam made me swear not to tell anyone – especially his daddy. His daddy woulda skinned his hide if he knew Adam was sneakin' around. Didn't matter who with. Even if it'd been a girl. He was just controllin' like that." She stares off, likely conjuring up memories of Tom Walker – a ghost of a man who still haunts Vera's parlor from his place on the mantel. "Adam said they were gonna run off together. Him and Coach Dunn." She shakes her head with a wry smile. "Lordie, Adam was in love with that man…"

"So, whatever happened to Adam?" Quinn asks plainly. "Do you stay in touch? Or have a way to reach him?" He has no guesses as to what she'll say next. The day is turning out to be rather unpredictable.

Jenna's face falls. "No. He just vanished one day. He wrote me once, sayin' he was in New York doin' some modeling. He told me the name of the agency, but I forget. He was always talkin' about seein' the world, goin' to Europe and stuff – even before the whole thing with Coach Dunn." She sighs and seems to have trouble with her next words. "Of course, the timin' was a little weird though."

"How do you mean?"

"Adam disappeared the same night Coach Dunn lost his wife." She visibly swallows her gum. "Folks started sayin' Adam had somethin' to do with it. Or maybe Coach Dunn killed them both." She throws up her hands. "Honestly, folks 'round here didn't know what to think, they were just convinced the two were related somehow."

"What do *you* think happened?" Bailey perks up in his seat.

Jenna takes a moment. "I don't think Adam would hurt

her – Mrs. Dunn, I mean. I never knew him to be violent or nuthin', you know." Despite this, her face is pickled with doubt. "I mean, Adam could be downright as tough as a pine knot though. When he wanted somethin' bad enough, he usually got it."

Quinn and Bailey share a look.

"Think he might have wanted the wife out the picture?" Bailey raises an eyebrow, happy to play bad cop in this scenario.

"Umm… no…" Jenna shakes the darkness from her face. Her high-voltage diner smile returns, and she's suddenly back to being their lovable '50s waitress. "*Listen*, that was all so long ago, and I've just been talkin' y'all's ears off… Why don't you finish enjoyin' your pie and I'll be back with your drinks."

"I'm a reporter," Quinn says quickly.

Her eyebrows shoot up. "A reporter?"

"I'm covering a story I think you could help with. Adam might be involved. That's actually why we're in the area. I bet you could help us out."

She rests a hand on her chest and a laugh escapes. "You wanna interview *me?*"

"I think you could be a big help." Quinn smiles, hoping it looks as charming on the outside as it does in his head. "I'd quote you in the story. Unless you'd rather be an anonymous source."

"Uh, well, no…" she stammers, "I mean, I've never been interviewed for nuthin' before. I'd want people to see it was me, you know? Otherwise, they'd never believe me!"

"Good point." Quinn laughs along with her and reaches for his tape recorder. Her eyes go wide at the sight of it, filing it as further proof she's about to be interviewed by a real New

York journalist. The fact that it has to do with Adam is of little consequence. Quinn could ask her questions about the patty melt the menu and she'd be just as obliged. "Do you have a break coming up?"

She glances at the clock and says, "In about an hour." Her face has gone flushed. It's just too much excitement for one day.

"How about we chat on your break?" Quinn smiles. "I wanna hear your take on things, since you knew Adam best."

"We were besties," she nods. "We told each other everything."

"Right." Quinn holds his smile and goes for another bite of pie. "Your insights would be invaluable."

She gives them a determined smile. "Right. Great! I'll go get those drinks and be right back. We'll talk."

Quinn watches her leave and Bailey shoots him an amused smirk. "My, my. Bewitching the locals." He winks. "It's so much fun watchin' you work."

"We only have half the story," Quinn reminds him. "And Adam's out there alive with the other half." He narrows his eyes and licks his fork clean. "We have to find him."

12 / BLACK MAGIC

Levi Chandler is nineteen minutes late to their interview. If this were a real interview for the *London Herald*, Adam would have long left by now, but it isn't. It's his first and perhaps only chance to speak to Levi alone, so he must wait and plaster on a smile as Levi makes a hurried entrance into the room, full of apologies.

"So sorry, mate. My interview with *London Architecture* ran late this morning, and I've been behind ever since! Can I offer you something to drink? A coffee, perhaps, or some sparkling water?" Levi marches straight to the bar, never looking up, and undoes the remaining button on his jacket. He wears a black shirt and a sleek gray suit that emphasizes his height and lean swimmer's physique. A two-way radio dangles from his belt. They've arranged for interviews to be held in the penthouse suite of The Chandler so that Adam and the next reporter scheduled can see the hotel's most opulent suite up close. The interior is designed in tufted gray furniture and gold accents. There's a chef's kitchen adjacent to the full bar and the living room includes surround sound, smart lighting, and seating for eight. Larger-than-life canvases with splashes of black and gold hang on the walls while the bedroom boasts heated floors and a spa-inspired bath leading to a balcony with an outdoor shower and Jacuzzi.

"A coffee sounds great," Adam sits up in his club chair. He's gotten comfortable waiting, but it's showtime now. It's time to do what he's been hired to do.

"Coffee it is! I hope you're enjoying the suite," Levi says, his back turned as he pours a coffee for Adam and a scotch for himself. It's been a full press day that started early with the news circuit. Levi hasn't had a moment to breathe, so he figures he's earned this scotch.

"It's a beautiful suite," Adam nods at Levi's back, observing the way Levi's trousers cling to his tight glutes. "How many does it sleep?"

"Only two," Levi adds sugar and cream to a saucer and takes a breath. "Despite its size, it's designed as a couple's hideaway – inspired by a resort I used to frequent in Puerto Vallarta, which is truly one of my favorite romantic cities." His accent sounds heavy and full of memories, perhaps of himself and Lauren on vacation back when their love was fresh and new. "You know, Puerto Vallarta's known for its sunsets, so many of the hotels and resorts in Olas Altas are built to face the ocean."

It's a fun fact only a hotel mogul like Levi might fully appreciate.

"Puerto Vallarta's on my list to visit," Adam says, ensuring there's a smile in his voice. "Perhaps you can give me some tips on where to stay."

"Sure. I'd love to open a resort there—" Levi finally turns to deliver their drinks and stops cold in his tracks. "Oh." His eyes go wide upon seeing Adam. "It's you… with the, uh… green eyes."

"Sorry, what?" Adam laughs, off-guard.

"From the pool the other day. I remember your eyes. You, uh…" Levi hands Adam his coffee with a sly smile and sits across from him in a matching chair. "You almost knocked me in."

"Right, that." Adam meets Levi's blue eyes, sparkling like the infinity pool above them. "I was hoping you'd forgotten," he winces.

"I might have taken you in with me," Levi teases.

Adam smirks. "I suppose there are worse things."

There's a pause as Levi absorbs his words.

Levi goes for a quick sip of his scotch before clearing his throat. "So, um, Jonathan Morgan, is it? From the *London Herald*?"

"Indeed. Nice to meet you officially." Adam's dressed the part of a reporter in jeans, leather loafers, and a fitted shirt with the sleeves rolled up. A pair of black chunky glasses are the final touch; a five-dollar buy at a vintage shop downtown.

"According to my publicist, I'm all yours for the next fifteen minutes."

"Lucky me." Adam flashes a perfect smile and a recorder before launching into his first set of questions. They're legitimate questions that any reporter might ask; questions he pulled from the internet in a matter of minutes to prepare for his time with Levi. Levi answers each question like a pro, almost from muscle memory at this point in the day.

"Aside from its location, now bringing the Chandler brand home, what would you say sets this property apart?" Adam's improvising a bit now as he sips his coffee. He can see that Levi's grown a bit bored with his questions.

Levi runs a hand over his dark, wavy hair. "Innovation and luxury are what the Chandler brand is known for, but we've truly married the two in a way that's seamless and integrates into how people travel. You can order room service, request a massage, or even request your car from valet through the room's tablet or our app. Also, eighty-seven percent of the technology in this suite can be controlled by your voice. Allow me to demonstrate." He stands and says in a clear voice, "Turndown service."

On cue, the sheers and the blackout curtains begin to close one by one. The lights dim to a warm glow and the sleek, stone fireplace in the living room ignites. The heated floors in the bathroom turn on and the speakers in the ceiling start to play an ambient lullaby.

"Impressive." Adam takes it all in with a gleam of wonder. "Does it also tuck you in?"

"That's in the next software update." Levi winks and stuffs his hands in his pockets.

Adam absorbs the ambiance. It's startling how quickly the room has gone from day to night. If he didn't know better, he'd swear it was nine o'clock at night. "I enjoyed your speech," Adam says, breaking the silence hanging between them.

"Thank you." Levi absentmindedly rubs the back of his neck. "I can talk to reporters and don't mind live television, but speeches still get me a bit edgy."

"I thought you were great. And that part about 'the life you chose for yourself' and 'having the life you want'…" Adam nods slowly. "It really resonated."

Levi narrows his eyes. "Thank you. I'm glad that landed, at least with someone."

"So why did you do it?" Adam asks. "Why did you leave home in the first place? The whole yacht story, I'm assuming is true."

194

Levi rocks back onto his heels and slowly inhales through his nose. No one's asked him about this in a long time. He exhales and gives Adam a listless shrug. "Guess I'd had enough."

Adam is silent, watching Levi's mouth shift and battle with itself before forming his next words.

"*There must always be a struggle between a father and son, while one aims at power and the other at independence.*" Levi gives a bitter smile. "Samuel Johnson said that. I think it's very fitting to the relationship my father and I have." He starts to pace as he talks now, his hands stuffed deep in his pockets with his gaze outward, reminiscing on the past. "My father is a brilliant man but he can also be a tyrant. I was scared to death of him as a child."

"I know the feeling," Adam hears himself say.

Levi pauses, waiting for Adam to say more, but he doesn't. "It sounds like we have something in common," he offers.

Adam doubts Peter Chandler is anything close to being as abusive as his own father, and he's certainly not the devil Andrew Dunn is. His encounters with his father and Andrew Dunn have left him broken and mutilated. Every time he undresses and peers at the scars on his body, he's reminded of their touch.

"Jonathan?"

Adam jolts to, remembering he's on assignment. "Sorry." He gives a dry smile and shakes the darkness from his eyes. "Mind if I ask you something off the record? It's a bit personal."

Levi regards him for a moment, then nods.

"What's the deal with the hot bellboys in the elevator?"

Levi releases a hearty laugh and returns to his seat, crossing his long legs. "That's probably the best question I've received all day." He locks eyes with Adam and takes a long, slow sip of his scotch. His copper skin shimmers against the glow of the fireplace.

"I go for the tough questions," Adam says with a wink.

"Let's just say I paid a ridiculous amount of money for a marketing survey that tells us people feel copious amounts of anxiety when surrounded by 'too much' tech. A nostalgic nod to the past, like a lift attendant, never hurts when you're asking people to check in with an app for example."

"Also doesn't hurt when said lift attendant's particularly handsome."

Levi gives a knowing smile. "I take it you met Wade."

Adam thinks back to his ride to the rooftop pool. "He was cute. Not very chatty, but cute."

"Guess he's rather fit," Levi shrugs. "Shall I introduce you?"

"Not *quite* my type." Adam makes a point for his eyes to travel from Levi's lips down to the bulge in his trousers.

Levi swallows the lump in his throat. He says, "Duly noted," and shifts in his seat. "Is your coffee alright? Or perhaps you'd like something harder?"

"Harder sounds tempting, but it's a little early." Adam opts to play coy – but not too coy. "How about a drink later? You could tell me more about this *fascinating* survey and your audition process for these bellboys."

Levi raises a playful eyebrow. "Off the record?"

"Off the record," Adam promises.

"What room do we have you staying in?" Levi pulls out his phone and the lights in the room grow brighter. The suite slowly returns to daylight, back to the confines of their fifteen-minute interview as the music fades.

"I'm actually at The St. Langham," Adam confesses.

Levi looks wounded. *"The St. Langham?"*

"There's not much of a budget from the paper," Adam thinks fast. "It'd take an act of Parliament for them to spring for a room here."

"Hmm. Come with me." Levi springs out of his seat. Before Adam can react, he's out the door and marching down the hall with his scotch.

Adam aborts his coffee and swiftly follows.

"The St. Langham's nice," Levi calls over his shoulder. "But it's not The Chandler."

Adam can't help but smile at Levi's cockiness. He's like a big kid, traipsing down the hallway of his multi-million-dollar hotel. He shoots Adam a roguish grin as he passes a housekeeping cart and snags two mini bottles of Jack, tossing one back to Adam.

"Where are we going?"

"Your fifteen minutes are up, green eyes," Levi taunts. "I'll be asking the questions from here."

Adam returns his wicked smile and follows him into the elevator.

Perhaps, fittingly, Wade is there in full bellboy regalia, ready to push whatever button they request like it's his life's mission. He straightens at the sight of Levi and gushes, "Good afternoon, Mr. Chandler!"

"Afternoon, Wade," he says, shooting Adam a secret smile. "Mr. Morgan and I were just talking about you."

Wade blushes. "I hope all is well?" There's a hint of panic beneath his sugary smile as his mind races. *What's been said? Who is this 'Mr. Morgan' anyway?* He'll have to look into this new guest who Levi's escorting around.

"Just saying what a bang-up job you've been doing."

Wade gives an appreciative nod, but his eyes narrow at Adam. "Will you be heading to the rooftop, Mr. Chandler?"

"Actually, down one level, please. We're on official business. I'm taking Mr. Morgan from the *London Herald* here on a little detour." He nods dutifully.

"Splendid."

Adam meets Levi's gaze, and Wade's face turns a rosy red. It's a tense few seconds, but finally the doors chime open and Levi leads the way out, giving Wade a nod goodbye. He lures Adam down the hall past the custodian quarters, until they reach the end of the hall. He flashes a key card at the handle, and the door to room 921 chimes and swings open automatically.

"What sort of black magic is *this*?" Adam teases as he inspects the door's hinges.

"Research tells us most people have their luggage with them the very first time they use their key card. I thought it'd be a nice touch to give them a hand with the door," he says proudly.

Adam can't help but be entranced by the brilliance of this. Levi Chandler is every bit as charming and intelligent as he's prepared himself for.

"I call this suite The Abbey," Levi says, ushering Adam inside and closing the door. "It's just over two-thousand square feet, fully automated with voice command, a personal concierge, a two-thousand-dollar mattress no one's even slept on yet, and the paint just fully dried *yesterday*…"

"Cutting it close to your grand opening?"

"You're the first person to see it finished." Levi salutes Adam with his mini bottle of Jack.

Adam does a lap around the suite, appraising the tasteful décor and furniture. There are hardwood floors throughout, a kitchen with stainless steel appliances, and a pool table off from the sitting area. The bathroom's jetted tub looks big enough for two, and he has a clear view of The London Eye from the living room. "Well, it's no penthouse," he laments. "But it's beautiful."

"You're welcome to it," Levi announces.

"Uh... *sorry?*"

Levi approaches with amusement and whiskey on his breath. "You're welcome to stay here."

Adam shakes his head. "I can't afford this, Mr. Chandler."

"*Levi*, please, and you'd be my guest. I insist."

"Levi..." He senses the distance closing between them and his voice goes hollow. "You don't have to do this."

Levi spreads his arms wide and grins like a car salesman. "You're writing a story on The Chandler, right? How can you write about something you haven't experienced?"

He has a point. Adam gives a defeated sigh and begrudgingly accepts the key card. "This is very generous. I suppose I'll have to write a rave review now, won't I?"

"It's not a bribe." Levi rests a hand on Adam's shoulder and shrugs, explaining, "I never read the papers. Could care less about reviews – no offense."

Adam would be offended were he a real reporter. "Then why are you doing this?"

Levi's eyes sparkle with mischief. "Think of it as a convenience. You'll be close to all the action during our opening week for your research, and now I'll know where to find you."

"Where to find me?"

"If I think of anything helpful for your article. Or should I need a drinking buddy to help get me through this week," he says with a grin.

"Right." Adam swallows and raises his mini bottle of Jack. "Cheers to that then."

Their eyes lock, and Adam makes a conscious effort to control the smile tugging at his lips.

· · ·

Adam's all smiles during the car ride to The St. Langham to pack.

Levi's just made his job immensely easier. It must be awfully convenient to carry on an affair when you own a hotel. He imagines he should have everything he needs for Lauren Chandler within a matter of days at this rate. Enough for a divorce and equal, if not more, shares in the Chandler hotel and resort empire. Of course, the fallout depends on what Lauren decides to do with the intel he provides her.

He thinks back to their initial consultation and the tearful case she presented that painted a portrait of a woman trapped, her wings clipped.

"He *refuses* to trust me with any aspect of the business," Lauren spat from her end of the phone. "I'm just a trophy wife to him! Something pretty he can wear on his arm like an accessory for the press. It's all about appearances with Levi. As long as I'm bouncing from hotel to hotel posing for pictures with him, he's happy. But when I bring real viable ideas to the table, he shuts them down! I *know* I could run this company better than Levi."

Adam distinctly remembers the fire and fury in her voice, and he almost feels sorry for Levi.

Then again, Levi's a big boy in control of his own actions. People make conscious decisions to have affairs. Before

200

Adam's targets jump into bed with him, the choice is always there to end things with their wives first or at least have a conversation about their secret desires. The choice is always there to walk away or simply say no. Adam's never held a gun to anyone's head. He's simply there as bait – a sacrificial lamb of sorts – and the rest plays out as the other parties deem.

Adam ponders over this, wondering how dismal Levi's fate will be as he arrives at The St. Langham. He walks into his room, scoffing at his door not opening automatically. He starts to pack when it hits him...

Something's off.

He steps back and has a look at his open travel tote... his clothes scattered about the floor...

Someone's been in his room.

It would be easy to dismiss it as housekeeping, but housekeeping would have made the bed. Housekeeping would have replenished his toiletries and folded the toilet paper into a perfect, neat triangle. Housekeeping might have been more discreet and left undetected if they'd rummaged through his belongings looking for valuables.

Adam feels a knot in his stomach as he scurries to collect his belongings, frantically tossing them into his bag. He curses under his breath and flees the room at lightning speed, not bothering to close the door behind him.

For the first time in a long time, Adam fears the worst.

13 / C'EST LA VIE

So far Paris is nothing like Quinn imagined. He'd pictured himself walking along the Seine eating warm croissants near the Champs-Élysées, a perfectly cliché introduction to France. Instead, he now finds himself cooped up in a strange apartment, hunched over his laptop and second cup of coffee.

James sits opposite him, his long legs stretched out on the sofa as he cradles his laptop. "It's like he's a ghost," he sighs and briefly closes his eyes to give them a rest. "There's literally no paper trail of Adam Walker having stepped foot in Paris."

"Which means he's using an alias."

"But why use an alias?" James closes his laptop and stands to stretch. His arms go over his head and his T-shirt rises to give Quinn a peek at his hard stomach and the soft trail of hair leading to his jeans. "Only people on the run use an alias."

"I'm telling you, I still don't think he was involved in the murder of Sara Dunn," Quinn says and squints at his screen. Adam's involvement in the death of Andrew's wife has been a constant debate since Quinn told James about his visit to Sweet Ridge and his interview with Jenna. "Did you fly all the way to Paris to fight me on this?"

"Nah." James grins and rubs the scruff on his face. "I've got some PTO to burn. Plus, how could I say no to watchin'

Bailey 'work the runway' at this André-whoever show?" He rolls his eyes.

"Mock all you want, but Bailey's agency paid for these accommodations. The timing couldn't be more perfect."

Their accommodations are nothing glorious. It's a modest studio apartment with a small terrace and equally small kitchen with white tile countertops. There's a writing desk that faces a pair of tall windows, a sofa, wood coffee table, and a bed just a few feet from the bathroom that's finished with white subway tiles. There are a few lamps and plants scattered about, along with some French fashion magazines Bailey devoured as soon as they unpacked. Furnished studio apartments abroad are a go-to for Bailey's agency, ensuring their models will be close to location.

James sprung for a room at a proper hotel not far away to commemorate his first time in Paris. "Guess you're right," he says. "Funny how things line up." He refreshes his wine. "Paris being Adam's last known location... Bailey's fashion show thing..."

"I like to think we're always *exactly* where we're meant to be in the world," Quinn says. "The universe has a way of keeping us on course." His eyes are glued to an old article about Taylor Barnes, a media baron of sorts who was once the toast of daytime television.

"So, you're sayin' you and me are meant to be in Paris together right now?" James gives a playful smile. "That the universe has destined us to be together at this exact time and place...?"

"You're here because you have a friend in customs who owes you a favor," Quinn teases back. "Hopefully they can give us a lead on Adam."

"Always a source, huh?" James scowls and walks over with two glasses of red wine. "It's our first night in Paris. Drink with me."

Quinn doesn't need convincing. He accepts the half-full glass of merlot and their fingers touch, giving off a spark hard to ignore.

James sits on the edge of the desk and takes in the starlit windows, a view of the Eiffel Tower glowing faintly in the distance. "Seriously, you know I'm here for *you*, right?"

Quinn leans back in his chair with a bittersweet smile. James looks so handsome tonight; it kills him. His edge-up is razor sharp against the collage of dark curls that crown his head, and even his nails look freshly manicured – far from what you'd expect from someone who works in a forensics lab all day. His jeans with the knees ripped out cling to his muscular thighs, and the burgundy polo he wears looks sculpted to his chest. Quinn has no idea how James finds time for the gym; he must somehow, or perhaps it's just his genetics. Every time he sees James, his body looks swollen as if he's fresh from a hard workout.

Quinn can think of hundreds of gym-inspired exercises he'd love James to introduce him to.

Glute Kickbacks.

Dive Bomber Push-ups.

Barbell Squats... right on top of his...

Ugh. If only things weren't so complicated at the moment.

"I know this story's important to you," James' voice cuts in, full of bass. "I'm here to support you however I can." He nods sincerely. "Even if that means sitting through Bailey's asinine fashion show."

"Such sacrifice!" Quinn smiles. "How sweet of you."

"I *am* sweet," James laughs. "Let me show you how sweet I can be." He licks his lips and reaches for Quinn's hand just as the front door bursts open.

"Bonjour, bitches!" It's Bailey.

James clenches his fists and forces a smile. "Bonjour. Votre timing est impeccable comme toujours." Of course, his French is the best in the group – far better than Bailey's, who just smiles in return.

"We thought you were at the venue," Quinn says.

"I'm runnin' late," he struts into the kitchen, takes a swig from the open wine bottle and pauses. "Is that what you guys are wearin' tonight?" It's not really a question. The alarm in his eyes tells them they've gravely miscalculated the dress code for an André Lefèvre couture fashion show.

Quinn touts, "What's wrong with jeans and a nice blazer?"

"I'm not changing," James shrugs.

"Well," Bailey takes another swig and shrugs back. "C'est la vie. What are you boys workin' on?"

"Digging a little deeper into Adam's past." Quinn turns his attention back to his laptop. "Aside from the postcards, there's not much of a trail, but I did an image search online and got a few hits."

"Seems he's been running in some well-to-do circles," James says.

"He shows up in two photos including one with *Taylor Barnes*!"

Bailey frowns and asks, "Who the hell's Taylor Barnes?"

"You're kidding. He was this big shot media mogul. Had his own network and a few satellite radio stations… WCVR… NBR?"

No bells are ringing.

"Quinn found a photo of Adam and Taylor Barnes together at some industry event. They looked cozy."

"I also found a photo of Adam rubbing elbows with Robert Tate."

Bailey's eyes go wide. "Should I know who *that* is?"

"He's a sports agent. Used to be *the* top sports agent in football," Quinn explains.

"Used to be?"

"Apparently, he went through a nasty divorce and his wife cleaned him out. Lost most of his clients."

"I remember that in the news," James says, taking a healthy sip from his glass. "And Taylor Barnes' wife now owns over half his radio stations."

Bailey's eyebrows flex. "Guess there's nothin' like a woman scorned." He chuckles, but Quinn's expression remains grim.

"There could be a connection. I don't know what yet."

"How do you mean?"

Quinn leans back in his seat at the desk. "We can only go on the intel we have, but as of now, the only documented appearances of Adam after his disappearance are with Taylor Barnes and Robert Tate – two rich, fat white guys who *both* had divorces that ruined their careers. It might be a stretch, but it doesn't seem like just a coincidence either."

Bailey can't digest what this all means, but he knows it has nothing to do with them changing for the fashion show. Their minds seem made up. "Well, I'm sure you'll figure it out, babe." He flashes a smile and heads for the door. "I better get my ass down to the venue. I'm leaving two passes for you guys at the door. *Please* don't be late."

"Are you playing the role of the *pot* or the *kettle*?" Quinn winces.

Bailey grabs his coat and waves on his way out. "See you boys there. Wish me luck!"

They oblige, and just like that, he's gone.

"Well, *I* think you're onto something," James says once they're alone. "I should look into who the divorce lawyers were, tonight after the show. Could lead to something."

"Good thinking, detective."

"Mmm," James growls. "I love when you call me that."

Quinn closes his laptop with a smile. "Think you'll apply when you get back to work?"

"It's a long road to detective. There's the entrance exam, police academy..."

"You've got to start somewhere," Quinn shrugs. "You've already got great connections at most of the precincts. Lots of people know and love you. I bet you'd climb the ranks quickly."

"Maybe cracking this case with you will grease the wheels," he says, half joking.

"You've been a big help since you arrived." He meets James' gaze. "Thanks for coming. I mean that."

"We're in this together now, right?" He reaches for Quinn's hand and gives it a squeeze. "Besides, I hear the French guys here are real Casanovas with their fancy accents and skinny jeans. *Someone's* gotta be here to look out for ya."

"Is that so?" Quinn grins. "So you're here to '*save*' me from them?"

"Yes, *and* you're welcome," he winks.

Quinn laughs, more than he's laughed in the past week since his near-death brush with Andrew Dunn. "Thank God you're here." He rests a hand on his chest. "Wouldn't want them sweeping me off my feet in their skinny jeans and, what else, *red berets?"*

"Okay, okay!" James resigns with a laugh, "I might have stereotyped them, but still... if anyone's gonna sweep you off your feet, I want it to be me."

The words make Quinn's knees go weak. It's a good thing he's sitting down.

They share a smile, and James reluctantly releases Quinn's hand with a sigh. "You think we should really change for this thing?"

They exchange looks, weighing each other's outfits, and decisively shake their heads.

"Nah."

• • •

The morning brings coffee, flaky pastries, and hangovers. Quinn licks his fork clean of the sweet, creamy tiramisu and red berries he's ordered. He watches Bailey cautiously sip his cassoulet – a casserole made with meat and white beans their waitress suggested as a cure for his throbbing hangover. The café is packed with locals, sipping coffees and conversing in oversized chairs. The French Country décor and delicate, mismatched china embody the local charm Quinn's been craving. Every mouthful of their brunch is a cultural orgasm. Even the faint melody of "La Vie en Rose" in the background is a thankful departure from the previous night's fashion show full of loud house music and strobe lights.

Bailey removes his shades and passes Quinn a near-death look. He's draped in a kimono over jeans and a white T-shirt that reads DON'T FEED THE MODELS. "I still can't believe I kissed André Lefèvre at the afterparty. Like some horny teenager."

"He didn't seem to mind."

"Guess things got a little weird," he says, grimacing at his bowl. "Even James looked like he had fun."

Quinn rolls up the sleeves of his lightweight gray pullover and can't help but smile to himself.

"He's so into you," Bailey scoffs. "Following you all the way to Paris like some lovesick puppy. Pathetic."

"I know you guys aren't 'friends' but he's been a huge help. You can't take that from him. He gets that this is important to me."

Bailey makes a questionable face.

"Oh, come on. You honestly don't think he's doing all this to get in my pants."

Bailey crosses his arms.

"You're the worst. I hate you for putting that in my head."

"Like it wasn't there already." He winks and stirs his Bloody Mary.

Quinn huffs and glances at his watch.

"Listen, I mean, sure, James is hot," Bailey concedes. "Even I wouldn't kick him out of bed for eatin' crackers, but I just want you to be careful. You fell so hard for Elson, and that fucker took that job and moved to San Francisco, without even talkin' to you about it first! James seems like a nice guy, but he reminds me of Elson," he says with a shrug. "Maybe that's why I haven't exactly warmed up to him. I just don't want to see you hurt again. You're a great catch. You don't even—" He glances at his buzzing phone. "Ugh. Shit."

"Is that your mother again?"

Bailey nods and watches it go to voicemail.

"Guess that makes two of us dodging phone calls this morning. Detective Bradshaw called. Not exactly thrilled

I've left the country."

"A fine mess we're both in."

Quinn peers around the café and exhales. "Gotta admit though, it beats being at the office writing stupid human interest stories under bad fluorescent lighting."

"Sure beats being in Paris *alone*. I'm usually by myself on these gigs, so having you here has been really nice." A smile crosses his lips. "And hey! Your first time abroad, right? Who else can say their first time abroad was full of *international mystery?*" He shimmies his shoulders. "You attended the hottest fashion event of the season last night and this morning you're eatin' tiramisu and back to solvin' a murder case. I mean, *who does that?* You're my fuckin' hero."

It sounds like a stretch, but Quinn accepts the praise. "I'm doing it for Travis, you know. And all those other boys everyone still assumes are missing." He shoots Bailey a weak smile. "I never told you this, but you remind me of him sometimes."

"How so?"

"He wasn't afraid to be himself."

Bailey smiles and strikes a fierce pose. *"I fuckin' love bein' me!"*

"You do." Quinn nods admirably, "But Travis got bullied a lot in school for being gay…"

"At least he had you to look out for him."

"A fine job I did at that." Quinn crosses his arms. "Thinking he ran away without telling me was hard enough. *Knowing* that Andrew killed him is…" He shakes his head, at a loss for words.

"Babe, I know you wanna protect everyone, but you can't. *Even with me.* You're *always* lookin' out for me, and I love you

210

for it... but you can't blame yourself for what happened to Travis. You can't save everyone."

Quinn releases the breath he's been holding. "I know it's too late to save Travis, but I can at least try to give him justice... he deserves better than how Andrew left things."

"Hey, sorry I'm late." James rushes to their table, breathless. "You won't believe who I just got off the phone with."

"Here." Quinn composes himself and pulls out a chair. "Catch your breath. Did you run here?"

"I guess I did." James plops down. His head is spinning. "I was on my way here when I got the call back."

"From who?" Bailey's patience is already wearing thin. He's mostly poking at his cassoulet with his spoon now. It's lost its heat and he's wishing he ordered a greasy burger instead.

"I found the divorce attorney, well Taylor Barnes' ex-wife's attorney, Greta Houck. I emailed her during the show and got a reply this morning."

"What did she say?"

"Wait." Bailey points his spoon. "You emailed her *during* the show?"

"Not that your show wasn't *riveting*," James frowns. "I've never seen so much latex in all my life, really. I just had to jump on this."

"Again..." Quinn presses, "What did she say?"

"It was a lot of back and forth. She wouldn't go into details about the case of course, but I sent her the photo of Taylor and Adam. Interesting thing? She recognized Adam, but not as *Adam Walker*."

"An alias."

"Right. She wouldn't tell me what name Adam used, but that's neither here nor there. We figured he's been using aliases." He eyes an empty coffee cup on the table. "She did let it slip that Adam had a part in the divorce. She told me to get in touch with a PI the wife hired."

"A private investigator?" Quinn chews at his bottom lip. "The wife must have suspected something."

"Well, this PI wasn't gonna talk unless I paid him, which I did."

Quinn's shoulders drop. "You didn't have to do that. I'll pay you back."

"Don't worry about it. This is important. And what he had to say was well worth the money." He motions to a passing waitress for coffee. "Turns out it was the easiest job of his career. The wife hired him just one day before she filed for divorce and *she* brought him the evidence!"

"Wait, *what*? What do you mean? And what evidence?"

James pulls out his phone and lays it on the table. "Let's just say Adam's been a busy boy. Here's the photo the wife *gave* the PI for his report."

Quinn and Bailey lean in, peering over plates of toast and jars of orange marmalade. There, on James' phone, is a photo of Adam and Taylor Barnes in bed. Taylor's naked and exposed, trying to shield his face from the camera. Adam's in the background under the sheets.

"Adam was sleeping with him." The words leave Quinn breathless. "Maybe with Robert Tate, too?"

James shrugs. "I wouldn't be surprised."

"We should reach out to both of them."

"I've tried. Tate's people aren't calling back, and when I finally got Taylor Barnes on the phone he hung up."

"Damn." Quinn hits the table. "I'd love to know what they could tell us about Adam. They might still have a way to contact him."

"Hey, guys?" Bailey leers at the photo from his side of the table. "Somethin's not right."

"What do you mean?"

Bailey points a finger at the screen, "Somethin's not right here. Look. *This guy* looks surprised, right?" He points to Taylor. "He looks genuinely caught off guard and embarrassed." He does his best to suppress a chuckle, peering at Taylor's less than epic erection. God knows he's seen bigger. "Now look at Adam's face…" He trails off, and a chill settles over the table. "You see it? Adam looks… *bored.*"

Quinn's heart starts to race. He sees it. He sees the dullness in Adam's green eyes. He sees his listless body language and how his eyes don't connect with the camera.

Finally, Bailey says what they're all thinking, "Adam just doesn't look surprised. It's almost like he was expecting it."

Quinn and James share a look as the weight of this sinks in, dropping to the pits of their stomachs.

Adam thinks back to the photos of Adam plastered on the walls of his mother's parlor, then takes another stinging look at James' phone. Long gone is the broken boy who disappeared from Sweet Ridge. Long gone is the sweetness in his yearbook photos and the innocence in those familiar eyes.

The question remains… what does Adam know that may unlock the mystery of Andrew Dunn?

But now a larger question has come into focus.

Who exactly is Adam Walker?

14 / CHERRY

Adam can't focus.

He's sitting in the front row of The Chandler's main ballroom among investors, press, and VIPs, half-watching Levi give a presentation on... *something*. It's unclear what exactly, but there are charts on the screen behind Levi and lots of talk about equity and stock. The ceiling drips with chandeliers that have been dimmed for the occasion and Levi is center stage in a handsome navy suit and black tie, pointing excitedly at the screen behind him.

Adam's mind is back at The St. Langham. He replays the scene over and over, wishing now that he hadn't fled in such a hurry. He'd been hasty. If someone did break into his room, he should have taken more time to discern what they might have been looking for. Perhaps he should have even reported it. But there's also a nagging thought – a conceivable explanation that shadows his reasoning and it is just as troubling.

What if his mind is playing tricks on him?

He'd been in such a hurry to be on time for his interview with Levi that it's possible he left the mess himself. He'd misplaced the prop glasses he bought and had searched frantically for them before leaving the room that morning. It's possible he only has himself and paranoia to blame. He's been on edge and ever since arriving in London he's felt the sensation of being watched. Then again, ever since leaving Sweet Ridge he's felt the itch to look over his shoulder…

Levi catches Adam's gaze, and his face immediately softens.

Adam hopes it looks like he's paying attention, and Levi won't quiz him later. He's supposed to be the reporter after all. If anything, he should have follow-up questions in mind, but he doesn't.

The lights soon return to their full glow, and the crowd applauds as if Levi has just announced they've all won cars. Adam's tempted to check under his seat for a prize of some sort, when a familiar face struts onstage. Adam instantly recognizes her as the red-lipped blonde from the lobby who ushered him to the rooftop elevator. She whispers something into Levi's ear, and Adam can only hope it doesn't pertain to himself. There's something about her that makes him uneasy. *What if she's checked his credentials and discovered he's not with the London Herald?* He doesn't have a plan for this, which was sloppy. Normally he'd have a plan B, but he's been laxer this time. This is his last big contract. His final job.

"You alright?" It's Levi. He breathes relief and smiles at Adam. "Bloody glad that's over with. What'd you think?"

Adam stands and shakes Levi's hand, which feels like it's mostly a show for the people lingering, somehow. "It was interesting." He plays it safe but has a feeling Levi's caught him drifting off.

Luckily, Levi doesn't challenge his reply. "I know it's a lot to take in," he says under his breath. His eyes gloss over Adam with a faint smile.

Adam's instantly glad he's worn his tightest trousers, however uncomfortable they may be. He's channeling a sexy

215

version of Clark Kent in his newsroom attire and glasses. He's even wearing a blue tie since Lauren confided that blue is Levi's favorite color. He might have guessed this on his own, but regardless, he's content to see Levi take notice.

"Today will be good for the article," Adam reassures him.

"About that," Levi says, making a labored face. "We should talk."

Adam's breath catches in his throat.

"We should talk privately, I mean." Levi leans in, giving Adam a trace of his cologne. The warm notes of citrus and spice are inebriating. There's a line of people waiting to speak to Levi now. "Perhaps you'll join me for dinner this evening?"

"Oh…" Adam teeters between relief and flattery. An obvious response might be to ask if *Mrs.* Chandler would be joining them, but he knows Lauren has told Levi she's flying to one of their hotels in Berlin for the weekend. It will be just the two of them.

Alone.

At dinner.

"Sounds good." Adam does his best to downplay his excitement, but a smile slips past.

Levi gives a boyish grin and nods. "Right. Well good. I'll arrange transportation and will send for you, say, quarter to seven?"

Adam's never been *sent for*. Should he expect a horse-drawn carriage or a royal escort? He nonetheless agrees and prepares to excuse himself as the line behind them grows. "I look forward to it, Levi," he says, noting how intimate Levi's name feels on his tongue now. There's something among the syllables and consonants that wasn't there before. A secret, woven into the language they now share.

· · ·

There's a knock on Adam's door just after six thirty. He's kicking himself for forgetting to record his interaction with Levi earlier. Normally he documents all conversations and interactions with a target as evidence. He keeps a journal of events. He has the tools to wiretap phones and plant tracking devices. He's even bugged his own room with mics strategically placed around the suite, behind paintings and the headboard. He's usually thorough, but somehow the simple task of pressing record on the tape recorder in his blazer eluded his memory at Levi's presentation.

Between that and the knot of paranoia in his stomach, he feels like he's unraveling.

Adam opens the door to find Wade in uniform, forcing a smile. "Good evening, Mr. Morgan. I've been asked to escort you to dinner."

"Right." Adam does his best to hide his surprise, but it's useless. Levi's clearly making a statement by bringing Wade into this. Adam wants so badly to ask who's manning the elevator but doesn't. Wade looks like he's in no mood for sarcasm, so Adam complies and follows Wade down the hall.

The silence in the elevator is deafening as they ascend. Wade looks like a watered-down version of the bright-eyed elevator attendant Adam first met. There's a hint of scornful defeat in his gaze as he stares silently ahead. It's clear that the pleasantries are over.

The doors chime open, and he shoots Adam a rehearsed smile. "Have a pleasant evening, sir." His words are frostbitten.

Adam starts to ask if he's done something to offend Wade

but settles on a polite nod as he exits the elevator. He shrugs off the encounter as sunlight warms his face, realizing he's been brought to the roof level.

Levi is at the far end of the rooftop terrace with his hands folded behind his back. He's changed into a pair of toffee-colored trousers and a white, tight-fit polo that looks stunning against the hues of gold in his skin. He's clean-shaven and his dark wavy hair looks as if he's had a trim since his presentation earlier.

Behind Levi sits a jet-black helicopter with the gold Chandler logo branded near the tail boom. For a moment Adam thinks he's hallucinating, but Levi's game-show-host smile confirms it. "Ready for liftoff?"

Adam nearly doubles over. Before leaving Sweet Ridge he'd never been on an airplane, and it had taken months to overcome his fear of flying. Still, he's never been inside a helicopter, and there's not a pilot in sight which can only mean... "*You're* flying?!"

"Of course." Levi grins with a shrug as sunlight catches his aviators.

Adam ensured Levi was vetted. He'd done weeks of research into Levi and his company before accepting the contract, but no amount of research could have prepared him for this. He slowly makes his way across the roof's terrace, past the pool, and leans into Levi with an awkward half handshake, half hug. His mind's too consumed with all the things that can go wrong to ask where they're headed.

"Shall we?" He feels Levi's hand on his back and before he knows it, he's sitting inside the chopper, buckled in. Levi hands him a headset, fixing it over his ears. Their fingers brush as Levi's voice comes over its speaker. "You alright?

Hear me okay?"

Adam nods mutely, numb from the neck down. The cockpit shakes as the chopper blades roar overhead. Levi confidently flips a few switches and does a pre-takeoff check. He gently pulls on the collective, and Adam feels his stomach drop as they lift off. He clutches firm to his seat belt, daring to peer down at the world dropping away below them.

Levi tosses him a smile as they soar higher, cutting through the rosy pink light of the sky. "You alright?" He nods encouragingly.

Adam mimics the movement with his head, but he is not good. Nothing about this is good. "Uh, how long—" His voice over the headset startles him. "How long have you been flying?"

Levi shrugs. "'Bout two weeks."

"Two weeks?!"

"*Relax.*" He throws his head back with a laugh. "I'm fucking with you."

Adam cuts his eyes and peers down at the city beneath them, spotting what looks like The St. Langham, but it's hard to tell. Buildings that once looked so massive and imposing now look *minuscule*. Bustling streets resemble streams of insects and toy cars. "Everything looks so small," Adam marvels.

"That's why I like it up here," Levi purrs. "Really puts things into perspective."

They share a look that's interrupted as the cockpit sways to one side. Levi grips the collective, adjusting against the turbulence. "Just some rough air," he says, seeing the panic in Adam's eyes. "It's just 'cause we're flying over concrete – the streets. It does that." His hand finds Adam's knee, giving it a squeeze. He senses the tension locked into Adam's thigh and his face softens. "Heeey... it's alright."

Adam feels his throat tightening and forces himself to swallow as his ears pop.

"It's alright. You're in good hands." Levi grips Adam's hand reassuringly. "I won't let anything happen to you."

The words hit Adam like a sledgehammer.

Adam feels the warmth of Levi's hand that lingers within his own for a second too long. He hears Levi's soothing voice in his ears over the headset. He sees the tenderness in Levi's face and allows himself to breathe.

Something within him finally breaks, and for the first time in a long time, floating eight thousand feet above the ground, Adam feels safe.

• • •

Levi touches down on a lush green lawn, miles from the clamor and flurry of the city. Adam has long lost his sense of direction but guesses from the picturesque English country-side that Levi has taken them to Besford. Although... as he takes in the sprawling Jacobean-style manor before them, he wonders if they could be in Oxshott.

He really should have spent more time looking over maps before this contract. He knows nothing about London.

Levi helps him down from the chopper, and Adam smooths his tousled hair, shielding it from the wind of the blades. He's glad he wore jeans now. Paired with a pale blue collared shirt and an off-white light jacket he looks like the quintessential weekender. Perhaps even a real Londoner, minus the accent of course. He'll leave that to Levi.

"This is home." Levi waves to the largest of the buildings on the property. It easily dates back to 1880 with its Renaissance-inspired architecture, detailed russet brickwork, and soaring columns. One-third of the structure is enveloped in tendrils of ivy that has crawled and tangled its way into the facade of the estate house, giving it an old-world charm. There's a large circular driveway with a running fountain and a row of stables sit to their right. To their left sits a greenhouse and yet another building Adam determines must be staff quarters or a guest house.

As they near the main house, Adam peers up four stories to the towering slate rooftop, half expecting to see gargoyles.

"This is where I grew up," Levi says, trying to read Adam's face.

Adam frowns to one side. "I've seen bigger."

"Ha!" Levi's dimples show as he shakes his head. He unlocks the oversized front door and ushers Adam inside.

Their footsteps echo eerily throughout the large foyer, half lit by a stained glass skylight overhead. The floors are a polished ornate design of oak and mahogany while dark wooden beams and hand-carved woodworking cover the walls. There are statues of Grecian gods and furniture, all covered in white sheets. The house looks beautiful but abandoned.

"I used to think it was haunted when I was little," Levi's voice echoes throughout the halls. He looks around, breathing in forgotten memories and dust. "My parents are in Monaco," he says, which explains why everything is covered. "I like to stay here when they're away." He motions for Adam to follow as they make their way deeper into the belly of the manor.

Adam listens to Levi's half attempt at a tour as they pass a library and indoor pool that's turned acid green without regular maintenance.

They finally arrive at the kitchen, which is a gaudy monstrosity of marble and stainless steel. Levi makes quick work of turning on the lights and opening a bottle of red wine.

"To Monaco!" He proposes a toast after filling two crystal goblets.

Adam swirls his wine and sits on a stool at the kitchen island, watching Levi rummage through the fridge. "When you said dinner, I didn't think you'd be *cooking*."

Levi produces a bag of groceries from the fridge with a receipt attached and pulls out two steaks wrapped in butcher's paper. "You can't be in the hotel business without picking up a thing or two from the kitchen."

It's not long before pots are bubbling and the air smells of spices. The sun begins to set, and its burnt-auburn glow starts to extinguish, leaving the manor in darkness with the exception of the kitchen's warm glow.

"How's your article coming along?" Levi asks out of the blue.

"Good!" Adam's eyes go wide. "Although I haven't worked out why you're giving me the VIP treatment. Helicopters... now dinner."

"It's called an exclusive."

Adam shoots him a playful glance over the top of his wine glass. "I bet you say that to all the reporters."

"Only the ones I like." Levi smirks and turns the steaks. They sizzle in the pan, one side now caramelized and charred to perfection. "Actually, I've rather enjoyed having you around." His accent sounds musical, blending into the Bach playing over the kitchen speakers. "It's been a hectic few days – anytime there's a new opening it's completely draining. These

222

press tours do me in, you know. Just meeting after meeting. Interview after interview." He pauses and points his tongs at Adam. "You're different though. You're not like the rest."

"You haven't seen what I've written so far," Adam teases.

"I'm not worried. I can tell you see through all the bullshit, you know? You see through all the smoke and mirrors. You see through all the pomp and circumstance at these things. Everyone always expects me to put on this *big show*. I've got to be *on* 24/7..." He frowns and starts chopping a handful of rosemary. "But with you, it's just... I dunno. It's like I can just be myself around you."

"It must not be easy bein' the Chandler 'gold standard', everyone expecting you to be like your father."

"Exactly!" Levi shudders and points the knife in Adam's direction. "That's exactly it. Or they're just waiting for me to fail, so they can say I should have become a plastic surgeon, like him! Miserable old git."

Adam can't help but flinch as Levi talks with his hands, waving the knife around.

"You know, I think he had my whole life planned out before I was even born. 'Born with a silver scalpel,'" Levi mocks, "just grooming me to take over his practice one day."

"But you started your own empire, without his help."

"I refused to take a cent," Levi spits with fire in his eyes.

"Pretty ballsy."

"See? Like I said, you get me." Levi grins. "I think I'll keep you around."

Adam blushes and his eyes fall to a pile of cherries on the cutting board. "My family grows cherries. On our farm," he finds himself saying out loud.

Levi's eyes light up. "Yeah?" His eyebrows hover, waiting

for Adam to elaborate.

"Uh, yeah. I mean that's not all. We grow corn and cabbage and taters, and we have chickens and a few horses. I guess everyone in town knows us for our cherries though."

"Wait." Levi squints. "Did you say *taters*?"

Adam holds his breath.

"And was that an *accent* I just heard? Bloody hell, Jonathan, where are you *from*?"

"Oh, nowhere you've ever heard of." Adam quickly buries his face in his wine glass, but Levi's unyielding.

"No really, where?" He removes the steaks from the pan to rest.

Adam swallows hard before doing something he's never done with a target. "I'm from a really small town in Tennessee called Sweet Ridge," he hears himself reveal. "You won't even find it on most maps. There's not much there but farmland and bad memories. I haven't been home to see my ma in a while." Even as he says this, he can hear his southern drawl returning.

"And your father?"

"He died," Adam says unflinching. "Tractor accident."

Levi's face contorts. "God, that's *awful*." He's never heard of anyone being mauled to death by a *tractor* of all things. "I'm so sorry."

"He deserved worse." Adam's eyes dim. "He was a monster."

Levi slowly nods, noting the shift in Adam's body language. His folded arms and the pain rippling across his handsome face say more than any confession. "I'm sorry he hurt you," Levi says softly. "How old were you?"

Adam leans away. "What is this? You interviewing *me* now?" He forces a laugh, although there's a sheen to his eyes. "I'll be askin' the questions here, mister."

"I just wanna know who you are." Levi's voice remains level, but there's an intensity in his eyes that makes Adam's heart race. There's an intimacy in his tone that makes him want to reveal the small-town boy inside and put away the character he's been wearing over his skin. He wants to tell Levi that his name isn't Jonathan Morgan, and that he's not a reporter from The *London Herald*. He's just a boy who's been running from his past for as long as he can remember.

"You don't want to know the things I know, the things I've seen…" Adam trails off. "You wouldn't like me so much, I bet."

Levi smiles that charismatic smile of his and lowers the flame on the burner. "Everyone has a past. And hey, this might be hard to believe, but I'm no angel myself."

They both crack smiles, and Adam's thankful Levi's lightened the mood. "Is this where you play the billionaire bad boy card?"

"Something like that," Levi smiles coolly and scrapes the bottom of the frying pan with a spatula.

"I've got my eye on some land in Kentucky. It's perfect for a farm," Adam hears himself sharing. "I'm gonna buy it. Start over fresh with just my ma 'n me."

"That's your plan?" Levi squints. "You're gonna buy a farm on a journalist's salary? Bloody hell, I'm in the wrong business."

"I've been tuckin' some money away," Adam says confidently. "I've got a goal."

"It's good to have goals," Levi agrees, pointing the knife again. "When I was younger, I wanted to go to the Olympics, you know, as a *job*?" He cracks a smile, "Really I just wanted to do anything other than become a doctor."

"So, you swam?"

"Actually, yeah." Levi blinks. "Secondary school and university swim team. How'd you know that?"

"Lucky guess…"

Levi stares at him for a tense moment. "Huh."

"And the pool," Adam thinks fast and points over his shoulder. "Most people don't have indoor pools. I just figured."

"Guess that's like journalist instincts, huh? Like Sherlock Holmes?"

"Sherlock Holmes was a *detective*. You're English. You should know that," Adam laughs.

"Technically I'm only half English." He shrugs his wide shoulders. "Plus, I was never much on school and reading. Hating having to read all those medical journals…"

Adam's face lights up. "I used to love school. I was a science geek. I wanted to go into agronomy."

"Which *is*?"

"Think of it like… the science behind crops and soil. Agri-culture."

"Hmm. Okay. But you became a journalist instead." Levi squints. "That's quite a leap, innit?"

"You have no idea." Adam deflates in his seat and watches as Levi adds butter, rosemary, and a splash of beef stock to the pan. He cranks up the heat and grabs a handful of cherries, crushing them in the pan with the back of the spatula. "What's all that for?"

"It's a sauce for our steaks." Levi lifts the pan from the burner and douses the mixture with a cup of brandy. He expertly tilts the pan back over the flame and it ignites, sending a loud roar of flames into the air.

Adam leans back, mesmerized and frightened as he does a quick check for his eyebrows.

Levi shakes the pan, causing the flames to dance. "Are you impressed yet?" His English accent sounds more charming than ever as he shoots Adam a wink. "Us bad boys love playing with fire, you know."

Perhaps it's the flames, or perhaps it's Levi's unabashed talent for flirtation… either way, Adam feels blood rush to his cheeks and starts to melt in his seat.

Levi grabs a spoon and has a quick taste. "Mmph! I've done it again!" He shouts like a mad scientist. "A masterpiece. Here…" He takes another spoonful of the sauce and walks from behind the island. "Have some." He blows on the spoon before bringing it to Adam's lips.

Adam wets his lips and slowly opens his mouth, his eyes locked with Levi's. He feels a comforting warmth on his tongue, followed by a flood of sweetness and notes of tart cherry. He closes his eyes and relishes the bold flavors in his mouth as a moan escapes.

Before he can utter a reply, Levi leans in for another taste.

Adam's lips part and Levi's tongue rushes in, sending waves of desire and savory sweetness swirling within Adam's mouth.

Their kiss deepens, feeding an insatiable hunger, and Adam can no longer distinguish the taste of Levi's mouth from the sauce. Both are equally intoxicating.

He could drown in this kiss.

15 / DÉJÀ VU

James peers around the near-empty bar with a dismal expression. The space seems too dimly lit for five in the afternoon, and aside from a few locals perched at the bar, he and Quinn are its sole occupants. He'd suggested the lobby bar of his hotel, but Quinn had been strangely adamant about meeting elsewhere. "Sooo… *how'd* you find this place?" The octave of his voice indicates he's less than impressed.

Quinn tears his eyes from the football game playing over the bar and says, "I don't know, just seemed like a good choice. Inconspicuous, you know." He shrugs. "I saw the name and there was something familiar about it. I must have seen an ad for it somewhere."

"An ad. For this place." Doubt clouds James' eyes as the sound of a toilet flushing erupts from the bathroom behind them.

Quinn gears up to rebut when they're interrupted by a pencil-thin man with a wide cartoonish smile. "Would you gentlemen like for something to drink?" The bartender has trekked over, placing napkins on the table of their booth.

"Whiskey neat, please," James says.

The bartender's smile goes flat. "Ahh… '*Neat*'? I'm sorry my English is, uhh…" He waves a shaky hand. "What is 'neat'?"

"No worries. He'll just have a beer." Quinn smiles. "The cheapest beer you have on tap."

James glares from across the table.

The bartender nods steadfastly. "And for you, vodka with St-Germain, oui?"

Quinn blinks, taken aback. "Um, no." He can't imagine why the bartender has made the assumption. He shrugs it off and squares his shoulders back to announce, "Je voudrais votre meilleure bière artisanale locale!"

"Ah, très bon. Venir tout droit, monsieur." The bartender shakes off a sudden sense of déjà vu in his dark oversized eyes, gives a final nod, and traipses back to the bar.

"Someone's been practicing their French." James flashes a smile.

"Hold your applause. I only know how to order a drink and find the bathroom."

"What else is there?"

Quinn meets James' playful gaze before glancing at his watch. "It's after five. What if she doesn't show?"

"Mari wouldn't let me down."

Quinn hopes he's right. If James' contact has any valuable intel on Adam, it could change everything.

A few minutes pass until, finally, they hear the front door open followed by a rush of cool air.

In walks Officer Mari Hayes, doing her best to look unofficial in a pair of black slacks and a baby blue embroidered tunic top. Her coffee-brown skin seems to glow, even in the stale light of the bar, and her jet-black hair is cut into an asymmetrical bob that frames her face. There's the slightest hint of lip gloss and mascara but nothing more than that. Her nails are done in a high-gloss mauve finish. The purse dangling off her shoulder is designer but could easily be a well-done knockoff. She looks like any number of women who have just clocked off to meet their coworkers for $5 margaritas at happy hour.

You'd never guess she's a customs agent.

She slides into their booth and says, "I can't stay long, and if this meeting ever comes into question, I'll deny everything." With that, she pulls a book from her purse and glides it across the table.

"Nice to see you too, Mari." James makes a face and intercepts the book. The cover indicates it's an English to French translation book but tucked within its pages is an airport surveillance photo of Adam.

"Clocked him at the airport." She brushes a few strands of hair from her face and crosses her arms. "I ran facial recognition from the photo you texted and got a match through security. He's traveling under the name Jonathan Morgan and took a flight from Paris to London. No sign he's flown from there since."

Quinn shares a look with James and reaches for the photo. There, in grainy black and white pixels, stands Adam in line at security holding a passport and duffle. Quinn wishes he could decode the stoic look on Adam's face. He wishes he knew what was running through Adam's mind at that moment.

"Wonder what's in London?" James poses.

"Maybe he's meeting someone?"

Mari gives Quinn an uneasy look, "This a relative of yours?"

"No," Quinn echoes her unease. "We just look alike. It's sort of a thing."

Her neatly plucked eyebrows scrunch together. "I promised I wouldn't ask questions – and I won't." She narrows her almond-shaped eyes at James, "but please tell me this guy isn't dangerous. I've crosschecked him in our database and there are no warrants or priors but *still*. Anyone traveling under an alias is either running from something or up to something."

"He's not dangerous," Quinn says.

"We *suspect* he's not dangerous," James passes Quinn a hardened look. He doesn't bring up the death of Andrew Dunn's wife in front of Mari, but he hasn't ruled out Adam having a hand in it.

Mari looks between the two of them and throws up her hands. "I've done my part," she sighs, "and you're welcome. Now you can stop holding junior year at Howard against me."

"What happened junior year?" Quinn asks.

Mari sighs in James' direction and folds her hands on the table. "I broke up with him."

"On my birthday," James adds with a salty half smile. "In front of all of my friends and my parents. It was a surprise birthday party."

"Apparently *full* of surprises," Quinn gags.

"I did you a favor," Mari shrugs. "I mean, obviously…" She nods at Quinn, whose shock has turned into a blush. "But, hey, he's cute! Really. You guys look good together."

"Oh…" Quinn's heart nearly ejects from his chest. "We're not…"

"It's complicated," James winces.

Mari looks at each of them and shrugs. "Whatever. I have a nail appointment to get to." She stands and slings her purse strap over her shoulder. "Wait ten minutes before you leave and remember—"

"We know, we know," James waves a hand at her. "You were never here."

231

The stern look on her face slowly gives way to a smile. "It's been a long time, Jamesy. I'm glad to see you're doing well."

James matches her smile and a quiet acknowledgment passes between them. "Good to see you haven't changed a bit."

Mari rocks back with a chuckle, "Me? Never." She then winks before striding off.

The front door slams shut and Quinn's left facing James with a teasing smile. "Well, *that* was interesting. You failed to mention your 'contact' is an ex-girlfriend."

"A story for another day," James says as the bartender returns with their drinks.

"I like her style," Quinn decides. "Kind of a badass."

"More like a pain in the ass."

"How long did you guys date?"

"Oh God, here we go."

Quinn tilts his head. "You can't blame me for being curious, *Jamesy*."

"How 'bout I tell you about it over dinner?" James leans in and the bass in his voice deepens. "Just you and me tonight. No Bailey. No crazy fashion shows. Just us."

"Hmm." Quinn's gaze tilts to the ceiling, "That sounds an awful lot like a date."

"You said it, not me."

"Guess I walked right into that one."

James smirks, sips his beer, and his entire face contorts as if it's possessed. "Gugh! What the hell *is* this? Tastes like skunk water."

Quinn laughs. "Not enjoying the local libations?"

"You owe me one." James circles his tongue around in his mouth and gapes at the frosted glass. "That's just wrong."

Quinn bites his lip and dives into James' bottomless brown

eyes. "Maybe I do owe you one. Dinner's on me tonight. Just don't bring flowers or anything," he teases. "I'm not that kinda guy."

James' hand finds Quinn's from across the table. "Fine. And don't think you're gonna kiss me on the first date either," he warns and slowly drags his thumb across Quinn's knuckles. "I'm not that kinda guy either."

They both nod with resolve… and share a smile.

• • •

Darkness has fallen upon the City of Light, leaving the skyline glittered with stars that curiously peer down at Quinn and James as they stroll the riverbank of the Seine. The Cathedral of Notre Dame and the city lights beyond dance across the glossy black river, and the air is thick with the smells and sounds of Paris after dark. Their hands occasionally brush as they wander the cobblestone streets on their way to dinner, inhaling the magic of the evening.

James finally seizes Quinn's hand, lacing Quinn's fingers with his own.

"Sorry." Quinn glances down abashedly. "It's been a while since I've done this," he says, giving James' hand a squeeze. He's wearing jeans, a blazer, and a new shirt Bailey helped him buy that's surprisingly tame. He's also managed to finagle his wild hair into something sleek and fitting of a proper first date.

James looks good enough to eat in a pair of white jeans and a tight black button-down revealing wisps of chest hair. He casts Quinn a curious look. "You know there's no rulebook to any of this, right? I mean, you think I know what the hell *I'm* doing?" He laughs softly. "I flew over three thousand miles to be here with you, and now I feel like I hardly know what to say."

Quinn watches James' face falter. For once, he looks just as lost as Quinn in all this. For once, it looks like he doesn't have the answer.

"You're fine, James. I'm the one who watched my high school crush bleed out on top of me. If that's not the definition of damaged goods, I don't know what is."

"You're not damaged goods." James gives their arms a gentle swing as they walk. "You're amazing. You don't even see it."

Quinn fights the urge to roll his eyes. "Careful. I'm not used to compliments and boys treating me nice. I might pounce."

James laughs. "I *promise* not to put up a fight."

They pass an open shop and a rack of postcards catches Quinn's eye from the window.

"I almost forgot! I should get a postcard while I'm here. For my collection."

"How did I not know you collect postcards?"

Quinn's face sours. "Probably because I never go anywhere. All my postcards are from other people's travels." The weight of this hits him as they peer at the display case. "I guess I never thought I'd find myself in Paris one day."

"But here you are," James says, nudging his shoulder. "Gonna buy one?"

Quinn purses his lips and reflects for a moment. "I'm not," he decides. "I think I'll hang onto the memories instead. There's nothin' like the real thing, right?"

James gives a nod, and they move on.

Soon they find themselves on the Pont des Arts, overlooking the Seine. Lovers glide over the bridge holding hands, taking photos for their social media feeds. It's crowded. Not knowing where else to turn, Quinn looks to the stars and is relieved to find them shining back.

It's suddenly clear that they've never left him.

"Funny story. When I was younger, I wanted to be a *legit* astronaut," Quinn says. "I thought I had it all figured out," he laughs. "I had this whole plan, and I was so sure that was what I was meant to do. To be among the stars," he says.

James follows Quinn's gaze toward the heavens. "What happened?"

"I had to take a flight test. I had to do 1,500 flight hours and on the day of my very first test, I *landed*, skidded off the runway... and crashed the plane."

"Oh, shit."

"Yeah. Oh, shit," Quinn says ruefully. "I walked away without a scratch but I also walked away thinking... fuck. *Now what?*"

James has fallen silent.

"Sometimes, I wonder what if I'd *died* in that plane crash, you know?" He forces an ironic smile. "I've never told anyone about that."

James gives his hand a squeeze. "I don't know what kind of astronaut you'd make, but I know one thing," he sizes Quinn up with sultry eyes. "I'm glad you walked away from that crash. Plus, if you weren't around, you wouldn't have been there to save Henry, right? Your whole 'we're always exactly where we're meant to be' mantra?" He half-smiles. "Andrew would still be out there murdering innocent people if it wasn't for you."

"I guess that's one way to look at it."

"You know, I can tell you're different here," James says.

235

"Since coming to Paris."

"It's hard to explain. It's like we've been chasing this ghost, but when I'm here – and I even felt it in Sweet Ridge – I just feel closer to him somehow, like I'm walking in his footsteps." He searches James' face for any sign of understanding, "I can't explain it, but I *know* he's the key to all of this. I can feel it."

James' hands find Quinn's waist, pulling him closer. "I believe you. And I get that this story is important to you, and that you have this... *connection* to Adam – and I guess to the others." He takes a ragged breath and says, "I just hope you find what you're looking for here."

"We know where Adam is." Quinn's face brightens. "Thanks to you. And your ex-girlfriend."

"I'm never gonna hear the end of this, am I?"

"Probably not." Quinn's fingers travel from James' forearms to the width of his biceps.

"I guess you'll be taking off to London?"

"About that..." Quinn deflates. "I'm being called back to New York by a certain detective we all know and love."

"Bradshaw?"

"She's asking questions. I need to reassure her I'm *not* writing a scorching expose on Ted Collins' closeted gay son who unwittingly had a tryst with a serial killer she knows nothing about."

"Tall order."

"If only she knew the half of it. I should also check in with work, and I got this really weird message from Jenna."

"The waitress?"

"Yeah. She told me back in Sweet Ridge Adam wrote her from New York once, that he was doing some modeling there. She remembered the name of the agency but it sounds sketchy.

Could be worth looking into. But after that, I'm hightailing it to London."

"The clock's ticking," James warns. "Based on what Mari told us, we know Adam was in Paris for a few weeks, but who knows. London could be different."

"Right. It'll just be a day trip. In and out." His mind goes back to Vera in Sweet Ridge, opening her mailbox to receive a new postcard with a new location from Adam.

"I guess I don't need to tell you to be careful," James says. He pulls Quinn close and furrows his brows. "I hate not knowing what you might be walking into."

"Hey, I've survived a plane crash and Andrew Dunn's clutches twice," Quinn smirks. "I'm still standing, right? I'm still here."

"And no one's happier about that than I am." James smiles.

"Yeah? Why's that?"

"Well…" James hugs Quinn's waist. "If you weren't still here, I wouldn't be able to do *this*…" He closes the gap between them with a searing kiss.

They lose themselves, caught in a whirlwind of their own making. James' fingers find their way into Quinn's hair as their kiss deepens. Strangers walk by with amused smiles as Quinn cups James' face in his hands, tasting the sweetness of his lips unfolding like a delicate rosé. They forget where they are for the moment. They forget about their dinner reservations at the Michelin star restaurant James painstakingly selected. They forget about the trauma and the body count that's led them halfway around the world to a place Quinn once only knew in his dreams. They forget who they are for the moment and allow themselves to get lost in one another.

Under the stars.

16 / SCARS

Adam awakes to the sound of his own scream, tearing out of the depths of his throat like a phantom from his past. He kicks and thrashes, fighting limbs and hands that seem to come at him from all directions.

"Jonathan... Jonathan! It's alright!"

The accent registers and Adam's eyes peel open, bringing Levi into focus.

"You were dreaming." He rests a hand on Adam's bare heaving chest to calm him.

Adam sighs heavily and quickly examines both sides of his hands, then curls them over to check his fingernails.

No blood.

It was just another dream.

"That musta been one hell of a nightmare." Levi can feel Adam's heart racing full throttle under his touch.

"I'm okay," Adam sighs, exhausted. As he looks around, taking in the safety of Levi's bedroom, it begins to feel true. Daylight filters through the curtains of the room, slowly revealing everything it touches in muted grays and blues. There's a large armoire, two armchairs, and a Victorian style sofa – all covered in white sheets, occupying the room like ghosts.

Their clothes lie littered across the floor, and the sheets smell like sex and Levi's cologne.

Levi props himself against one of the six pillows that reside on the bed. "You scared the hell out of me." He softly rakes his fingers down Adam's chiseled chest. "I couldn't wake you. You just kept yelling and *clawing*…"

Adam whispers, "Sorry."

"I didn't mind the clawing so much *last night*." Levi shoots him a wicked smile, feeling the sting Adam's nails left down his back.

"Sorry. I get a 'lil rough sometimes."

Levi shrugs a shoulder and admits, "It was actually sort of nice to just let go, let someone else take charge for once."

They're quiet for a moment as Levi's eyes wash over Adam. His fingers idly graze up and down Adam's chest. "What's the story with this?" He pinches the charm on Adam's necklace between his thumb.

Adam smiles. "I never take it off. My ma made it for me. It's like a hobby of hers, makin' jewelry." Like a spell, he conjures Vera in his mind, slumped over her craft table, a coffee cup of moonshine within arm's reach. "She sells 'em at the country fair every year."

Levi beams with his usual charm. "Think she'll make me one?"

"Doubtful." Adam smirks.

"And where did *these* come from?" Levi points to each of Adam's scars, connecting imaginary lines between the scar tissue.

"Motorcycle accident." The lie slides off Adam's tongue with ease. He's told it so many times it sounds believable now, even to him. But of course, he knows better.

He can never forget their sordid origins.

Levi surprises Adam by tenderly kissing each scar on his chest. One by one. From the peaks of Adam's chest leading down to his navel and the slight rise of his hipbone, Levi makes his way down.

"Careful," Adam says, raising a brow. "Don't start sumthin' ya can't finish."

"God, I love that accent." Levi's blue eyes dance. "Where've you been hiding it?"

Adam takes in Levi's lean swimmer's build peeking from under the sheets. His copper skin looks warm and inviting against the harsh concentrated rays of daybreak filling the room. "You just bring it out of me, I guess."

Levi peers at him mindfully. "So, let's see... a motorcycle accident... your mother makes jewelry," he notes. "Anything else you feel like sharing or want to tell me?"

"Well, *I like you*." Adam shrugs. "But you prob'ly figured that out by now." He leans in, swiftly capturing Levi's lips with his own.

A flicker of disappointment passes over Levi's face as Adam pulls him tight. He flinches as Adam's hands graze the angry cuts on his back, but the pain is quickly replaced with pleasure as their tongues intertwine. He presses himself hard against Adam, who moans in return. Their bodies entangle in the Egyptian cotton sheets, and Levi feels the heat kindling between them, quickly sweeping itself into an inferno. Then with as much restraint as he can gather, Levi slowly pulls away, breaking the current fizzling between them.

"What's wrong?" Adam glares back, his face muddled with desire and confusion.

"You're sure there's nothing else you want to tell me?"

241

Adam feels his heart sink as the air between them grows thick. There's a heaviness that threatens to pull them both under. He's already told Levi too much, he realizes.

"I should go," Adam says.

Levi watches, stunned, as Adam unearths himself from beneath him. "You're leaving?"

"I shouldn't be here." Adam sits on the edge of the bed and scans the floor for his underwear. "I never should have come here."

"And why's that?" Levi's voice has a chill to it.

"Because I don't *belong* here, Levi. I'm not the guy you want me to be." He frowns and concedes that things have officially gone off the rails.

How did he let things get to this point?

"I know you don't work for the *London Herald*," Levi says.

Adam suddenly feels sick. He turns to meet Levi's stare that's peppered with anger. His voice cracks as he asks, "How long have you known?"

"Does it matter?" Levi glares. "What is this anyway – you're some sort of corporate spy or something?"

"No," Adam shakes his head desperately. "I'm not a spy."

"You wouldn't be the first."

"I'm not a spy."

"Are you some sort of headhunter or, uh…" Levi cuts his eyes and reads deeper, "No." He straightens his spine and his voice goes cold. "No, I know what this is. Lauren put you up to this."

Adam's gobsmacked.

"She did. *Didn't she*?!"

It's the first time anyone's guessed.

Levi deserves a prize, Adam thinks to himself. He tries to

242

keep his expression neutral, but it's useless. Now that Levi's spoken the words aloud, it's written all over Adam's face.

"Wow. Are you fucking serious?!" Levi's head spins. "Are you fucking serious? Is any of that shit you told me yesterday even true? The cherry farm and that shit you told me about your dad?" His face is strained as his lips struggle to keep up with his runaway thoughts. "Hell! Is, uh, is Jonathan even your real fucking *name*?"

Adam sighs.

"You're joking." Levi throws up his arms. "You're fucking with me, right?"

"It's Adam. My name's Adam – and I didn't lie about yesterday. Everything I told you was true." The words come flying out. "That was me yesterday. In the kitchen and at dinner – and in the helicopter – that was all me. And yesterday, with you, was one of the best days of life. Levi, I've never told anyone the things I told you yesterday, about my dad, about where I come from… When I'm around you, you make me feel like I can be myself, too. I *am* myself when I'm with you." He gulps and searches Levi's face. "It scares me to death how you make me feel sometimes. That's the truth."

Levi looks away.

"I never meant for things to go this way."

"Right, a little late now, innit?" Levi glowers. "I guess you and my conniving wife just meant to, what, blackmail me? Having feelings for me must be *such* an inconvenience, assuming that part's even true!"

"Wait." Adam's face goes dark. "What time is it?"

"Why?" Levi looks more flustered than ever. "You have somewhere to be? We're not quite done here, you know."

Adam reaches for the watch on Levi's wrist. He glares at the gold-plated hands on the timepiece, ticking and whirling in a foreboding countdown. "We need to get out of here. *Now*." Adam starts to flutter about the room and tosses Levi his pants.

"What are you talking about?"

"You have to fly us out of here." Adam hops into his jeans. He has no clue where his underwear might be.

"*What makes you think—*"

"Lauren's not in Berlin," Adam says. "In nineteen minutes, she's going to walk through that door."

Levi cuts his eyes, glancing between Adam and the bedroom door.

Could Adam be telling the truth?

Levi doesn't know what to believe.

"If she finds us together…" Adam winces. He doesn't need to finish the thought.

Panic rises in Levi's eyes as he slowly registers the gravity of their situation. "You set me up."

"She set you up."

"I brought you into my home," he snarls. "I opened up to you, and you lied to my fucking face!"

"I *am* sorry," Adam says. "And I can explain everything, I promise! But later. If we don't—" He stops and whirls his head towards the door.

"Your promises don't mean shit. I can't believe I—"

Adam holds up a hand to silence him.

Levi scoffs, then begrudgingly follows Adam's gaze towards the door.

They hold their breath, remaining perfectly still as they lean in.

Suddenly, past the stillness of the room and beyond the

244

bedroom door comes a sound. It's so faint that Adam thinks he's imagining it at first.

It sounds like hammering.

Adam cocks his head to the side and closes his eyes, listening to the hollow rhythm, tapping and echoing within the foyer, growing closer. Louder.

It's a sound he knows.

It's the sound of heels stomping down the hallway – but it feels like a runaway freight train barreling towards them. Destined for collision.

Adam's heart takes a nosedive as he opens his eyes to meet Levi's stunned expression. He draws his lips into a tight line, then whispers in a strained voice, "She's early."

17 / BONES

Quinn can barely think over the sound of children yelling and tearing through the indoor playground. Why Detective Denise Bradshaw has suggested they meet at a Mighty Burger is beyond him.

He gives her a faint nod as she joins him at the bright yellow table he's procured in front of a ball pit spilling over with toddlers. The ground beneath them is green AstroTurf carpet with loose balls and French fries scattered here and there.

"You came."

"As if I had a choice." He smiles mockingly.

Denise gives him a pointed look before glancing over each shoulder. Her locks are down today, reaching the middle of her back, and her nails are painted a shiny cartoon purple. "Hungry? It's $5 Mighty Meal Day," she says this enticingly, as if the prospect of deep-fried chicken nuggets may disarm him.

"I guess that explains the horde of children." He makes a face and digs his fingers into his dark hair, grabbing a handful.

"What? You don't want kids one day?" She gives a wide amused smile and waves a hand. "I used to say the same thing. You'll change your mind."

He doubts it. "What can I do for you, Detective Bradshaw?"

"Denise," she insists.

Quinn deflates in his seat, clearly not in the mood for this game of pleasantries. The red-eye back to New York had been murder. He'd almost missed his flight and now the jetlag is settling into his weary bones.

"So, you've been doing some traveling." She raises an eyebrow.

"I wasn't told I couldn't." He sees where this is headed. "I gave my statement, so unless I'm under arrest for something—"

"Far from it," she waves a hand. "In fact, I've been asked to hand deliver this to you by the Collins family." She produces a thick envelope from her purse and slides it across the table. He gets a clear read of the tattoo on her wrist this time.

Deandre.

Something within him had secretly hoped it was the name of another woman, which would have given them something in common, but no such luck.

Quinn doesn't have to open the envelope to know what's inside. Still, he's dying to know how much his silence is worth. He opens it with his thumb, takes a peek inside, and whistles.

"You don't have to publicly accept the reward money." Her hazel eyes sparkle, "I'm sure that might be seen as a conflict of interest, given your profession. But at the end of the day, you did earn it. You did find Henry."

"Funny you say that. There was no mention of it in the news." He says incredulously. "It's almost like Henry just reappeared out of thin air! No explanation of where he's been or how he was found. Certainly no mention of being taken by a sadistic psychopath who tortured him for days on end…"

"The family wishes to keep the gory details out of the press."

"You mean Ted Collins wishes to keep the truth from the public."

"I didn't come here to argue with you." Denise shakes her head. "I came to deliver that as a thank you from the family, which I've done." She pulls her purse strap onto a shoulder to leave.

"You know I can't accept this, Denise."

Her face is crestfallen as she folds back into her seat. "I thought you might say that." She gives him a flustered look. "You journalists and your high morals." She can't help but laugh. "It must be nice to be in a position to say no."

"You know why I can't accept this."

"Quinn," she leans in and her voice becomes hushed. "You *don't* want to insult him. Collins is one of the most influential men in this city. He's everywhere. Trust me when I tell you, you don't wanna tango with this guy. And when he wins the election – *which he will* – you won't want to be on his bad list. Just take the money and walk away. And whatever you're planning to write, let it go."

"I can't do that, Denise." He slides the envelope back across the sticky ketchup-stained table. "He might own *you*, but he can't buy *me*."

She raises a finger in anger and says, *"You have no idea—"* but is interrupted by a tug on her arm.

Quinn and Denise look to find a boy, no older than five, hovering by her side. He faces Denise and makes a rhythmic motion with one hand curled into a fist in front of his face. He bobs his head to meet it, making a licking motion, then stops as his large hazel eyes spot Quinn. He gives Quinn a shy smile and cuddles next to Denise, peeking from behind her arm.

"Honey, we'll get ice cream in a minute. Go find your brother and put your shoes on."

His eyes are glued to Quinn, who gives a small wave.

"I like your shirt!" Quinn does his best to look excited as he points to the bright orange and purple dinosaur plastered across the front.

The boy pulls at the hem of his shirt and glances down at the design with a smile. He does a little dance, yanking on the fabric and flashing part of a feeding tube port that's lodged into the side of his stomach.

Denise soothes a hand over his curly hair to calm him and leans in to whisper something close to the hearing aid in his ear. She backs it up with a quick slew of hand gestures and without a second to spare, he runs off to find his shoes.

"It's CHARGE syndrome," Denise says once they're alone. "He's had his feeding tube since birth, but he likes the taste of ice cream." She shrugs. "Who doesn't?"

Quinn makes a mental note to look up CHARGE syndrome on his phone later. "Seems like a brave little guy."

"Hell, he's got no choice," she says, her eyes distant. "He's a kid *now*, but one day he'll be a man – a deaf man of color, trynna survive navigating his way through this world." She slings her locks over one shoulder and confides, "I think he also might be gay."

They share a look, and Quinn can't help but pass her a vibrant smile. "He's been chosen!"

She laughs.

"Deaf, black, *and* gay?" Quinn grins. "Come on. That kid's gonna be a force!"

"Let's hope so, cuz the other one's just like his father." Denise gives a ragged sigh, showing her age for the first time since they've met. She looks tired and weathered suddenly, showing hints of age at the creases near her eyes.

"If nothing else he'll be a tough motherfucker like his mom." Quinn offers another smile.

She issues a return smile that dims with distress as her eyes fall to the envelope on the table. "Think about what I said." She reaches for her purse again. "It's easy to say no from that high horse, but you never know what you'll do when your back's against the wall. Ted Collins and his money may be as low as it gets in this city, but there's no end to what *I'll* do to take care of my kids," she says. "They're all I've got."

Quinn shrinks in his seat. "I didn't mean… I'm sorry." He bites his lip and watches her rise to leave. "I shouldn't have been so quick to judge."

She makes a face. "I know you're workin' on a story, Quinn. You're not gonna convince me you flew to Paris just to see the damn Eiffel Tower."

He's careful not to react, channeling one of Bailey's patented poker faces.

"I just hope you and *The Chronicle* don't write a check your ass can't cash. I won't be able to help you if you go behind Collins' back, or if you're withholding information related to this investigation."

He remains silent. If Denise discovers the true depths of Andrew Dunn's carnage it could derail everything… and he's *so close*.

She raises an eyebrow as if to say, "Last chance," then shrugs her shoulders. "Guess I better get these kids some ice cream now, or I'll never hear the end of it. *Want a cone?*" Her tone is light like sunshine now, and motherly in a way he suddenly misses.

250

"I'll pass," he says with a weak smile. "Hey, I meant to ask about Henry. How is he?"

"He's back at work. Back to normal, I guess."

"There's no such thing as normal."

"I think he's just mostly confused. Confused as to why this happened to him."

"Well, I'm working on that." Quinn runs a hand over the stubble on his face and watches her eyes go wide. "Don't worry. You can tell Collins I won't mention Henry by name." He gives a taunting wink.

"You're playin' with fire," she warns, again sounding more motherly than even she intended. "Andrew Dunn is dead. It's case closed." She shakes her head and saunters off to gather her children and reward their good behavior with frozen custard.

She leaves behind a faint trail of perfume that smells of patchouli and jasmine, along with the envelope on the table.

· · ·

Quinn hops out of a cab and jogs up to Bailey, who stands before a row of elegant brownstones in the heart of Renaissance Harlem.

"Ha!" Bailey points a finger and grins *"You're late!"*

"Bullshit." Quinn checks his phone. "By two minutes!"

"Doesn't matter." Bailey shakes his head adamantly. "You late, bitch. Finally! The mighty have fallen." He pounds two fists in the air triumphantly as if he's just stuck the dismount.

"This is the first time I've been late in the history of our friendship."

"And I shall never let you forget it," he says, pulling Quinn in for a hug.

"This also means it's the first time your ass has ever been on time," Quinn mumbles into his neck.

Bailey rolls his eyes. He's in cutoff jean shorts, combat boots, and an oversized Fendi sweatshirt from last season.

"Have you heard from your mother lately?"

"Only every other day," Bailey says.

"You know you can't avoid her forever."

Bailey's face goes blank.

"Fine," Quinn sighs. "So, is this it?" He scans the series of brownstones before them. They all look the same, with their intricate brickwork and identical staircases.

"This should be it. I mean, I did exactly what you told me," Bailey says. "I looked into the name of the modeling agency Jenna called you with but couldn't find any info, so I started askin' around. *No one* had heard of this place." He swivels his neck. "So, the other day Aubrey was home – she just got back from doin' a flight to Portland – and I mentioned it 'cause I remember her sayin' a few girls she flies with used to dance and 'model'." He makes air quotes. "Turns out one of the girls she knows, who now flies with Skyline, heard of this place, which led me here."

It's a long-winded explanation – much more than Quinn was expecting – but fine. If there's any chance Adam worked for this agency, it warrants looking into.

"How was your meeting with Detective what's-her-face? Is that why you were *late*?" Bailey purrs.

"Fruitful," is the word that comes to mind as Quinn feels the weight of the envelope in his jacket.

"Did you get to talk to your boss?"

"Not yet. I need to go see him after this, so let's go."

They march up the steps to the brownstone marked 219 and ring the bell. A moment later there's a long buzz and a click at the door that cues them inside.

They enter and instantly feel as if they've stepped into another era. The room reeks of cigarette smoke and resembles more of a rundown waiting room in a doctor's office than a living room. The floor is a neutral tan color with stained carpet, gray herringbone chairs, and side tables stacked with old magazines. A large chandelier suspends from the ceiling with a few burnt bulbs, an original fixture of the house, hung between speakers in the cracked ceiling that play soft jazz. The space might have been beautiful in its glory days, but time and a lack of repairs have taken their toll.

Quinn and Bailey exchange looks as they absorb their surroundings and approach a desk at the far end of the room. There's a receptionist wearing a headset, staring intensely into a computer screen. She looks European with her flawless olive complexion and dark brunette bangs that keep slipping behind her glasses.

It takes her a while to acknowledge them, and when she does it's a mere glance over the top of her glasses, flashing a set of dark gray cat eyes.

"Yes?" There's a trace of an accent, but Quinn can't place it. "Can I help you?"

"We're here to see 'Nina'…?" Bailey offers this like a Cold War spy, speaking in code. Or as if "Nina" is slang for some new designer drug that only this receptionist in this unsuspecting brownstone is dealing out.

"Do you have an appointment?" She doesn't bother looking up.

"We're here about someone she once employed," Quinn says.

253

"Adam Walker...?"

"I'm sorry, but there's no—" Her eyes look to Quinn and go wide, having a better look at him now. Her whole body goes stiff and her mouth forgets how to work, the muscles in her jaw suddenly seizing up. "Oh... uh, yes." She blinks and swipes her bangs from her face. "One moment please." She quickly dials with her free hand and gives Quinn another strange look. A voice comes over her headset, and she answers in another language.

Bulgarian. Quinn's sure of it now. His ex, *Ivan*, has parents who migrated from Plovdiv and invited them over for dinner once. They spoke little English so Ivan did the translating that night over Gyuveche, which his mother promised him the recipe for but never delivered on after they broke up. Quinn has no idea what she's saying into the headset because Ivan never took the time to teach him any Bulgarian. (He was much too busy fucking around.)

Her words sound hushed and urgent as she speaks, keeping her eyes trained on Quinn.

"What's happening?" Bailey whispers nervously.

Quinn doesn't answer, trying to memorize as many words as possible to look up later.

"You can go back now," she says, releasing the call. Another buzzer sounds, and she motions to a door behind them.

On the other side they find a room that resembles an office, except there's no desk. The walls are a faded Chinese red with no windows. There's a black leather bench in the center of the room, along with a coffee table, all facing a large, ornate, cracked leather chair that resembles a throne more than anything.

There, sitting in the chair, is a woman who Quinn surmises

is in her late fifties. She's dressed in a long, simple black gown that matches the razor-sharp bob that dusts her shoulders. Her ears drip with diamonds, and her face is painted in makeup much too dramatic for a daytime look. Her red lip twitches, clearly startled at the sight of Quinn. Her eyes go big and a hand instinctively clutches the arm of the chair.

Quinn wishes he'd worn a hat now. He'll have to remember to be more careful. Being mistaken for Adam may have gotten him this far, but he can hear James' voice in his head telling him Adam might have enemies he doesn't know of.

"Have you found him?" These are her first words. Not hello or any semblance of a welcome or introduction. She poses the question in her thick Bulgarian accent as if she's been waiting for them to arrive with some sort of report.

Quinn's taken off-guard but is careful with his words. "We have an idea where he is."

She smirks at this and crosses her legs, resting her hands in her lap. The room is quiet for a moment. Each side regarding the opposition until she abruptly reaches for her cigarette case on the coffee table. "You're here for information." There's a flicker, and she pauses to blow a stream of smoke into the air above them. "Are you cops?" She says this with a smile, as if joking, although something inside her must ask the question. *If they are cops, they must tell her. Right?*

"Family." Quinn's the first to think of a good answer. An angle he should have thought of before. "Cousins."

"Right. Clearly," she says, but still looks spooked. She's not sure she believes them, but here they are. Her afternoon is free and more than anything she wants to know what they have to say about Adam. She hasn't heard his name in years. She no longer speaks it, and the rest of her staff knows better than to speak it in her presence. Adam's name is a curse now. Like poison on her lips. She's thought of him often though, more than she'd like to admit… "I'll tell you what you came for. Then you tell me where he is." It sounds like a command.

Bailey wets his lips as he inhales her secondhand smoke. He'd love to bum a cigarette off her but knows what Quinn will say.

"You have a deal," Quinn agrees and watches as she takes another slow drag before speaking.

"He was all bones when I found him – well, not when *I* found him," she backpedals. "Sasha, one of my girls, discovered him at a party. She went out to smoke and there he was in the alleyway, homeless and scrounging for scraps!" She says this with disgust in her mouth, like she wants to spit the words onto the floor.

It's hard to imagine Adam outside of school pictures, but Quinn tries.

"He was bones," she says, flicking her wrist for a dash of drama. "I saw potential in him though. He had something. He was smart. He had something you just can't… teach." She pauses to gauge the room. So far Bailey and Quinn are with her. "So he came to work for me," she continues. "He went on a few runs. Did a few parties." She's choosing her words carefully in case she's being recorded. *You never know.* "He did very well, but he was bored." She smiles like a proud mother, remembering clearly now. "He got bored easily."

"What happened?" Quinn presses.

"There was a call. Madeline Larson," she recalls with a grimace. "She was having a soiree and had a very specific… *request.*" It's getting trickier to choose the right words. "A lot of my clients have events," she explains. "Big events with

256

wealthy and powerful guests to appease, and they want to fill the room with *friendly faces*."

The boys nod. They get it.

"Well, darlings, Madeline had a very peculiar request, you see. She wanted just *one* extra for the party. A male. Good looking. Savvy. Someone who could hold a conversation in a room full of heavy-hitters."

They're perfectly still, allowing her to continue.

"Adam fit the bill. Only Adam wasn't there to entertain her guests." Nina pauses for dramatic effect. Her dark eyes sparkle as she glances between them, waiting to see if anyone can guess what she'll say next.

She's killing them.

Just come out with it, Bailey wants to scream, but he bites his tongue.

Quinn uses his journalist voice, calm but straightforward. "Who was he there to entertain?"

"She wanted an extra to entertain *her husband*." Nina raises an eyebrow. "Adam was bait."

The air in the room grows dense.

"We didn't quite realize it at the time of course. Adam was brilliant though. Charming. Beguiling." She chuckles to herself. "He did very well that night indeed."

The two have no idea what might come next.

"The problem…" Nina suddenly lashes forward to ash her cigarette, "The problem was that the assignment went beyond the party. It turned into an affair with Madeline's husband."

Quinn tosses Bailey a quick glance.

"It turns out Madeline had grown rather tired of her husband. She had a hunch that his tastes might lie with the same sex and my little Adam not only proved her right, he gave her all the evidence she needed to blackmail her husband, divorce him, and take fifty-five percent of his company."

This is what they came for. What Nina is telling them somehow makes perfect sense as Quinn recalls the photos of Adam with Taylor Barnes and Robert Tate.

"Ohh, but it didn't stop there!" Nina laughs to herself. "It turned out Madeline belonged to some hoity-toity southern sorority. A whole network of women married to powerful men who paid them little attention, had affairs, and, well, you know what they say..." She waves a finger at them, "One in five?" She's less sure about Quinn, but figures he must be gay like Bailey. Guilty by association.

Bailey gives a little nod. "More like two in five these days, I'd say. Given inflation."

Quinn shoots him a look.

"Next thing you know, everyone's asking how Madeline did it!" Nina laughs wildly. "They all wanted to test their husbands and catch them in the act! Like it was a game. So *we* gave them what they wanted, darlings. Supply and demand."

"It became a business?"

"It *became* my business. No more hotels and dates." She's getting sloppy now. She shouldn't have said hotels. Or dates. "We were in it for the long haul. The stakes were higher. The rewards were higher."

Quinn sees it clearly now. Women were paying Nina to bait their wealthy husbands with her employees, often with it ending in an affair the wives would be privy to. They'd have all the ammunition they needed for blackmail or a lucrative divorce. Nina could provide audio, video, or even arrange for the wives to "accidentally" walk in on their indiscretions. The hardest part often fell on the wives to act surprised upon "catching" their husbands with another man.

"An affair is one thing." Nina purrs. "Who hasn't had a little tryst?"

Quinn flinches a little.

"When women are together it's 'sensual' and 'sexy' and society hardly bats an eye. But when a man has an affair with another man…" She shakes her head. "It's something very different. Something very shameful and…" She searches for the right word.

"Emasculating." Quinn fills in the blank and Nina's red lips form a sinister smile.

"Yes! There's something very threatening about the concept."

Threatening. Like an unstable stick of dynamite.

"How long did Adam work for you?" Quinn asks.

"Until I found out he'd been moonlighting, running his own operation," she says, her voice bitter, vexed with vinegar and spite. "We had a fight and the next day he's gone with my client book, a gun, and all the cash from my safe. Just like that!" She snaps her fingers. "Gone."

Quinn knows Adam's talent for disappearing well; a stunt he's apparently perfected since leaving Sweet Ridge.

Nina uncrosses her legs and snuffs out her cigarette, apparently done with her ghost story. She appraises Bailey and Quinn once more, letting her stare linger on Quinn's green eyes. "Cousins, you say." It's clear she's not buying it. "You know, if it wasn't for your voice, you could very well pass for him."

Quinn and Bailey exchange uneasy looks.

"I've told you what you came for, cousin." She rocks back in her chair and snarls. "Now you tell me what I want to know."

Quinn can only imagine what Nina will do with this information, but he's confident he can get to Adam first.

He must.

Also, a deal is a deal, right?

He takes a breath as if he's about to dive into an icy pool and utters the words before he has a chance of psyching himself out of taking the plunge. "London," he says, watching her razor-sharp lipstick spread into a devious smile. "Adam Walker is in London."

18 / BANG

The elevator doors chime open, and Adam slumps down the hallway toward his suite at The Chandler.

The past few hours have been hell, but, thanks to his fast thinking, he and Levi managed to evade being discovered.

It had taken the two of them working together to quickly make the bed – something Adam has always loathed, even as a child. Adam helped Levi into the armoire and covered it again with its dusty sheet, then rolled under the covered Victorian sofa just as Lauren walked into the bedroom. He can only imagine her shock at finding the room untouched and empty, but the slew of voicemails and texts that have flooded his burner phone since make it clear she's not a happy customer.

So much for a 5-star review.

It's only a matter of time before Levi confronts her himself, the final nail in the coffin.

Adam fishes for the room key in his pocket and suddenly brushes past Wade in the hallway, who offers no apology or greeting. Before he can react, Wade is swiftly making his way back to his post at the elevator.

He wants to tell Wade that he can have Levi if that's what this is about. It'd been a cold silent flight back to The Chandler with Levi, who clearly wants no part of him now. As soon as they arrived at the lobby, Levi made an excuse to go to the front desk without even a goodbye.

Adam flashes the key card at the door and is surprised to see the light turn green. It's a wonder Levi hasn't canceled his reservation, but he wouldn't be surprised if security comes to escort him off the premises soon.

He wastes no time packing.

As he enters the bedroom to gather his belongings, he pauses in the doorway.

Something's off.

It's clear that housekeeping has been inside since the bed is made and his shoes are aligned in a neat row near the closet, but something beneath the surface stabs at his gut.

He rushes to the closet to find his travel tote unzipped. He empties its contents, tossing handfuls of clothes over his shoulder and frantically checks the lining of the bag.

The gun is gone.

His legs give out from under him as he clutches his chest, feeling for the charm on his necklace. His mind races, resurrecting his worst fears as he pulls himself to his feet and races to the bathroom. "He found me," he mutters, conjuring up visions of Andrew Dunn. "How did he find me?"

He splashes water on his face and closes his eyes to stop the room from spinning. The last thing he needs is a full-blown panic attack. There's no time for a proper meltdown either. He has to leave.

Now.

He wipes at the hot tears streaming down his face and throws his clothes back into the bag. He makes quick work of packing and zips the last of his luggage, just as another wild thought crosses his mind.

"Wade!"

He had just passed Wade in the hallway.

What if...

He grabs his bags and rushes to the door. Just as he reaches for the doorknob there's a thundering knock from the other side! Adam lunges back, his heart lodged in his throat.

Is he losing his mind?

He slowly approaches the light streaming through the peephole of the door.

Levi glares back from the other side impatiently. "Open the door."

He hesitates but does as he's told.

Levi strides in and stares at Adam's luggage. "Where are you going?"

"I haven't gotten that far," Adam admits. His accent has returned in all its glory. He imagines he must seem like a total stranger to Levi now.

Levi frowns and rubs the back of his neck. "Do you, uh, have someplace to go?"

"Why are you acting like you care?"

"Damn it, Jonathan – I mean – *Adam*..." His face looks tortured, haunted by the memory of the man he went to bed with only the night before. "I don't know. I don't know anything anymore." His blue eyes are piercing, but weary. "I was planning to leave her, you know."

"Lauren?"

"Who else?" He throws up his arms, exasperated. "I was just—"

"Waiting for the right time?" Adam crosses his arms. It's an excuse he's heard before.

"More like waiting for the right person. I guess I thought

263

this was different, you and me. I guess I thought lightning struck twice."

"I don't understand."

Levi starts to pace as his hands find his tie, crumpling it into his fist, "Casa Helena," he says.

Adam shakes his head at a loss.

"Casa Helena, that dilapidated little hotel in Italy I bought and fixed up. You know the story," he says hastily. "I left home, bought that place to fix up and that was the start of everything, right? Headlines read, 'Son of Peter Chandler, famed plastic surgeon to the stars, goes rogue at sea and dives into hotel business.' Great for selling papers. But what people don't know is that something else happened that summer at Casa Helena."

Adam holds his breath.

"I met someone."

"That's the summer you met Lauren."

"Before Lauren, there was someone else." Levi rolls his shoulders. "The family that owned the hotel had a son my age, Gabriele. He was always around. He even helped with the renovations after I bought it." He trails off and shifts his weight from one foot to the other. "We became close."

Adam's face softens, watching Levi dig through the memories.

"It was the first time I'd been with another man." His words are a whisper. "It just felt natural, it felt so… right." Levi smiles and his eyes shimmer. "But then my father found me, I ended up marrying Lauren and, well, here we are."

"Why are you telling me this?" Adam glances at his suitcase, knowing he should leave. His cover's blown and his gun is missing. It's officially a shit show.

"Because saying goodbye to Gabriele killed a part of me that summer. And I've never felt anything like what I felt for him since." He swallows and adds, "Until I met you."

Adam's heart pounds in his chest.

"Look, Adam, I don't know why you're doing this or what you're running from," he says, drawing closer, "but before I say another goodbye, I just have to know if any of this was real?"

"You're asking if this was all just part of the job."

He nods, sadly searching the green depths of Adam's eyes. "When I met you – as soon as I saw you in that interview, *I knew*. I felt it. There was something bigger than the interview, something bigger than the both of us at work. I need to know if you felt it too."

"It's been a long time since I've allowed myself to feel anything *for anyone*, Levi," Adam says, wringing his hands. "The last time nearly killed me. I barely made it out alive. But, with *you*…" He can't help but reach for Levi's hand. Their fingers lace together in a perfect fit. "If I didn't feel anything for you, I would have let Lauren walk in on us." He swallows and inches closer. "You have to know that. If I didn't care for you, I would have let it all just explode like all the other times."

"What other times?"

"You were more than just a job," Adam says, changing the subject. "Yesterday was real. And this might be hard to believe, but trust me, you know me better than anyone, Levi. You're the only one I've allowed to get this close in a long time." He gives his hand a squeeze and reels him closer. "I care for you."

Levi leans in, touching foreheads with Adam, and sighs.

The moment is bittersweet as they grow still, savoring each other's warmth and the remnants of the fire that once burned

265

bright between them, quietly wondering if this is goodbye.

There's a burst of static and a hurried voice over the radio clipped to Levi's belt.

"Shit. One of our servers just went down. I must handle this – but don't go," Levi says. "Don't run. Just stay here tonight, and let's continue this over dinner, shall we?"

Adam peers up at him with hopeful eyes. "You mean you still want me around?"

"I just don't want you to leave like this, not when I still have so many questions." He frowns. "Also, it seems I'm a glutton for punishment." His face softens for the first time. "I'll see you at dinner, okay? I'll send for you."

Adam nods. He's prepared to tell Levi everything over dinner. The details of the contract, how Lauren had contacted him through a past client, whatever Levi wants to know. With this slight glimmer of hope, he wants more than anything to kiss Levi in this moment, but he doesn't. He knows there's a long journey to regaining his trust if it's ever to be had again.

Levi gives Adam's hand a squeeze before rushing off to address the call over his radio.

Adam rests his forehead against the door as it clicks shut and sighs. He's exhausted but suddenly hopeful. He knows he deserves far worse than the tongue lashing – if you can even call it that – Levi dished out. The fact that Levi hasn't punched him or kicked him to the curb remains a wonder.

Whether the fire is still burning or Adam's simply still under his skin, Levi Chandler isn't ready to say goodbye.

Adam faces the closed door and smiles, just as there's a loud click behind him… and the unmistakable pressure of a gun barrel being pressed to the back of his head.

• • •

The sound of the gun's hammer being cocked back, clicking into position to fire, could have come from any revolver, but somehow Adam knows in his gut that it's his missing gun, the one he bought from a dealer once he arrived in London. He's never fired it. He's never had to. Now he can't help but appreciate the irony of being on the receiving end.

Gun? Found.

The person standing behind him remains a mystery, however. In his panicked mind, it could be anyone. It could be Andrew Dunn, the monster from his past who has finally caught up with him. It could be Wade with his own jealous vendetta, or even Lauren, scorned but looking fabulous in a pair of red bottom heels. Perhaps she'll kill him first and then Levi, becoming a widow to the Chandler empire and inheriting it *all*. For a fleeting moment, Adam wonders if he'll ever find out, or only see the red, mangled splatter of his brains coloring the front door before him.

"Don't shoot," Adam forms the words calmly. His instincts tell him to turn and fight, but he resists the urge and remains still. "I have money if that's what you want! It's yours. Take it."

"You mean the money you *took* from me?" The voice instantly registers and sends a chill down the small of Adam's back. "You mean *my own money*? I can have it back now? How generous." There's a sharp laugh, and Adam feels the gun press harder against his skull.

"How? How did you find me?" Adam blinks and a tear streams down his cheek.

"Never mind that." The gun presses harder. "Let's talk about that poor sap who just left."

"Leave him out of this!" The words tear recklessly from his lips.

"Sounds like he fell for you too, for all your charms and *lies!*"

Adam silently wonders how long they've been hiding in his suite, waiting for Levi to leave. He closes his eyes, waiting for the gun to go off at any second. It's better if you close your eyes, he thinks. He's heard this somewhere. Likely in a movie. Perhaps it'll be so quick that he won't even hear the gun go off. "You don't have to do this."

"Shut up! *Shut the fuck up!*" The voice shakes with rage, and Adam can feel the pistol jittering. "There's no talking your way out of this. Turn around. I wanna see the light go out in those pretty eyes when I pull the trigger."

Adam's heart drops as he turns and comes face to face with Vaughn Parker.

He's lost a little weight. The suit he's wearing looks a size too big for him and his beard, once the perfect mix of salt and pepper, is longer and noticeably more white. His shirt is half tucked in sloppily, and Adam can smell the alcohol and disdain on his breath.

"Your friend Wade let me in," he says, reading the confusion on Adam's face. "All I had to do was show him your picture, slip him a few pounds, and he was more than happy to let me in."

Adam makes a mental note to punch Wade dead in his face the next time he sees him.

"It's all over," Vaughn says, unhinged. "Tonya leaked the video of us to my job and the press, even after I agreed to a divorce settlement. After everything I gave that bitch!"

Adam thinks back to that morning in Paris – the sunlight

streaming through the bedroom window of Vaughn's flat, the smell of frozen waffles and eggs, and Tonya bursting through the door with her pink phone case, taking pictures of them in bed.

"I didn't know she would do that!" Adam swears. "I don't have any control over what—"

"I'm a laughingstock! I was the COO of one of the largest solar technology corporations in Europe. Now I'm on 'indefinite suspension'. When they finally do let me go, *no one*'s gonna hire me since those photos of us have been passed around. I wanna know how much of my money that bitch paid you to set me up, '*Michael*'…" His handsome face contorts into a snarl. "Or is it '*Adam*' now? If that's even your real fucking name!" He rushes Adam with the pistol.

Adam feels his back hit the front door of the suite. "I'm sorry this happened to you, I am," he says, squirming under the weight of the pistol pressed tight to his forehead.

"You know the worst part?" Vaughn wipes the sweat off his bald head with his free hand. "I loved you, Michael – or whoever the fuck you are. I fuckin' FELL IN LOVE WITH YOU!"

The words hit Adam like a shotgun blast.

"I fell in love with you, and it was all a scam."

"I was doing what she hired me to do," Adam tells him, raising his hands in surrender.

"I'll never meet my son." There are tears in Vaughn's eyes now. Dark, angry tears that trickle down his face. "Not after this. She said she'll never let me meet him. *I don't even know where they are!*" He wipes at his face and leans in with a breath that's stale with bourbon. "But I found *you*."

"That was you at The St. Langham," Adam realizes now.

"You were in my room."

"Looking for you and any sign of where Tonya went. *I know you know where she is!*"

"I don't!" Adam moves to shake his head, but the weight of the gun holds it in place against the door.

"Don't fucking LIE TO ME!" Vaughn clenches his teeth, foaming at the mouth with spit and fury.

"I swear I don't," Adam cries out. "It's part of the agreement. No forwarding addresses."

"I've lost everything because of you..." Vaughn's holding the grip of the gun so tight that his knuckles are losing their color. "*Goodbye, Michael.*"

Adam seizes Vaughn's wrist with both hands, pushing the aim of the barrel above his head. They wrestle and knock into the door, each fighting for possession of the gun. Adam knees him in the gut and they double over onto the floor, refusing to release their grip on the gun's handle.

"I'm gonna fucking... *kill you...*" Vaughn breathes into Adam's ear as they scuffle on the floor. It's a deadly promise he intends to keep.

Adam cries out as Vaughn rolls on top of him with the gun. He feels Vaughn's weight pin him down, followed by the gun's discharge... a piercing bang.

19 / GOTCHA

Quinn's taxi dodges a pothole as he scrambles to answer his phone.

James' deep baritone voice rings through the line, "Just making sure you landed okay."

"Just touched down. It's gray and raining here like everyone says. I kinda like it though."

"You would. Where are you?"

"In a cab." Quinn locks eyes with the driver in the rearview mirror. He looks barely nineteen with pale skin, a nose piercing, and an overbite. He lowers the trap music pumping over the speakers as a courtesy.

"So, what's your plan?" James asks.

"God, you sound like Marcus. Headed to the hotel. Coincidentally, it may be a lead." Quinn rubs an eye and yawns. "Adam has a thing for the Taylor Barnes and Robert Tates of the world. It's all a scheme for money, so it makes sense he's come to London for a similar mark. He's after someone big," he says, furrowing his brow. "I've been scouring the news from the last few weeks to see if anything jumps out. It's mostly politics, but I saw a slew of headlines about this swanky new hotel opening. The CEO's this guy, Levi Chandler. They call him 'the golden child,'" he smirks. "He's handsome.

Obscenely rich. Flashy. He's the only one in the news lately who seems right up Adam's alley."

"Handsome, you say?"

"At ease, soldier," Quinn smiles. "I'm on the clock."

"Just don't want you gettin' seduced by those London 'blokes' with their fancy accents and—" He stops to think of something witty.

"Fish and chips?"

"Exactly," James retorts. "Their crunchy, delicious fish and chips, the bastards."

"Well, I promise to come home to you. Unless the fish and chips are, like, really good. I do love a beer-battered crust."

"That's fair." James smiles into the line. "So you think Adam's after this Chandler guy? What if you're wrong?"

"It's still a nice hotel. I'll get a good night's sleep, maybe go see The London Eye. Might as well see the sights while I'm here."

"I wish I could be there." The tone of his voice is melancholy. "Or even that Bailey could have come, so you're not alone."

Quinn can't help but smile, still feeling James' phantom kiss on his lips. "Bailey has some family business he's tending to. His mother keeps calling about, well, it's a long story," he sighs. "What are you up to?"

"Aside from missing you? Up to my elbows in blood. Runnin' samples for a toxicology report. Gotta label all this stuff and submit it to evidence."

"Good times."

"Yeah," James exhales into the line. "Promise you'll be careful?"

Quinn feels his stomach flip. He's been too preoccupied with travel to think about what he might be walking into. He

272

pictures James' face, riddled with worry, and he forces a smile. "I'll be fine. It's just an interview with Chandler, assuming he'll even see me. What's the worst that can happen?"

The driver's eyes meet Quinn's in the rearview mirror forebodingly as he pulls into the hotel entrance. He brakes and Quinn's door is instantly opened by the valet staff who don crisp black uniforms with gold lapel pins of the Chandler's iconic C logo. "Good afternoon, sir. Welcome to the Chandler!"

Quinn glances toward the rooftop as he exits the car with a whistle. "I wish you could see this place," he whispers into the phone.

"Well, enjoy. You've had a long day of travel," James says against the sound of test tubes clicking in the background. "Just stay sharp and call me later. Come back to me in one piece, alright?"

Quinn can feel James' smile over the phone. He promises and hangs up as he enters the lobby. The ceiling, glittering with chandeliers, stops him in his tracks. He's never seen so much opulence. Everything about the Chandler feels new and expensive, including its well-dressed clientele, who strut by, rolling suitcases in tailored suits and designer threads.

He suddenly feels out of place in jeans and his favorite gray hoodie he's worn for the long flight. The NYC baseball cap he's thrown on isn't helping either.

A blonde at the front desk that's wrapped in hammered gold invites him over with a razor-sharp smile. "Checking in, sir?"

He clumsily rolls his luggage over and matches her smile. "Yes. Last name Harris."

She punches a few keys on her screen and stops short, giving him a closer look. "*Harris*, you say?" Her eyes scan him suspiciously as if this is some sort of joke.

He lowers his head and tips the bill of his cap. "Here for two nights."

Her lips part to speak but press into another tight smile as she continues searching her screen. "Looks like we have you on the seventh floor in our Berkshire suite. I can have one of the bellboys deliver your luggage if you like?"

"I'll manage. There is one thing though." He smiles, full of charm, "I'm here on assignment with *The Chronicle* and was hoping to grab some time with Mr. Chandler."

She looks thoroughly confused. "*The Chronicle.* Not the *London Herald?*"

It's Quinn's turn to look confused. "I'm with *The Chronicle*," he repeats.

"You're a little late for the press tour. Things just wrapped yesterday," she says with a hint of annoyance. She tilts her head to get a better look at him. "I'm sorry, but are you *sure* you're—"

"Is there any chance I can meet with him – just for a few minutes? Or perhaps you can help me with something else," his voice peaks. "I'm looking for someone, a *Jonathan Morgan* who I believe is staying here." It's a clever alias Quinn realizes now, the name of Adam's old high school, John Morgan.

The name only appears to upset the blonde further, who looks more confused and agitated than ever. "I can't divulge information concerning our guests," she manages. "I'm sorry, Mr. *Harris.*" She gives another tight-lipped smile and shoves a room key at him. "Let's get you checked in and I'll see if Mr. Chandler is available for comment. If so, I'll ring your room."

It's clear from the ice on her red smile that she has no such intention. It's also clear that she's rattled, despite his flimsy

274

disguise.

"I could use some coffee. I think I'll wait at the bar."

She nods patronizingly, the tight bun on her head following suit. "Please, relax and enjoy some coffee. Your room is ready whenever you are and I'll keep you posted. Welcome to The Chandler."

An interesting welcome indeed.

Quinn leaves his luggage and makes his way to the bar, plopping down on one of the tall leather stools.

"Wait, don't tell me..." a friendly voice calls out, "I never forget a drink..."

Quinn looks up to see a bartender grinning in his direction. He has a brawny build, a full beard, and skin the color of midnight.

He points a finger, like a gun, "Vodka and St-Germain on the rocks!"

Quinn looks like a deer caught in headlights. This is the second time he's heard this order from a bartender. First in Paris and now here in London. It can only mean one thing. Quinn plasters on a smile and points a finger back. "I'm impressed. *Good memory.*"

Dupree proudly smiles and grabs a shaker. "How's your stay been?"

Quinn tips his cap down and shrugs. "Good. It's a beautiful hotel."

"How's your story comin'?"

"My story?"

Dupree grabs the neck of a vodka bottle and cocks his head to the side. "I thought you said you were doin' an interview or somethin' – on the grand openin', right?"

"Right!" Quinn says quickly. "It's coming along." He does

his best to cover his disbelief.

Is Adam here under the guise of being a reporter? The irony's almost painful.

Dupree grabs an ornate gold-hued bottle from the top shelf. Quinn watches him work his magic from his side of the bar's counter until he's presented with an illustrious cocktail on a crisp gold and white napkin.

Dupree pauses as he sets the glass down and asks, "Garnish?"

It feels like a test. Quinn's never even tasted the drink before him to guess what garnish would be appropriate. Guessing what Adam chose in the past is an even bigger gamble.

If only Adam was a beer drinker...

Dupree raises an eyebrow, waiting.

"Not this time." Quinn snags the glass and takes a sip. Rich floral notes of sweet, musky elderflower flood his mouth. He rolls it over his tongue thoughtfully. It's not... *awful*. He can see the appeal, but it's not a drink he'd order himself. "You've done it again," he says, giving Dupree a thumbs-up. He coughs as the vodka burns the back of his throat.

"Cheers. Wanna start a tab?"

Quinn's eyes light up. "Actually, can I charge it to my room? Room 445."

"Of course." Dupree heads to his register and punches the screen. "445?"

"Right, under Morgan. Jonathan Morgan."

Dupree punches in room number 445 and makes a face. "Hmm. That's not comin' up, mate."

"Shit. Sorry," Quinn huffs, "I keep forgetting what room they moved me to."

"No worries." Dupree smiles. "I'll just look you up by name." He punches the sticky computer screen, stained with traces of grenadine, sugary syrups, and mixers. He punches in MORGAN and produces a smile. "Room *921*?"

Gotcha.

Quinn manages a calm smile and jokes with Dupree, "I should write that down."

He does his best not to appear anxious but can't help but chug the cocktail. Before he knows it, he's placing the empty glass on the bar and waving goodbye to Dupree on his way to the elevator.

He steps inside and is shocked to see an attendant.

"What floor, sir?" He's handsome in a boy-next-door way with tousled brown curls peeking from under his bellhop cap and a square, clean-shaven face. His eyes narrow at the sight of Quinn.

"Ninth floor."

He can't tear his eyes from Quinn as he pushes the ninth-floor button. He leans in slightly, as if squinting into a funhouse mirror. The sight before him looks familiar, but there's something off about it he can't place.

Quinn glances at the gold name badge on his uniform that reads *Wade*.

It's clear Wade's crossed paths with Adam, but there's a scornful sheen to his eyes. The look on his face is far different from the confusion the blonde at the front desk held. It's also clear that Wade is not as easily fooled as the bartender.

The air suddenly feels dangerous between them as they ascend. Quinn can only guess how many enemies Adam has made in London, but apparently he's come face to face with one of them.

Wade's fists clench by his side. "No." he sneers under his breath, "You're not him…"

The doors chime open and Quinn rushes out, giving Wade a long look over his shoulder.

They're at a standoff until the doors slowly glide shut, giving him one final look at Wade's haunting glare.

"Definitely taking the stairs down," he says to himself.

He travels the length of the hall until he finds room 921, and takes a second to absorb the moment.

The man he's been searching for is very likely on the other side of this door. The boy who ran away from Sweet Ridge, escaping God knows what, is just on the other side. The boy who quite possibly holds the key to more than a decade of unsolved murders is within reach.

What if I'm wrong, Quinn suddenly thinks.

What if Adam isn't the source Quinn thinks he is? What if Adam's no help at all, and this whole thing has just been a wild goose chase. All for nothing. Even worse, what if Adam doesn't answer the door?

He has no plan for that. He's been walking by faith this whole time, trusting his instincts and quietly praying for the best. It's brought him this far… but what if it's a dead end?

He reaches to knock just as the door bursts open and Vaughn comes barreling out! Quinn catches a fleeting glimpse of him as he tears down the hall. His face is full of panic.

What could he be running from?

There's no time to speculate. Quinn sticks his foot into the doorframe just as it's about to swing shut. He leans into the door and offers a low, "Hello?" as he makes his way inside.

The first thing he sees is blood.

There, in a pool of blood lies Adam, clutching his side. Bleeding out.

Quinn rushes over and drops to his knees. Their eyes meet

and it feels explosive and oddly destined, like the universe folding in on itself.

Adam gasps at the familiar stranger above him and gives a gurgled cry.

Is he having a vision? Is this what death looks like? A mirror image of yourself coming to coax you into a peaceful slumber? Between the pain and the tears in his eyes, it's hard to process what he's seeing.

Quinn eyes the dark red stain soaking through Adam's shirt, growing larger under his trembling fingers. He feels the panic rising in his throat as he peels off his hoodie and covers the wound, applying pressure.

Adam groans and writhes beneath the force.

"You're a hard man to find, Adam Walker," Quinn says. "Don't you dare die on me now."

A tear streams down into Adam's ear as he reaches for Quinn, gasping for breath.

How could this stranger who looks so much like him possibly know his name?

His fingers brush Quinn's cheek, leaving red strokes of blood on his skin. He can barely believe what he's seeing.

This is real.

"Stay with me, Adam." Quinn fishes his phone from his pocket and tries to control the alarm in his voice. "Stay awake, look right here!" He points two fingers at his face, directing Adam to focus on his eyes. Eyes so much alike. Green like Sweet Ridge's rolling hills and farmland. Green like Central Park in springtime.

Adam's breath grows shallow as he blinks away tears, straining to focus. He hears Quinn's voice grow muffled, sounding further away than before. He feels the warmth of his blood pooling under him. He feels the end growing near.

"*My mother,*" he mutters, "tell her... I, I forgive her, and..." but the rest falls short, reaching only the peaks of his lips. He gets one last glimpse of Quinn Harris hovering above him... and slowly succumbs to the darkness.

20 / BAD BLOOD

Quinn eyes the roses before him. Delicate blush petals destined to wilt and fall from hardened stems sprouting angry thorns. He inhales their sweet, musky cologne and frowns. He's never been much for flowers. It's easy to be fooled by their colors and beauty, but he knows, like with all things, death will one day embrace them, leaving him to dispose of the frail corpses in the trash and recycle the vase.

He's returned to The Chandler, two days after Adam was shot. He sits in a comfortable armchair, eying a bouquet that seems to taunt him at the center of the long conference table.

Levi paces the room, occasionally throwing him troubled glances. The resemblance still distresses him, but he's trying to move past it. *He's not Adam*, he tells himself and glances at his watch. "It's after two."

"He'll show," Quinn says calmly. He glances around the luxurious conference room, a showcase of plush gray furniture with cream and gold accents opposing the chestnut conference table. There's a crystal pitcher of water on the table, a fruit platter from room service, and Quinn's tape recorder.

Levi starts to offer Quinn a scotch when his phone buzzes. He gives off a relieved expression and signals to Quinn with a nod.

Quinn takes a deep breath and watches Levi leave the room.

Levi steps into the hall to greet Adam, who looks like a pale, fatigued version of himself. They half-hug awkwardly, and Levi is careful not to squeeze too hard, as if Adam might break.

"You just got out of the hospital." His eyes lower to Adam's belly. "You don't have to do this if you're not up to it."

"He saved my life," Adam shrugs. "He wants an interview, it's the least I can do, right?"

Levi shrugs back. "How long will you be?"

"You're not staying?"

Levi's blue eyes go wide. "You want me to stay?"

"You said you had questions," Adam takes a slow breath. "What better way to get answers?"

Levi loves and hates the idea in equal measure. He dreads what further truths Adam might reveal but knows he can't live with the unknown. "Here." He hands Adam a room key.

"Ohh la la." Adam grins. "The penthouse?"

Levi rubs the back of his neck. "You got shot in my hotel. It's the least I can do, assuming you even want to stay here."

"I don't think I have to worry about Vaughn for a while."

"At least he didn't get far after what he did. The hall cameras caught him running out of your room, and we got a clear shot of him entering the lobby. Security submitted footage to the police."

"I hear he's awaiting trial. These things take a while."

"In the meantime, you're welcome to stay. Think of it as a get-well gift until you figure out your next move." His face falls and his hand finds Adam's. Their fingers intertwine loosely. "Any idea where you'll go?"

"I've still got my eye on that piece of land in Kentucky," Adam says wistfully. "Maybe you'll come visit one day?"

"Me on a farm," Levi laughs. "Sure, why not?"

Adam takes a deep breath with resolve and leads the way back in the conference room.

Quinn stands and the two meet eyes. "Thanks for agreeing to speak with me, Adam. I've come a very long way to meet you."

Levi pulls out a chair for Adam and pours everyone a glass of water.

"Why me?" Adam asks. He tosses Quinn a downcast look. "I'm no one special."

"Actually…" Quinn bites his lip. "I think you might be more special than you realize. You see, I'm investigating a situation in New York involving Andrew Dunn, who I believe you knew."

Adam's face goes ghost white as he shifts in his seat. "You can say there's some bad blood there," he confirms.

"I'd like you to tell me about that. On the record." Quinn shoots a look to the tape recorder between them. "Tell me about the last time you saw him alive."

"Alive?" Adam balks at the word. "You mean, he's…"

"He's dead," Quinn says evenly. "He was killed by, well, someone he was holding captive. It's really the whole reason I'm here." Quinn wrings his hands and tells Adam the details of his encounter with Andrew. How they met in the bar… the car ride home… Andrew snapping and attacking him… and Andrew's death ending in too many stab wounds to count. "He was a murderer – a serial killer, best I can tell. He had photos, Adam. Photos of boys, his *victims*. One was even a friend of mine. He was a sick, sick man."

283

"Wait." Adam's shaking in his seat. Tears stream down his face as he puffs his cheeks and exhales a mixture of relief and sadness. "He's dead? He's really fucking dead?"

"I was there." Quinn blinks and finds himself back in the yellow kitchen. He can still feel Andrew's dead weight on top of him; Andrew's warm pool of blood, swallowing him whole.

Adam sniffs and wipes his eyes. He leans in, and his voice is deep with something ominous. "Was it slow? Did he *suffer*?"

Levi and Quinn exchange uncomfortable glances, noting the darkness dancing in Adam's eyes.

"It was slow," Quinn nods. "He didn't go easy."

It's cold comfort.

"Good." Adam leans back in his seat and grabs his glass of water. He chugs half the glass and slams it back on the table. "He had it comin' for what he done." He takes a moment to collect himself as Levi calmly rubs his knee. It seems unreal. He reflects on the years he spent running and looking over his shoulder… "You say this happened recently?"

"Yes. I'm hoping you can tell me about your last encounter with him. Was it back in Sweet Ridge? Did he get violent with you?"

"Wait…" Adam sits up in his seat and his eyes dart around the room. "What was that you said about *photos*?"

Quinn's clearly struck a nerve. "He, uh, kept photos. Photos of his victims – and they all looked like us! Well, *like you*," he corrects himself.

Adam furrows his brow and squints. "He took photos of me," he recalls. "With his Polaroid camera."

"Tell me what happened." Quinn leans in. "Start from the beginning."

Adam stumbles as his mind races, "He um… he…"

"He was your teacher, right?" Quinn gives him a start. "He taught you science, right?"

"Right. He was my teacher," Adam says with a shrug. "It all started out innocent enough, I guess." He sighs heavily and thinks back, transporting himself to the year 2006, back to his hometown. He's younger now. He can almost feel himself growing more youthful as his accent returns. He can almost see the details of Andrew's face clearly. "He was everyone's favorite teacher." He can't help but half-smile. "Everyone had a crush on him. Even me. He just had this... way about him. He could charm the dew right off the honeysuckle."

Quinn frowns, relating.

"He took a likin' to me early on. He even offered to tutor me – not that I needed it really, but I guess I just liked the attention. It sure as hell beat bein' at home." He stops to swallow the lump in his throat.

"Things were rough at home?" Quinn envisions the family photo on Vera's fireplace, Tom Walker's firm hand on Adam's shoulder.

"Rough's puttin' it mildly," Adam says. "I took every chance I got to get away from *him*. Coach Dunn made that easy. I kinda became his teacher's aide, and there was Science Club... I even helped him out at football practice. That was the year we won the state championship."

"Go Panthers," Quinn says wryly.

Adam pauses, impressed. "Someone's done their homework."

"All part of the job."

Levi looks away, stung by the words.

"One day I was helpin' him put away equipment after practice. I remember it was just us on the field. It was so hot out. The cicadas were singin'. He asked me about a bruise on my arm…" He trails off and rubs one of his arms, remembering. "He knew who done it. I didn't have to say nuthin'. I remember he told me he'd never let anyone hurt me again." His expression goes soft. "It felt so good to hear that – and I believed him! He said he'd protect me. He wrapped me in his arms and hugged me so tight I could feel his heart beatin'. It was like our heartbeats matched." Adam's face goes tight. "And then I kissed him. My first kiss. *Just like that.*" His fingertips brush the peaks of his lips as he stares blindly at the table. "Then I turned and ran. I ran off the field, all the way home, cryin'. I don't know what came over me. He was the only man in my life worth a damn, and I'd just ruined everything."

Levi rubs a hand over his face. It's hard to listen to. He wants to bolt out of the room, but he can't.

A glutton for punishment.

"The next day he asked me to stay after class, of course. I knew it was comin'. He asked me why I did what I did."

"What did you say?"

"I said I did it 'cause I loved him," Adam shrugs. "I suppose in my own way, I did."

"A lot of people loved and looked up to him," Quinn offers, reminded of his own admiration for Andrew Dunn. He may have been a monster, but he had once helped shape Quinn into the man he is today.

"Well, time went on and it was like nuthin' had happened. School. Science Club. Football practice. He was the same ol' Coach Dunn. Then, one day after practice, I was about to leave when he stopped me. He said he couldn't stop thinkin' about what happened. He couldn't get it out of his head."

286

"Then what happened?" Levi cuts in.

"He kissed me," Adam says with bittersweet delight. "Just like that. He kissed me. Of course, I knew he was married." He meets Levi's eyes, almost apologetically. "Everyone knew Mrs. Dunn. She was always at school droppin' off sweets… chaperonin' the school dances. I didn't do it to hurt her, but Andrew told me he *loved* me. He said one day he'd leave her when the time was right and we'd leave Sweet Ridge, go someplace far away where my daddy couldn't hurt me and no one knew us." Adam wets his lips and presses on, saying, "*He said we'd be together.*"

"What happened then?"

"It was all fun and games at first. *Secret rendezvous*… he'd leave little gifts in my locker," Adam smirks. "If there was an away game, I'd take my ma's old pickup and meet up with him out of town. It was like this dangerous game we'd play, pushing ourselves to the edge of bein' caught."

"Did he ever make you do something you didn't want to do?"

"Never," Adam says. "If anything, I was the reckless one. Leavin' love notes on his desk, on the back of my homework for him to find…"

Levi frowns.

"But we never went to his house. The house was off limits," Adam recalls. "I really thought he loved me. He said I'd 'awakened' something in him, that I'd 'bewitched' him." He laughs but Levi is deathly silent.

If anyone in the room can vouch for Adam's gift for seduction, it's Levi.

"For the first time in my life, I didn't feel powerless. It felt like I could do anything, you know?"

"Love will do that to you," Quinn says softly. For a split second his mind conjures up James' smile. It flashes before his eyes like a premonition.

"Well... of course all things must come to an end," Adam's tone changes as he rocks back in his seat. "Andrew kept promisin' we'd leave. He kept sayin' he'd leave her, but it was just one excuse after another. Finally, homecoming was comin' up. He said we'd leave right after the game, but I knew he was just lyin' to me again. He didn't *love* me," he sneers. "I finally saw things for what they were. I was just a boy toy, something for him to play with when he got bored with his wife." Adam swallows and lowers his head. "So I swore I'd leave with or without him. I was bold and young and stupid, and I... I did something I shouldn't have."

The room is quiet. One of the ice cubes in the pitcher on the table splinters and pops, startling Quinn.

"I packed a bag," Adam says. "I kissed my mother goodbye on her forehead while she slept, and I snuck out." His lips form a grim line. "I didn't just leave town though. That would have been too easy. In true teenage-rebellion, I just *couldn't* go quietly," he laughs under his breath bitterly. "I went straight to Andrew's house and rang the bell."

Quinn stops breathing.

"His wife answered. She recognized me from his class and invited me in. You shoulda seen how fast Andrew jumped off that couch," he smirks. "I told him I was leavin' town, and as a parting gift I told his wife we'd been havin' an affair." He nods solemnly, as if confirming Levi and Quinn's disbelief. "I told her everything, and watched his face just... *crack*!" Adam makes a fist. "I wanted to hurt him. I wanted him to feel what I felt."

"What happened next?"

"She lost her shit. I mean just completely lost it! She believed me right away. She must have had her suspicions," he says snidely. "She was inconsolable." Images of Tonya and the women before her flash before his eyes – distraught and thrashing about the room like wildcats. "The next thing I know there's a scuffle and she goes down. I thought she just tripped, *but the blood…* she must have hit her head on the coffee table because there was so much blood – it just wouldn't stop!" His eyes tear up again.

"Was she pushed?"

"I wasn't near her." Adam throws up his hands. "I swear I never touched her. But it didn't matter. Andrew said it was all my fault. He went crazy. He just snapped!"

Images of Andrew flash before Quinn's eyes. He can still see him in the living room of his kill house, his eyes wild as he came undone, spewing words like a broken robot.

"Next thing I know, he grabs me by the neck and throws me down the basement stairs. I must have hit my head." He blinks and his eyes go pitch black. "I woke up tied to a chair in the basement… and that's when the real fun began."

Quinn's blood turns to ice.

"Days went by. I lost track of time. All I remember is the pain and begging to make it stop."

Levi turns his head. He doesn't want to hear any more.

"Did anyone come looking for you?"

"He drugged me off and on. I remember waking up once in the attic, gagged and hung up by my wrists. I could hear Sheriff Bates downstairs, askin' about what happened the night his wife died. Guess they come 'round askin' questions. Then I blacked out again. Andrew hid me up there until

Sheriff Bates left. I never heard him come back 'round again."

"What happened after the police came?"

"He made it clear that I was to blame for her death, and there was no convincing him otherwise. He said I was poison, and he vowed to make sure I never hurt anyone again." Adam tosses Levi a sideways glance. "Maybe he was right about the poison part."

Levi makes a face, "You're not poison."

"Aren't I though?"

The two share a complicated look as Quinn fidgets in his seat. Having Levi here was a mistake he realizes now, but it's too late to ask him to leave. Plus, he can't help but be fascinated by the relationship before him. It's clear that Levi was indeed a target but perhaps there's hope for something bigger.

"I know this is hard, Adam, but please continue."

Adam presses on, eager to get it over with now. "He liked to go slow," he swallows and wipes his eyes. "He'd cut into me so slowly I'd black out from the pain. I'd wake up thinkin' it was a new day, but just a few minutes had passed and he was just gettin' started. It was a game to him. He used anything he could get his hands on… knives, his power drill… but the belt sander was one of his favorites. One day he stripped half my back bare of the skin and told me my face was next. Every day brought some new twisted torture. The only way I knew he was done for the day was cause he'd take a photo. Like he was… I dunno… documentin' the whole thing? He'd carve into me a little more each day and show me photos so I knew what I looked like. 'Not so pretty now, are ya?' he'd say."

Levi wipes at the anger on his face. Unable to sit still, he stands, smooths out his tie, and he starts to pace in the background.

"He used to threaten to slit my throat all the time. That's the thing I was most afraid of. I knew he'd be done playin' with me then."

Quinn's mind flashes to the Polaroids. Twelve boys, all with their throats slit in the same manner.

"He was havin' too much fun to finish me off though."

"How did you survive that?" Quinn can't imagine how long he'd last in Andrew's chair. The fact that Adam is sitting before him now seems like a miracle.

"I just kept thinkin' about all the places I wanted to go... the things I wanted to see. I kept tellin' myself this wasn't the end."

"How long did this go on?"

"Had to have been weeks. Between the starvation and Andrew, it felt like I was wastin' away. Some days I barely had strength to lift my head."

"Did he ever say anything or did you get a sense that he'd done this sort of thing *before*? Were there others he'd hurt?"

Adam thinks for a moment, "No. No, I mean, it all felt... like he was makin' it up as he went along. He wasn't this skilled killer if that's what you mean. He didn't know what the hell he was doin'. He just knew he wanted to make me hurt."

"Adam... he did this to twelve boys after you," Quinn says. "Only they weren't as lucky. He never said anything about other boys or other students?"

"No," Adam shakes his head. "Jesus. *Twelve?*"

"And no one has been able to find their bodies. That's why what happened to you is so important, Adam. It set off a chain reaction. Andrew kept repeating this same pattern with boys who fit your profile."

291

Visibly upset, Adam jostles in his seat. "I don't know how to help you," his voice cracks. "I don't know what you want me to say."

"Just keep talking," Quinn says softly. "Tell me what happened next."

Adam hunches his shoulders. "It was just more of the same until…" Something in his expression shifts. "Until the day I woke up in the dark."

Levi stops pacing.

"At first I thought he just blindfolded me or that he'd moved me again. It was hard to tell up from down, but then I realized I was on my back. There wasn't much space to move and my voice sounded different, like it was bouncin' back at me…" he struggles to explain. "I reached out and hit somethin', and that's when I knew. I was in a box."

Levi gasps.

"The fucker buried me alive. I must have screamed and kicked for hours. I kept beatin' my fists against the box. When dirt started fallin' in my face that's when I knew I didn't have much time. I kept workin' at it. Scratchin' and clawin' until my fingers bled." He lifts his hands, then curls them over to check his fingernails. No blood. "I still have nightmares about bein' trapped in that box."

Levi looks sick, thinking back to the morning Adam had awoken so rattled and terrified.

"Once I had a crack in the box, I just kept clawin' my way out," he says as a tear trails down. "It seemed to take forever, but I just kept thinkin' about all the places I wanted to go. How much of this world I still hadn't seen. Andrew's mistake was not slittin' my throat before he threw me in that box. Now I had a chance! *I just kept moving*," he says. "Thank God it rained that night because it made the ground soft and muddy. The earth got softer and softer until I broke through the surface. I crawled out and laid in the mud, feelin' the rain beat down on my face."

"Where were you?" Quinn asks. His eyes find the tape recorder on the table, confirming it's still running.

"The lights. That's how I knew. Right away I knew where I was," he smiles ironically. "I looked up, right into those stadium lights and laughed. I was at school, on the football field. Probably right at the 50th-yard line!"

"I don't understand."

"Homecoming was comin' up and Andrew had convinced the school board to *finally* lay down new turf on the field – which meant they had to *dig up the old field*. The timing was perfect. It really *was* the perfect place to bury me," he says, almost appreciatively. "In a day or so new turf would've gone down and no one would think to look for me there."

The thought of the whole town convening to watch the game happen right over Adam's dead body is chilling.

"You escaped," Quinn says, more to himself than anyone. "I knew it."

"I called the sheriff's office once I got some distance. I knew it was no use though. Everyone in town loved the air Andrew breathed. He was like a fucking god, since he turned that loser football team around – and he'd just lost his wife. They thought it was a prank when I called and hung up," he sighs. "I almost can't blame them. Who would believe he was even capable of the things I accused him of? *No one*."

"The police never investigated further?"

"Everyone just assumed I ran away, accordin' to my friend Jenna. Since he took me the day his wife died folks started

293

thinkin' *I* had somethin' to do with it," he shrugs. "And soon enough they just stopped lookin' for me. Figured I'd ran away so I wouldn't be arrested."

"That's awful," Levi says, returning to Adam's side. "So, he just got away with it?"

"I figured he would come looking for me, so I kept movin'. I hitchhiked, and I did things..." He trails off. "Things I never thought I'd do for food. I finally made my way to New York, and I met someone who taught me how to survive."

Nina.

"I didn't have a thing to my name when she found me. I had no money. No car. And outside of *farm work*, I had no real skills or resume. I never finished high school," he says with a pang of remorse. "All I had was my face... and my body, once that finally healed. She showed me how to survive off that."

Levi folds his arm uncomfortably.

"I owe her a huge debt," Adam says. "Literally. I crossed her, and I need to make amends one day and repay her. I'm not proud of the things I've done." Adam's eyes plead with Levi. "But I did what I did to survive. Once I got on my feet, I started sendin' my ma some money to keep the farm runnin' after that bastard she married died. Then I started savin' to buy some land and move her away from there. Away from all the bad memories. I just want a fresh start." Adam breaks down and cries.

Quinn stops the tape recorder and gives Levi a pointed look. "Why don't we take a break?"

Levi nods and collects Adam. "You did good. I know that wasn't easy." He wraps Adam in a warm, protective hug. The expression on his face is conflicted, more confused and intrigued than ever with the man in his arms.

Quinn slips out into the hallway. He clutches the tape recorder to his chest and sighs, feeling the color return to his face. He had been right to trust his gut about Adam. Not only is Adam "the original", but Adam has given him a testimony far darker than he could have imagined, outlining the catalyst for Andrew's murderous past. With Adam escaping and out of reach, Andrew never had a chance to finish the bloody job he started. Then came Damon Porter, the first photo in the timeline from 2007, and Andrew's actual first kill. Damon looked enough like Adam with his green eyes and familiar face. He reminded Andrew of Adam so much that the temptation bled into reality.

He slit Damon's throat for good measure.

Only the kill wasn't truly satisfying.

Time went on and the body count grew taller, proving there was no substitute for the real thing.

No one could ever replace Adam.

Quinn hugs the tape recorder Marcus gave him to his chest and thinks back to something Adam said earlier. He imagines Adam crawling from a muddy hole in the ground. He imagines Andrew – or Anderson Doyle, as he knew him – leaning into his ear at SKY to speak over the crowd… kissing him passionately on the sofa… strangling him from above as sweat and blood rained down. He imagines him at the front of the classroom in his tight corduroys. He imagines him yelling from the sideline at the players on the field at his school… and that's when it hits Quinn.

It's suddenly so painfully clear that tears come to his eyes.

It all makes sense as he reaches for his phone to dial Marcus. He can't dial fast enough, thinking back to Adam's words and how deviously clever Andrew had been this whole time.

The phone rings twice before Marcus answers, and before he can say a word Quinn blurts out, "I can prove he did it! I know how to find the bodies!"

21 / THE PRODIGAL SON

The seat belt sign goes off and a flight attendant swoops in to give Bailey a cautious smile.

"Mr. Alexander? Sorry to wake you. Before lunch comes out, would you like another vodka cranberry?"

Bailey removes his pink glitter sleep mask and sighs, saying, "Glenda, honey, I'm on my way to see my *mother*. Keep 'em comin'."

She nods dutifully, says, "You got it, hon," and returns to the galley.

The landing is bumpy, but Bailey arrives in Savannah feeling relaxed and ready for almost anything. The drinks took the edge off, but the moment he exits the jet bridge he curses his decision to come home. Still… he can't ignore her messages any longer.

Time is indeed running out.

He rents a yellow convertible from the airport, throws his travel duffel in the trunk, and speeds down the highway. Half an hour later, he's walking the halls of Goodrich Hospital searching for room 1215.

His mother, Candice, jumps at the sight of him and clutches her pearls.

The hospital room smells of antiseptic and her perfume.

The blinds are open, casting the afternoon glow across the faded yellow linoleum floor while an old episode of Judge Hathorne plays on the mounted TV. Bailey's father lies motionless in the hospital bed, wheezing as the ventilator does its work.

Bailey takes a good look at the man he's thought of as indestructible for so long. He's much smaller now, frail even. The handsome features that once captivated his mother have sunk and faded into the lines on his face. Bailey softly gasps at the way his skin looks discolored under the fluorescent lights and how his hair is all but gone.

"The prodigal son returns!" Candice gawks at Bailey in disbelief.

"You're *surprised*?" He crosses his arms. "You only called and texted one hundred billion times, lady. I'm here so you'll finally stop."

"Your father's very sick. He's on his deathbed," Candice swoons theatrically. Her face is grave with concern. Her hair is beauty-parlor fresh; the bright blonde curls swept into an elegant updo. She's wearing a demure pink sundress with a white sweater tied around her shoulders. The only thing missing is a mint julep. "The doctor says he can go any time now, within the hour for all we know. I told the girls at the country club and everyone at church to just keep him in their prayers. The Lord could take him any day now!"

"So it would seem." Bailey can't help the frown on his face as he glances about the room. "Where's Mason and Sawyer? Where's Violet?" He glares at his mother in disbelief.

"Mason's in The Hamptons, Sawyer's in LA closing a very important business deal, and your sister can't fly because she's in her third trimester. Did you even know she's due to have

298

the twins any day now? Have you called her?"

"So, I'm the *only one* who came." He arches his brows and laughs. "The black sheep of the family's the only one to show up. Priceless."

"Your brothers wanted to be here, but their schedules simply won't allow it."

"You know, I have a life too, mother. I have a whole life in New York you know nothing about. I've made something of myself. I have a job and *friends* who need me, but I'm here. I came." His mind flashes to Quinn, wondering how things are progressing in London with his investigation.

"I know aaaaall about what you've been up to in New York," Candice sneers. "Your brother said he saw you *shirtless* in some magazine, and ugh, you're livin' in that rundown building. *I looked it up on the internet!*" Candice cocks her head proudly. "It looks *condemned.*"

"It's a loft, mother, it's supposed to look like that. It's part of the charm…" He waves her off. "Anyway, I don't need your judgment. And I don't need your money," he says sternly. "So you can stop sendin' me checks while you're at it. I'm doing fine on my own."

"I sent you money to make sure you're at least eating!"

"Oh, *now* you care if I eat or starve?! You let him kick me out the house at sixteen!" Bailey bellows. "I left with the clothes on my back. I was *homeless*! Do you understand that? I had nothing!"

Candice wilts in her chair. "Well, there'll be plenty to *divvy up* from the franchise once your father passes!" She turns her head, and the tears turn on like a running faucet. "All this talk about *money* while your father is laid out dyin' in front of ya." She hisses, "You oughta be ashamed!"

"Oh give me a fuckin' break—"

"Don't you dare use that language with me, Bailey Langston Alexander!" She's on her feet now, looking like a wild, aged film star. It's amazing how quickly her makeup has been ruined. Mascara bleeds from her eyes like a leaky oil rig. "I may not have been the best mother, but I am still your mother nonetheless."

There's a grunt from the hospital bed. His father's eyes dart groggily between the two of them, and the monitor next to his bed beeps.

"Now, look. You're upsetting your father!" She shakes her head and rushes to his side.

"You know what?" Bailey laughs bitterly. "I didn't come here for this. You said he didn't have much time, so here I am. I'm sorry to see him like this, I am – but I'm not gonna stand here and be punished when I am the *only one* of your children who cared enough to show up." He turns to leave but spins back to address his father. "You kicked me out of my home… the only home I ever knew growin' up. *No child* should be abandoned or mistreated because of who they are." He feels his throat tightening, but refuses to cry. "I am who I am, and I will never apologize for that. You were wrong for what you did – and when I think about all the time we've lost it breaks my heart." He sniffs and stares deep into the eyes of his father. Eyes so much like his own. "None of this is about money. Money comes and goes and you can always make more of it, but I only get one father." He blinks away an annoying tear and turns his gaze to the ceiling. There's a moment of silence, filled only by a commercial blinking from the TV screen. "I still love you, despite everything – even if you hate me for what I am." He lets a tear fall and gives his father a final bittersweet smile. "Despite everything, I'll always love you, Daddy."

Bailey spins on his heel to leave when there's another faint grunt.

He turns back to see his father remove his oxygen mask, and a tear streams down his face. Slowly, with as much strength as he can muster, he reaches out a hand to Bailey.

Bailey stifles a sob. He thinks back to the day he left Savannah. He thinks back to the struggles he faced alone at sixteen. He thinks back to all the nights he cried himself to sleep, hungry and wondering if he'll ever have his father's love again. He meets his mother's wistful gaze, walks back to the hospital bed, and takes his father's hand.

22 / HOME

The air in Tarrant's is thick with the smell of French toast and bacon, while ambient house music plays in the background and an infantry of champagne bottles pops behind the bar like cannons. It's a full house, but luckily Quinn and James have arrived early to secure a table near the stage.

James rests his arm across the back of Quinn's chair as his fingers play in Quinn's hair. "You hungry?"

Quinn dives into James' sultry gaze, and his lips curve into a mischievous smile. "Starving."

James eyes Quinn's bottom lip. "I coulda made you breakfast at my place, you know."

"Leftover cold pizza does *not* 'breakfast' make," he nudges James' knee with his own. "Besides, it's second Sunday. I haven't seen a show in a while."

James eyes the empty stage and winces at the buzz of conversations swarming about the room.

Meanwhile, a server seats a foursome of attractive men at the table ahead of them and one dares to glance back at Quinn with a luring smile. He's one-part golden skin, one-part gray eyes, with dreadlocks tied into a messy bun.

Quinn instantly recognizes him as Tomas, his crush from the yoga class he's long since abandoned.

James wraps his arm around Quinn's shoulder and leans in to kiss his earlobe.

Quinn suppresses a smirk, ignoring Tomas' curious stare, and gives James an adoring smile. "Should we order a pitcher for the table?"

"Hmm? Sure." James finishes shooting daggers at Tomas and waves down a server to order a bubbly pitcher of grapefruit juice and champagne.

"Ohh they have frittatas!" Quinn swoons over his menu. "That's gotta be the best breakfast mashup ever. Picture it! One day, an unassuming uptown omelet and a quiche from the wrong side of the tracks have a torrid one-night stand... nine months later, the frittata, in all its glory, is born on brunch menus everywhere!"

James chuckles and pulls Quinn close. "It's good to see you in a better place."

Quinn's smile fades as he studies the emotion in James' face. "Yeah," he slowly agrees. "I can't believe it's been three months since I found Adam." His mind instantly spirals back to the conference room at The Chandler. Back to Adam's harrowing testimony.

"I saw your interview last night," James says.

"James. I told you not to watch."

"It's like your third televised interview this week, how could I not?" James smiles. "You're a hero."

"I'm not a hero."

"You survived a serial killer and solved twelve cold cases in a single blow, Quinn. You got justice for all those boys, just like you said you would."

Quinn rubs a chill on his arms. "Justice for Travis. I'm glad I got to be the one to tell his mother... I couldn't have done it

303

without you, you know… and Adam."

"How do you mean?"

"It was what he said in London," Quinn recalls. "That whole thing about laying down new turf on the football field? I suddenly remembered the field at *my* school got redone at one point! I didn't think of it as a big deal. I didn't care anything about football, you know, so it all just went over my head back then – but I went back and checked and lo and behold it was redone the same year *Travis* went missing." Quinn frowns. "It got me thinking. I dug a little deeper and sure enough, every school Andrew coached at had their football field redone or maintenanced the year a boy went missing."

"He buried them in plain sight."

"Adam said it was the 'perfect place' to bury him, and he was right. Andrew went to great lengths to find reasons for the school to lay down new turf. Sometimes preparing for the championships or the homecoming game was enough, but there were even some cases where the field was 'vandalized' with graffiti. People thought it was a senior prank or a rival school…"

"But it was Andrew, giving the school a reason to dig up the old field."

"Right. The schools basically provided the open graves. All Andrew had to do was find a window to bury the bodies before the job was completed. Once Marcus and I brought our findings and Adam's taped interview to the local authorities in Bristol, the dominoes started falling. Once they realized Andrew wasn't who he said he was, the school districts and universities he worked at launched investigations. Then, city after city, town after town, they found them buried. One by one."

"And connected Andrew with their deaths."

"Well, thanks to a certain handsome and daring forensic analyst scanning the photos onto Andrew's computer the police confiscated here in New York," he winks. "I didn't know *how* we were gonna get those photos into evidence where they belonged."

James groans. "It wasn't easy. I had to call in a favor, but it was the right thing to do. And now that the truth's out, the story you broke's gettin' national media attention."

"It's been a little crazy."

"Are you still getting job offers?"

"They keep coming, but I can't leave *The Chronicle*. It's where I belong, at least for now," he says. "Things are good. No more fluff pieces, Marcus is giving me first crack at the top stories, and he's even connected me with this agent he knows! They want me to write a book about my investigation into the murders."

James nudges him with a bright smile. "I'm proud of you, know that? Today a book, then someday they'll make a movie out of it!"

"I love your optimism," Quinn laughs. "Speaking of job offers, congrats again on passing your entrance exam. Your brother would be proud..."

James crumples in his chair. "Thanks, babe."

"Next stop, police academy, right?"

"How do you feel about having a cop for a boyfriend?"

"Hmm. Cops and reporters don't mix," Quinn reminds him playfully.

James concurs with a slow nod. "Oil and water."

"Good thing I'm a sucker for a man in uniform." Quinn leans in to deliver a searing kiss that deepens as he rests his hand on James' chest.

"Ugh! Get a room!" Bailey grins, appearing out of thin air.

"Wow, look who's actually on time."

"You had me at bottomless mimosas," he teases and removes his jacket. "Saw you on the news last night." He gives Quinn a pointed look. "Next time, don't wear stripes. They make you look ten times heavier on TV."

"Now you tell me."

Bailey grabs a piece of toast from the basket on the table and stuffs his mouth.

"Hey, Bailey," James clears his throat and extends him a sympathetic look. "I was real sorry to hear about your dad."

"You know what?" His voice raises an octave. *"It's okay.* Really. I got to spend some time with him at the end. Time I didn't think I'd ever get, so…" He shrugs. "I'm glad we got the chance to talk, set things right between us."

"Some people never get that chance," James says. "Are you gonna help fill 'Big Daddy's' shoes now that he's gone?"

"Nah. I'll let Mason and Sawyer run the franchise," he says, waving a hand. "Violet's busy breastfeeding in suburbia… I spoke to her yesterday. The twins won't stop cryin'. She's 'bout to slit her wrists from no sleep," he muses. "As for me, I figure I'll buy a condo with my part of the inheritance. It's time. There's no place I'd rather be than New York, you know? Work is steady. Hell, maybe I'll even start a fashion line. Who knows," he says with his mouth full. "Anyway, enough about me." He leans over the table with a salacious smile. "What's new with you lovebirds?"

"We were just talkin' about the investigation and how Quinn's a hero. He's bein' modest though."

Quinn gives James a dubious look as their drinks arrive.

306

"You boys order a pitcher?" A six-foot-tall drag queen with a cotton candy beehive and a voice deeper than James' smiles at them.

They each grab a glass and ask her to change some $1's for the show, then watch as she sashays delicately away in a pink, glittering, floor-length ball gown.

"God, I love drag queens," Quinn sighs. "They just make everything better."

"Amen," Bailey sings. "But hey, seriously? Back to the investigation. You really did a good thing." Bailey winks sincerely, and sips from his champagne glass. "I'd say you've earned your wings, hon."

"Hmm. Think heaven has a place for dangerous right-wing politicians?" Quinn directs everyone's attention to breaking news on a TV near the bar. Ted Collins grimaces at them from the screen as speaks at a rally, dressed in a stiff black suit and angry red tie. He's addressing an audience who all look the same in their red ball caps with his campaign logo embroidered on the front. His wife and Henry stand to his right with glazed-over expressions and matching smiles.

"He's down in the polls," James says.

"It's looking like he'll need a miracle to bounce back." Quinn gulps his mimosa.

Bailey gasps, "Shit. That reminds me! Whatever happened to that 'reward money'? Don't tell me you blew it all on craft beer and *lube*?" He rolls his eyes in James' direction.

"I donated it. Half to a local LGBTQ youth shelter and half to Stacey Marek's campaign."

"His opponent?"

"Yep. The state's first female African American candidate for Lieutenant Governor!" Quinn glows.

"You used Collins' own money to make a contribution to his opponent's campaign? *Savage!*" Bailey approves and raises a glass, "To Stacey slayin' this election!"

"To Stacey!" They all clink glasses and toss back their drinks.

"What are y'all doin' after this?" Bailey asks. "Wanna catch a movie?"

"We're going to visit my mom." Quinn slides James an anxious smile and clinches his teeth. "She's been asking to meet a certain someone…"

"And I'm dying to meet *her*." James kisses the back of Quinn's hand.

"Yuck." Bailey's face sours as he tosses a piece of his toast at them. "You guys make me sick. Maybe I'll just go to SKY after this… find some old goat to keep me company tonight…"

Quinn's face ignites bright red and Bailey cringes…

"Too soon?"

"You are literally THE WORST!" Quinn bellows before they explode into laughter. "God, I hate you…"

They blaze through the pitcher quickly as they catch up on each other's lives. Their adventures abroad suddenly seem like a distant dream from a past life.

Soon the queens take the stage, one beautiful, proud glamazon after the next, and the trio find themselves clapping and singing along with the crowd. For the first time in a while, Quinn's life feels simple again.

Drink and be merry.

Live and let live.

Enjoy the day as if it's your last and be thankful for life because the alternative is a dark dismal grave, full of the missing. Full of boys long gone and stories longing to be heard.

Quinn pours the last of the pitcher into James' glass as Bailey leans in with a puzzled look.

"There's one more thing I meant to ask," he winces.

Before the words spill out, Quinn knows what he's going to ask. How could he have been so foolish to think the subject wouldn't arise?

Quinn will always be tethered to the memory of what's occurred. He'll always be reminded each time he looks in the mirror. He'll always ponder over what Bailey is about to ask.

Bailey gives him a piercing stare and utters the words that will haunt Quinn for years to come...

"Whatever happened to *Adam*?"

• • •

Vera's in the kitchen.

Her hands are stained blood-red as sugary syrup drips off her fingers. She fills a mason jar with plump pitted cherries and sighs wearily as Gus suddenly bursts through the screen door.

"You got another one, Miss Vera!"

She drops everything and wipes her hands on her apron, smearing it red. She moves as fast as she can in her house slippers to meet Gus in the foyer, forgetting to turn off the large pot bubbling on the stove.

Her hair is down today, making her feel young and girlish despite its steel gray color. Tom always hated when she wore her hair down.

Gus holds a stack of mail in his callused hands. He's sweaty from working outside and smells like the animals. The tart fragrance of warm cherries drifting from the kitchen masks the stench until Vera is upon him.

She wrinkles her nose and snatches the postcard he hands her with a nervous smile. She holds it to her chest for a moment and takes a breath. She can only guess what glamorous destination the 4x6 tiding has traveled from this time.

Spain?

China?

She doesn't know much about either country but she's willing to put her money on China.

How exotic would that be?

Guessing has become half the fun during this ritual.

The postcards arrive and she always reads the back first, savoring the handwriting – trying to imagine where it was written. (Sometimes she smells them, but she won't today because Gus brought in the mail. Lord knows where his hands have been.) She flips them over to take in the bright colors and picturesque landscapes, always stunned by the beauty of landmarks she's only seen on TV and in books. She reads the back of the postcard again, sometimes twice more. Then it's added to her collection, in order of its arrival.

Gus leaves her to her silly ritual, returning back to the midday heat and his work in the barn.

The goats aren't gonna feed themselves, he thinks, although that sure as hell would be nice.

The screen door slams shut.

Vera goes to read the back of the postcard when her mouth suddenly goes dry.

It's blank!

She utters a cry as she stares at the empty space where his handwriting should be.

There must be some mistake.

She fears the worst as she grazes her fingers over the empty space, smearing the cardstock with the sticky residue from her hands. She can hear the pot in the kitchen bubbling over, splashing and sizzling on the hot burner. She catches a whiff of burnt sugar.

In a panic, she flips the postcard over and is met with a familiar view.

It's Sweet Ridge.

A rolling green landscape fills the background, set against a winding road and trees that bloom with crimson red cherries. Vera instantly recognizes it as the road just outside. It's clearly her farm, although she's never seen it photographed so beautifully. She's driven the road hundreds of times and never once thought of it as postcard-worthy. Yet, here it is in her hands.

There's a creak from the screen door and Vera looks up in time to see Adam walk in.

With green eyes brimming with tears, Adam drops his duffle on the floor and says…

"I'm home."

BOOK CREDITS

Developmental Editors
Emma Keegan, Theresa Kostelc,
Samuel Smith, Truniece White

Cover Design / Art Direction
Matt Davies
Christopher Murphy

Interior Design
Christopher Murphy

Special Thanks
Suzanne Goodrich, Columbus Coleman, Brett Quinn,
Samuel Smith, William Smith, Gloria Sprow

ABOUT CHRISTOPHER MURPHY

Christopher Murphy is an activist, artist, and author of the new novel, *Where The Boys Are*. Christopher is a graduate of Virginia Commonwealth University and the Hurston/Wright Foundation. As a graphic designer/copywriter/marketer by day and author by night, Christopher can usually be found behind the bright neon glow of his laptop. When he's not writing, he enjoys reading and traveling to new destinations. He is a shameless thrill-seeker, lover of roller coasters, and all things that go fast. Christopher lives and works out of his home in Georgia with "the hubs" and their two dogs, and is currently writing his next novel, *The Other Side of the Mirror*, to be released in 2020.

If you enjoyed this book, please leave a review on Amazon, Barnes & Noble, and Goodreads.

For more information and works by the author:
www.ChristopherMurphyBooks.com

Follow on social media: @ChristopherMurphyBooks

CPSIA information can be obtained
at www.ICGtesting.com
Printed in the USA
BVHW031917190920
589206BV00001B/33